For Dad,

We inherit a lot more than just possessions from our parents. I'm thankful for the laughter, stories, and lessons you've passed down to me over the years.

"I never ask a man what his business is, for it never interests me. What I ask him about are his thoughts and dreams."

H.P. LOVECRAFT

GRAVE SUSPICION

a novel

AARON MAHNKE

CHAPTER ONE

SAM FELT THE LARGE pane of glass shatter against his back, followed by a brief moment of weightlessness before he landed hard on the concrete sidewalk. Fragments of glass ground into the thick fabric of his canvas coat, and he felt more than a few of them bite through to the skin. His body rolled with the momentum of the fall, sending his feet over his shoulders. A moment later, he was laying face-down in the gutter, gray snow and run-off clogging his nose and mouth.

"I don't want to see you around here anymore. You got it?"

The voice came from a large man who stood in the center of the broken window, just inside the bar. His shoulders were broad and he had a chest that seemed to be built from spare barrel parts. There was an intense fire in his eyes, as if hatred burned somewhere close to the surface. The man clenched his jaw, and even though his face was covered in thick stubble, Sam could still see the muscles beneath it ripple.

"I don't think he heard you, Repo," said a much smaller man behind him and to the right. "Maybe he needs to be told again."

"Shut it, Joey," barked the man called Repo.

Joey quickly shut it, backing up slightly for good measure. He was a weasel of a man, easily outweighed by his larger friend two-to-one. His face had the tired look of someone who had run too hot and fast most of his life, and there was very little of him left to show for it.

Sam lifted his head and spit out the filthy slush. He could still feel bits of sand on his tongue and lips, grateful for once that the town had already blown through its salt budget for the winter. The split in his lip hurt more than enough without a bath in cold salt water.

He glanced at Joey, but quickly shifted his gaze to Repo. Joey wasn't the problem. Joey was just a loudmouth with a big friend and very little courage. Repo, though, needed to be watched.

"No one talks about my girl that way," the big man growled. "I didn't like you the minute I saw you. You picked the wrong town to wander into, buddy, I'll tell you that. I don't know what you got away with before coming here, but you ain't gonna run your mouth off about my girl."

Repo had earned his moniker because of his evening job. By day, he and Sam worked together for a home builder —Sam preferred the detail work inside the houses, while

Repo spent his shift on back-breaking labor better suited to his physique—and by night the large man worked with the local savings and loan, repossessing automobiles from delinquent account holders. While most people in his profession worked clandestinely, Repo had a reputation for instigating confrontation with the people he took things from.

Sam struggled to his knees. The pieces of glass that were embedded in his coat shifted and tore at his flesh as he bent, then eased off again as he straightened. He could feel the blood pulsing in his lower lip where Repo's fist had connected moments before, and he ran the back of his hand across the cut. There was a lot of blood.

"Repo, I'm not making things up to trash-talk your girlfriend," he pleaded. "She's running around behind your back, man. You've gotta believe me."

"Believe you?" Repo's voice was thick with sarcasm. "You said yourself you've got no proof. Either you're the one poking her on the side, or you're making it all up. I'm guessing you just want a chance at her yourself, so you're trying to split us up. Unless you got some proof, that is."

The burly man's expression shifted from hatred to contempt. He knew Sam had no proof. Sam wished he did, of course, but he had nothing to go on except what he saw in a vision. No photos, no letters, no nothing. Claiming that his only source of proof was a waking dream wasn't going to satisfy a man as dense and untrusting as Repo.

"You know I can't prove it," he replied. "I just...I just know it's true, that's all."

Repo closed both hands into fists the size of Christmas hams. Veins stood out on his bare forearms, and he leaned farther out the window. The noise of laughter, loud music, and clinking glasses drifted out from the room behind the man.

"If you don't get out of town tonight," he intoned through gritted teeth, "I swear you'll be staying a lot longer than you ever expected. And I'll make sure they *never* find your body."

Sam exhaled with frustration. He didn't want to leave town, not yet anyway. He'd managed himself so well here, and while no place ever felt like home, he had grown comfortable.

Why'd you have to go and open your mouth, Sam? he asked himself. *You always think you're helping people, but you only end up making things worse.*

Joey pumped his fist and flashed his best attempt at a victorious grin. Sam didn't wait to see what Repo would do, though. He simply shook his head in disbelief, then turned and walked north, setting his sites on the traffic light ahead. Half a block from the bar he could still hear laughter and the familiar sound of REO Speedwagon blasting from the speakers.

…heard it from a friend who, heard it from a friend who, heard it from another you been messin' around…

He walked quickly and was climbing the stairs to his third floor apartment by ten minutes to midnight. His back ached from his fall to the sidewalk, and he was wondering if he might have broken more than just glass. When he reached the top of the stairs, though, he stopped. Something didn't seem right.

The dim, solitary light fixture hanging from the ceiling, a relic from another era by the look of it, flickered on and off for a moment before resuming its half-hearted attempt at illuminating the hallway. The walls and dirty, thread-bare carpet were cast in a sickly orange glow.

"Hello?" he tried calling out, but his voice broke and barely came out as a whisper. He could feel the hair on the back of his neck stand on end. "Wh-who's there?"

Nothing. Sam didn't like that. The hall was still silent, yet something felt off. Cautiously, he rounded the corner to face the entrance to his apartment, expecting to find someone standing in the shadows waiting for him. Instead, he found an empty corridor and the peeling surface of his door.

The door, however, was ajar.

He ran a hand over the strike plate in the door frame and felt a large splinter bite at one of his fingers. *Broken,* he thought. *Probably used a crowbar. Or just kicked it in.*

Sam leaned closer to the door, straining his neck to peer through the narrow gap and see inside, but it was too dark to make anything out. Had Repo and his friends somehow gotten here ahead of him, breaking in to wait for him in his own home? Sam doubted that. Repo was a strong man, and notoriously violent, but he wasn't known for his speed. No, if someone was inside his apartment, it wasn't his angry coworker.

He reached out with one hand and pushed the door gently while his other instinctively threaded his keys between the knuckles of his free hand. It was an old trick his father taught him when he was in middle school.

"You might not think you have a weapon, but there's always a solution handy if you think creatively," he had told Sam one night as they walked through a dark parking lot after leaving a restaurant "It's not the strongest guys who win the fight, Sammy, but the smartest."

Sam didn't think it was very smart to step into a dark apartment after finding the door busted open, but he didn't know what else to do. It was midnight on a Friday night, and towns like Benton didn't have the police staff of the larger cities like Carbondale or Mount Vernon. He would be lucky to reach a receptionist at this hour.

He steeled himself for whatever might be waiting for him on the other side of the door, and after taking one final deep breath, he kicked out at the door and jumped through, arms raised in defense. The door bounced off the wall and swung back with enough force to close itself, sending the room into darkness. No sound could be heard, but there was an odor in the air that he did not like. It was acrid and slightly metallic and reminded him of the violence earlier that night.

Sam backed up, blindly moving away from the center of the room. When his body connected with the wall, he reached out to where he thought the light switch might be, found it, and flicked it on. He had been ready to find a stranger waiting for him, perhaps near the window on the far side of the room, but what he saw instead chilled him to the bone. His feet froze in place, and he stared open-mouthed at the wall to his left that separated the living area from the only bedroom.

Blood had been smeared across the bare surface of the wall in wide, dark strokes. Thin rivulets ran downward in the places were it had been applied the thickest. Nailed to the center of the wall, about eye level, was the source of the blood, and Sam shuddered when he saw it.

A black cat, limbs spread wide, had been crucified with long, vicious nails before being cut open. Wet entrails hung alongside the dead animal's tail, and Sam felt his stomach lurch at the sight of it. That's when he realized that the blood on the wall was more than vandalism; it was writing.

The words nearly covered the entire width of the wall, their letters formed with broad strokes from some morbid brush. Sam struggled to read them before finally realizing that they had been written in Latin.

LUX SUSPICIONE

Sam didn't know what it meant, but the macabre medium spoke clearly enough. This wasn't the first time he had read those words, though it had been over a year, and never in such a gruesome manner. He thought he had slipped their net, but he had been wrong. Whoever his stalker was, they had returned.

Repo was right: it was time for Sam to leave town.

He turned quickly and bolted into the next room. Two large duffle bags were laying beneath the bed and he pulled them out as if the building were on fire. He had stayed in Benton for seven months and had grown complacent. Now it was time to run.

As he stuffed his clothing and the few possessions he owned into the bags, he began to do a mental inventory of his best route to safety. Before Benton he had been in Carbondale for a few weeks, and Paducah prior to that. South was probably a dangerous direction to travel, so he would head north. Interstate 57 would take him far away as fast as possible, though he would have to leave it eventually. They always seemed to find him, but he could take certain steps to make that a challenge for them.

Sam took the key off his keyring and placed it on the counter along with a small stack of twenty-dollar bills. He hoped it would be enough to cover the remainder of his rent, as well as the cost of cleanup and repairs to the apartment. He preferred to leave town on better terms, but tonight he had no choice but to leave fast.

With the bags packed and slung over his shoulder, Sam looked around the apartment one final time. He avoided looking at the wall in the living room, though; he had seen enough of that. He did, however, take a moment to pull out a small notebook he carried in his back pocket and write down the words he had found there.

Once he was certain he wasn't forgetting anything important, he switched off the light and headed back downstairs to the cold, dark street. His truck, an old Ford Ranger that had served him well for years, sat parked across the street, and he quickly climbed in and slapped the lock down tight.

Despite the cold, the engine turned over on the first try—thank God for small victories—and he pulled away from the curb. After two right turns he reached Main Street, took a left, and began his long drive north. He didn't know what waited for him at the end of this trip, but he hoped that it would put as much distance as possible between himself and whoever it was that had left the message in blood.

If only everything else could be so easily left behind.

CHAPTER TWO

THE SKY HAD BEGUN to bleed light from the edge of the horizon when Sam finally pulled off of Interstate 39 just south of Minonk, somewhere in the middle of Illinois. He sat at the stop sign for what seemed like an eternity, his truck idling with a monotonous hum that threatened to lull him to sleep, while he tried to choose which direction to turn. Left, toward the north, seemed the most logical choice as it took him farther still from his abandoned home in Benton, and so he eased off the brakes and turned the wheel.

He had been on the lookout for a small town, something out of the way and isolated, yet large enough to afford him a chance to find work and a place to stay. If he played his cards right—which entailed minding his own business as well as not attempting to help anyone, seeing as how Repo had reacted to *that* the previous night—he might just be able to start his life over again.

He had been living a nomadic life for a very long time now, and the years had taught him more than a few hard lessons. First and foremost, as he had been reminded in Benton, was to keep a low profile and mind his own business. Second, he needed to keep his visions to himself. It didn't matter if the things he saw might be able to help someone; those revelations were often seen as a threat and were treated as such. Repo wasn't the first angry recipient of news Sam knew very well to be true.

He passed through Minonk as quickly as the speed limit would allow. It was too close to the interstate and would be an easy target for whoever was tracking him. When a green destination sign appeared in on the edge of his headlights ahead, telling him that the town of Holden—population 9,531—was located ten miles to the northeast, he smiled. It sounded promising, and he was ready to be done driving.

The night had been thankfully uneventful, but also long and boring. It had taken him a little less than five hours to drive from his apartment to where he was now, and those were five hours that he would rather have spent in bed.

He had worked hard the day before, helping the foreman install casings on all of the downstairs windows in the house that was being built. Detail work was something he loved, but it took a lot of out him mentally, and when he had cut out at the end of the day he was ready for rest and relaxation.

The latter came first and consisted of a sandwich at the local sub shop. After that, Sam had wandered down the street to Bradley's Place, where he hoped to enjoy a few drinks, rest his bones, and take in a game or two of darts. Maybe if he hadn't stopped to take a piss in the restroom— the restroom where that vision had rushed at him out of the dark places in his mind and left him nearly helpless to ignore it—perhaps he would have walked out the door that night rather than getting tossed out the window.

He didn't, though, and mostly because Sam had a hard time learning from past experiences. Did he know, deep down in his gut, that telling Repo about his cheating girlfriend would get him busted up, perhaps killed? Absolutely. After all these years he had become a great study of human nature, and the big construction worker struck him as the type of man who enjoyed killing the messenger. Why, then, hadn't he kept his mouth shut?

That was a mystery for the ages, as far as Sam could tell. Perhaps it was the alcohol, although he'd only had three beers. No, he was fairly certain that it was his inner sense of duty that drove him to it. Repo was a good guy when he wasn't shit-faced and angry, and while he wouldn't have called the man a friend, he *did* feel like he had earned the right to speak frankly with him.

So he did it. He walked out of the bathroom and made a beeline for Repo, who was playing pool with Joey the Weasel while a few other rough-looking men watched on.

In retrospect, Sam felt regret gnawing away in the back of his mind, but he still knew it had been the right thing to do. It flowed from an unspoken conviction, a subconscious moral compass that seemed to push him along. He didn't know where these visions came from, and God knows he would probably have put a stop to them long ago if he could. But he wanted to be as responsible with them as he could—when it didn't threaten his life, that is.

Another sign appeared and Sam took a right turn onto Route 44. The fields to either side of the road were covered in snow and bathed in the pale light of the moon which hung low in the sky. He briefly passed through a tiny village where the county road bent north, but the sparse buildings vanished almost as quickly as they had appeared.

A moment later he could see the shape of a small town begin to fill the horizon, black against the dark gray of the sky. A sense of relief washed over him. His body was ready for a break, and perhaps some food.

Five hours north had better be enough, he told himself. *I don't want to have to do this again any time soon.*

Sam checked his watch and sighed. Not even 5:00 AM yet. That meant getting a hot meal was out of the question. Still, he could use the time to drive through the town and get a feel for it. The pre-dawn stillness would make it easy to scout the area without drawing suspicion, and he still had enough fuel, both in his truck's tank and in his gut, to move on if the place didn't seem right.

Holden, Illinois was a small and quiet town that sat at the intersection of Routes 44 and 47. A small bridge separated the northern half of town from the southern, crossing over a small, meandering stream that the sign labelled Long Point Creek. There was a Main Street, much like every other town throughout the Midwest, but it had seen better days. A quarter of the storefront windows were covered in paper, and a couple of the streetlights were out.

Aside from those admittedly small flaws, much of the town appeared as Sam expected it to, and that was a good thing. There were a number of larger businesses scattered through the central portion of Holden, and the residential areas seemed well-kept. He even saw two separate construction sites, both single-family homes that appeared nearly complete. He wondered if there was some version of himself in this town, or if his finishing skills would be welcomed by a needy contractor. Time would tell.

Time was not working in his favor at the moment, however. His brief tour ended in the parking lot of a tired old plaza near the western edge of town. A diner, The Sunny Side, occupied the center unit, but the lights were still off and no other cars were in the lot. It could be out of business, but at this hour of the morning it was hard to tell.

Sam decided to wait it out. He bunched his coat into a pillow and stretched out on the small bench seat of his truck. Next to a good meal, a nap seemed like just the thing he needed. As he closed his eyes, he briefly wondered how he would know when to wake up. Sleep, however, came swiftly, and before he could think of a solution, he was out cold.

———— ∞∞∞ ————

Sam awoke with a start, jerking his knee reflexively and banging it against the passenger-side dashboard. His coat, which had been wadded up into a makeshift pillow, had somehow slipped between the bench and the door, leaving him with a literal pain in his neck. To make matters worse, the small of his back was throbbing, and he instantly remembered why he never made it a habit to sleep in his truck.

He did not care about these minor aches, however, because his mind was occupied with more terrifying thoughts. His short nap had been uneasy and hollow, an empty gesture that failed to deliver on the promise of rest. Instead, he had dreamed.

Waking visions, such as the one that struck him in the greasy bathroom of Bradley's Place the night before, were clear and short with very little emotional content. They were quick and to the point, and he usually knew how to act upon them, if he was in a position to do so. But when those visions came during sleep, as this one had, the experience always seemed muddled and opaque.

Sam rarely felt more convinced that his gift was a curse than he did upon waking from dreams such as these, as if a noose had been placed around his neck, signaling his doom. This dream was no less damning. What little he could remember still lingered as mere flashes, bits and pieces of something larger. As always, it had left more questions than answers.

He closed his eyes and pressed the palms of his hands against his temples, willing himself to dredge up more of the images, but it didn't help. All he could see was blood. Not from his apartment, though, because this blood had pooled into a red circle, and the surface it rested on was darker. There had been a knife as well, he was almost certain, but he could not even summon an image of it. He simply *felt* it, as if it lay beneath an inch of debris and obfuscation at the bottom of his mind.

Sam could still hear the screaming. It might have been a female voice, but he wasn't sure. Perhaps there had been more than one person crying out. Either way, those shouts had been full of pain and fear. They left his stomach clenched and numb.

"Snap out of it, Sam," he said to himself. "No details, no solution. Time to move on. If it was important, you'll get another chance."

He reached toward the ceiling above the driver-side door and gripped the small vinyl handle there, pulling himself upright. The O-Shit Handle, as he had heard it called years before, for those moments when you needed something to grab ahold of while you shouted, "Oh shit!". His truck was still running, but he felt a sudden chill and retrieved his coat and began to pull it on.

While he did so he scanned the parking lot. The sun had come up and was well above the horizon, and although it looked cold outside, the light did wonders for warming his soul. Clustered in front of the entrance to the restaurant were three cars and another pickup truck, one of those enormous Fords that seemed as long as a yacht and too high off the ground to be practical. Aside from a small number of other vehicles that waited outside some of the other retail spaces, the lot was empty.

Sam zipped up his coat, turned off the truck, and then opened the door. The cold air slapped his face like an angry lover, encouraging him to lock and shut the door before his fingers froze solid. He walked as quickly as he could without breaking into a run, and didn't stop until he had reached the glass door of the Sunny Side.

A tiny bell jingled when he opened the door. It was most likely there to alert the staff that someone new had entered the place, but the blast of cold air he brought in with him could have done the job just as effectively. The two men seated in a booth about halfway down the left side turned and gave him a long, curious glance. Sam nodded in reply.

There was a counter to his right as he entered the restaurant, stereotypically topped with old linoleum and accented with occasional patches of chrome and coffee stains. Behind it, Sam could see the large window that separated the rest of the place from the kitchen, and the shape of someone moving within, most likely preparing meals for the other men. Before he could decide whether to wait and find his own seat, a waitress appeared, pushing her way through a swinging door beside the kitchen window.

"Hi, there," she said with a warm smile. "Welcome to Sunny Side. Booth or counter?"

She was young, most likely no older than twenty-five, and very attractive. She wore her long dark hair pulled back, but most of it still hung over her shoulders. Her work attire, a pair of well-worn black slacks and white polo shirt, were mostly covered by a large black apron. She pulled a menu the size of a paperback book from one of her pockets and motioned with it toward the restaurant.

"Counter," Sam replied. "And thanks." He did his best to smile, but the remnants of his dream were still wrapped around him like fibers from some hideous spider's web, and he could feel them tickling at his mind.

The top of the stool was round and covered with red vinyl, with sides trimmed in chrome to match the counter. The waitress slipped around to the server side of the counter as he took his seat near the door, and reached for the glass carafe that sat on one of two hot plates.

"Coffee, hun?" she asked.

"Yes, please," he replied with a smile. "It's a cold one out there this morning."

"Gosh, isn't it?" she agreed as she slid the menu across the counter to him while pouring his coffee. "My car needed a few extra cranks to get started this morning. They say it won't even get out of the teens today."

"Well, then," Sam replied. He cast a quick glance at her name tag, which was perched prominently atop one of her ample breasts, and then back down to his cup. "Looks like I'll be needing a hot breakfast to go with this coffee. Any recommendations, Susan?"

Susan pressed a finger to her chin and looked up in thought for a moment. "I'd have to say the Sunny Platter is the clear favorite around these parts. How do you want your eggs?"

Sam glanced at his menu. "It almost seems sacrilegious to do it, given the name of this place, but I'm going to order them scrambled. Bacon, not sausage. And wheat toast."

"You got it," she replied, scribbling the order down on a small pad before tearing off the sheet. "Holler if you need anything, hun."

She slapped the order slip onto the small metal counter in the kitchen window and then headed off to check on the other table. Sam was adding some cream and sugar to his cup when he heard the jingle of the tiny bell, and then braced himself for a gust of icy wind.

He turned to see an elderly man shuffle inside, one hand on the restaurant's door and the other firmly gripped around a cane. The man was neatly dressed and cleanly shaven, giving off the air of discipline and orderliness. Sam nodded politely, and the man smiled back before walking slowly to a booth near the door.

"Good morning, Mr. Olmsted," Susan said with a wave. She passed by the pair of men on her way to help the newcomer, and Sam watched as one of them grinned and pointed at her to his friend. Both men looked like they were closer to Sam's age, but their lewd behavior and invasive glances made them seem like high school boys.

Returning his attention to the coffee, he gave it a stir with his spoon and then sipped at it. The warmth ran down his throat and he felt a bit of the stress from his dream melt away. Good coffee had a way of putting a barrier between oneself and the realities of life. Unfortunately, this wasn't a good cup of coffee, but given how tired and cold he was, it was good enough.

His food soon arrived and he wasted no time shoveling it into his mouth as quickly as he could. His last meal, a sandwich down the street from Bradley's Place, had been half a day ago, before his exit from Benton. He hadn't wanted to stop during the overnight drive for fear of being found, but he felt safer here. Not completely secure, but closer than he had been all night.

Sam was just beginning to see the bottom of his plate when a small cry caught his attention. He turned to see the waitress slapping at one of the men's wrists. He was a lanky man with a head of thick, curly hair and a nose that seemed too large for the rest of his head. He had a recalcitrant grin on his face as he caught her hand in his, gripping it tightly.

"Let me go," she said through gritted teeth, tugging hard to free herself. "You're hurting me."

"Listen to the girl," called out Mr. Olmsted from the booth beyond them. "The lady deserves respect, and she's given you her answer."

"Shut it, old man," the lanky one spat.

"Sugar," drawled the other, a stocky fellow with a hairline that was in the final stages of a grand retreat, "we've been out salting the roads all night. We could sure use the company of a fine woman. Why don't you sit a spell with us."

Susan managed to pull herself away and took a step back from the table. The stocky one slid off his seat and stood up beside her.

"I think it's about time you boys got out of here," she said with a quavering voice.

"Frankie, she wants us to leave," the stocky chuckled. "I say we do as she says—and take her with us."

Sam watched to see what would happen next. He was a stranger in town, and needed to be careful about drawing attention to himself. He certainly didn't like how she was being treated, though, and had begun to weigh his options.

Before he could make a decision, though, the elderly man slowly rose from his seat. His pale hand gripped shakily at the gray metal cane as he rose.

"Get out," he said firmly to the young man beside Susan. "The lady has made it clear that you are no longer welcome, and if you do not do as she's asked, I'll escort you out myself."

Frankie laughed uncontrollably, his curly hair bouncing with each guffaw. "You hear that Pete? He's gonna help us leave!"

Pete didn't laugh. Sam could see a muscle in the stocky man's jaw twitching and he didn't like the way his

Aaron Mahnke

eyes had glazed over. Susan took another step back and this time Pete didn't seem to notice it. She glanced over her shoulder at Sam, and he motioned for her to get away while she had the chance. She complied gladly.

"Old man, I don't think you know your place here," Pete hissed at Mr. Olmsted. He took a step closer, and then sidestepped to allow Frankie to exit the booth and join him. "There's two of us, and we're a hell of a lot younger."

The elderly man, against all reasoning and better judgment, took a step toward them. "I killed more than two-dozen men in Korea, you little bastard." There was a fire in the old man's eyes as he walked closer. "Do you think I'm afraid to speak my mind to a couple of good-for-nothing crybabies that can't keep it in their pants?"

His words were a match that instantly lit a fuse somewhere inside Pete's head. The balding man's eyes flew wide, and he glanced incredulously at his friend. Frankie, though, seemed to be having second thoughts. He furrowed his brow and slowly tried to sit back down in the booth.

"Let's just finish our coffee, Pete," he suggested quietly. "No need to make a scene, man."

Pete, though, ignored his friend, and took another slow, deliberate step toward the old man. Sam still hadn't moved from his seat on the stool. He was afraid that doing so might mark him as the man's next target, but every fiber of his being was crying out for him to do something.

That's when he saw the younger man pull out a knife, and his dream resurfaced, rising up from the fog to become crystal clear once more.

CHAPTER THREE

SAM'S DREAM WAS SUDDENLY clear, as if the condensation had been wiped off the glass. The knife and the blood. He glanced at the feet of the men and noted that even the dark gray of the tile fit, and all at once the reality of what it meant hit him in the gut, taking his breath away.

Susan had retreated behind the counter, but had moved to a spot just across from Sam. As he slid from the stool—whether of his own volition or driven by some other power—she gasped and reached for his shoulder.

"Don't," she whispered harshly to him. "They're crazy!"

Sam didn't hear her, though. He was in another place; his feet were on the dark tile of the restaurant, but his mind was elsewhere, wrapped in dream and veiled truth. The vision that slipped into his mind earlier had grown, just as a crystal of ice quickly expands into a snowflake. And the images that had once been hidden, either by sleep or by fate, finally resurfaced.

He could see it all again. He knew that the knife—some kind of folding tactical blade—would be held upright before being drawn back. The elderly man would then ignore it, either because he could not see it or simply would not believe that the younger man would follow through. Then they would collide and the blade would be thrust forward into the old man's gut, releasing a flower of crimson that would stain his neatly pressed dress shirt before spilling through the material and pooling on the dark tile floor.

Sam could see it. He could sense it as a truth, only a heartbeat in the future. It was as if he had been given a preview of reality just one breath from now, and the urgency that came with that glimpse felt like hot coals in his stomach.

The waitress did not see the future that Sam did, but she saw the black blade of the knife.

"No!" she shouted.

"Dammit, Susie!" came the frustrated voice of a man through the kitchen window. "What's all the fucking yelling about out there?"

Sam did not wait for the cook to come help. The knife was already moving down and back as Pete's arm coiled for the killing blow. Sam reached back, gripped the long, oval plate that his breakfast had been delivered on, and then lunged forward.

AARON MAHNKE

There was a brief moment when Pete's arm was fully cocked, the blade of the knife pointed up toward the ceiling, and his head was completely exposed. Sam swung his arm around as hard as he could, gripping the plate tightly. He had intended for the edge of the white ceramic to connect with the man's head, but rotated his wrist at the last moment.

The flat surface of the plate collided with Pete's face. It shattered and came free from his hand, but not before knocking the man backward. Though he was short, he fell hard, and the back of his head struck the tile with a wet smack.

Frankie glanced up from the booth at Sam. The gears behind his slow, tired eyes were cranking, and Sam knew he had only a handful of seconds before the lanky man would stand and attack. A heartbeat later, he did.

He stopped almost instantly as the end of the elderly man's cane struck him in the side of the face.

"Sit down, you miserable bully," the older man said in a calm, steady voice. "Susan is going to phone the police now, and then you are going to wait patiently for them to arrive."

"Are you out of your—" the young man's words were cut off as Sam stepped closer, lifting a shard of the broken plate off the table.

36

"Listen to him," he hissed. "I wouldn't want to have to cut you."

Sam glanced back at the old man with an expression of relief mixed with panic. Mr. Olmsted smiled politely at him—the second time that morning—and then nodded.

"Well done, son," he declared quietly. "Well done, indeed."

———∞∞∞———

Sam worried about what would happen once the police arrived. In the past, acting upon one of his visions typically released a cascade of consequences that ended in his flight from the town he lived in at the time. He left, quite simply, because someone was following him, and publicity tended to make his trail more visible.

The police would most certainly make a big deal of his involvement in the restaurant, and that would put his name, or at the very least his description, into public channels. His goal was anonymity and subtlety—characteristics that allowed him to stay in one place for months at a time—and his rescue of Susan and the old man flew in the face of those qualities.

So Sam worried, but less than normal. Typically he would draw attention to himself by approaching a stranger and revealing a secret to them that no one else should know.

Repo was a prime example of this, though his aggressive response was certainly atypical. Sometimes it wasn't a secret so much as a truth that needed shared. Those were the moments that drew the most attention because they defied logic.

Those bits of information were, according to the people who received them, nothing short of a miracle.

There was the woman in Tulsa five years ago who had been about to step off the curb and hail a taxi when he stopped her. When the police cruiser rocketed past her a mere foot from the curb, she had simply looked back in shock. Sam made the mistake of telling her that he'd had a premonition. She told everyone she could find, and he left town the next day.

He had only been passing through Table Rock, Nebraska when he felt compelled to drive to a specific house. The man who lived there had been outside mowing his lawn, and as Sam approached him, his mind filled with the image of a young child in a dark well. He saved that boy's life, and soon everyone in the village was murmuring about the miracle he had performed.

Dozens of other episodes like this across the Midwest, spanning nearly two decades, had left Sam a little gun shy. His visions helped people, of course, but over time they had drawn enough attention to him that his own life seemed at risk. So he worried each and every time it happened.

Today, though, something felt different. He had taken action because of another vision, yes, but no one knew that he had done so. All Susan could tell the police was that Sam saw a confrontation about to take place and he had stepped in as any good citizen would. She had no idea that he had been driven by an urgency that only a man privy to the future could feel.

She saw a fight, but Sam saw blood and death.

Because of this, the police spoke only briefly to him. Mr. Olmsted quickly became the spokesman for the group, and made it clear about what had happened and who was at fault. The officers listened, nodded, made their notes on small paper pads, and then gathered lanky Frankie and bald Pete for a party in their cruiser outside.

As the door to the restaurant shut behind them, Sam sighed with relief. Perhaps there was a chance that this wouldn't need to be discussed in barber shops and mom's groups later today. Maybe, just maybe, he could pretend it didn't happen and begin building a new life here in Holden.

Susan had taken a moment to tell both men that their meals were on the house thanks to their heroics, and then slipped out back to find the mop. Sam, grateful for the meal, left a generous tip beside his coffee cup, and then tugged on his coat. When he turned to leave, the elderly man was standing between him and the door.

"I appreciate what you did, young man," Mr. Olmsted said to him as he slowly pulled on his long wool overcoat.

"I'm afraid I'm mostly bark at this stage in my life. All my bite got up and went decades ago."

Sam smiled. "Those jerks didn't know that, though. It was awfully brave of you to stand up to them, but you almost got yourself killed, you know that?"

The older man nodded. "Indeed I do," he replied. "And I have *you* to thank for my good heath this morning. What's your name, son?"

"Sam," he told Mr. Olmsted as he extended his hand. "Sam Hawthorne." The man shook it with a cold, soft hand that reminded Sam of one of those ice packs filled with gel.

"Henry Olmsted," the man replied. "Hawthorne, you say? I don't know that name. Is your family from around these parts?"

"No, sir," Sam replied. "I'm new to town. In fact, I only just arrived this morning. It was purely a random choice to pick this restaurant for breakfast. I don't know a soul in town yet." Then, after a pause, he added, "Aside from you, that is."

"I suspect it was more than chance," the man said wistfully. "Where are you staying?"

"That was on my list for after breakfast," Sam told him. Counting off on one hand, Sam held up two fingers in sequence. "Find a place to live, then find a job that pays. Hopefully both of those are things I can manage on a Saturday in the dead of winter, Mr. Olmsted."

"Please, call me Henry," he replied. The old man paused for a moment, studying Sam. There was an awkward silence while he appeared to be deep in thought, but it ended when he reached into the pocket of his coat and pulled out a small card and extended it to him.

"What's this?" Sam asked, taking it.

"My address," Henry replied. "I have a room for rent, and I believe you might be just the tenant I was looking for. Responsible, polite, and strong."

"And very handy with a tool kit," Sam added with a grin. "I can pay, of course, but I'm also happy to help with repairs if you need that."

"Excellent," Henry declared, and then picked up his hat from the table and set it gently on his head. "Take your time looking for work. Come by my address at noon and we can discuss the arrangement over a sandwich and cup of tea. Does that sound agreeable?"

"Absolutely," Sam replied with a smile. He was more than surprised by this unexpected offer. Life hadn't always been kind to him, and when gifts were offered, he was wise enough to accept them. "I'll be there."

Finding work turned out to be easier for Sam than he had first thought. After leaving the Sunny Side, he drove back around the areas of Holden that seemed to have some ongoing development. He had observed at least two active job sites earlier that morning, and was hoping that one of them might have a crew on-site today.

Sure enough, the first one he checked had the typical collection of pickup trucks, dirty compact cars, and loitering workmen outside. The sign in the yard, which matched two of the larger vehicles, proclaimed this particular home to be the work of Smitty's Home Development.

Alright then, thought Sam. *Time to find Smitty.*

He parked down the street from the property, behind the pair of blue plastic portable toilets, and began the walk toward the house. The crew had completed much of the exterior work, and probably had done so weeks before. Winter was a horrible season to spend outside, and the Midwest was notorious for harsh weather. The crew would have saved much of the sheetrock, electrical, plumbing, trim, and painting for the cold months.

Sam walked up the dirt path that would become a sidewalk in the spring, doing his best to step in the dark impressions in the snow left by hundreds of other feet. After climbing the front steps—temporary wooden risers and well-worn planks that were caked in mud and salt stains —he opened the door and stepped inside.

The air was warmer on the other side of the door. He could see at least three large industrial space heaters from the entrance, each placed in the center of the small groups of men who were working away at their various responsibilities.

"Shut the door," someone shouted from across the room. "It's not a barn."

"Sorry," Sam mumbled as he stepped in and swung the door shut. He glanced around to see if he could locate Smitty, although he knew finding the general contractor on the site on a Saturday morning was most likely a long-shot. Most of the men had their backs to him, the large orange Smitty's logo painted across each of their gray sweatshirts. One man, though, glanced over his shoulder and then stood up.

"Help ya?" the man asked with the low drawl of a man who had spent more time on a job site than in school during his life.

"I'm hoping to find Smitty," Sam replied. "Am I out of luck?"

The man motioned with his trowel toward the wide staircase off to the side of the room. "Master bedroom," was his curt reply before he returned to mudding the section of wall he was at.

"Right," Sam said to no one but himself. "I'll just show myself up, then."

He climbed the steps carefully, fully aware that they might not be completely finished yet. The upstairs was spacious, but he managed to find his way to the largest of the three bedrooms. Inside, an electrician was installing a ceiling fan from the top of a tall ladder while others hung more wallboard around him. Standing at the base of the ladder was an older man with much less dust and caulk on his clothing than anyone else he had seen so far.

Sam had met two kinds of general contractors during his years traveling from town to town and job to job. The first type always looked just as messy and filthy as the rest of the crew. Those guys didn't actually do any work, though; they simply wore clothes that looked like they did because they thought it earned them some credibility with their crew and subcontractors.

The other type never looked messy. They weren't ever perfectly clean, but they also didn't have large patches of white paint on their pants. This kind of contractor was more rare, but they were the good ones because they spent most of their time supervising and managing, as well as jumping in when needed.

Sam liked the second type of contractor much better.

"Can I help you?" the man asked as he turned away from the ladder.

He was older than Sam, but not enough to be his father's age. Gray had started to weave its way into his dark brown hair—both on his head and jawline—and the lines around his eyes and mouth were exactly what one might expect from a life in the harsh elements of a construction site. His eyes, though, had something that Sam could only think of as a twinkle, lending him a friendly, approachable expression.

"I hope so," Sam said as he approached. He extended his right hand in greeting. "I'm Sam Hawthorne. I'm new to town and looking for work. I was wondering if you had need of a skilled carpenter."

"Jim Smith," the older man replied, shaking Sam's hand with a firm grip. "Most of the crew just calls me Smitty, as you might have guessed. New to town, you say? Where from?"

Sam thought about this for a moment. He didn't like to leave a trail, whether that trail pointed in the direction he had gone, or the one he had come from. People talked and asked questions, and that was never a good thing for a man with a history of itinerant work like him.

"South," he replied, hoping it wasn't too vague of an answer. "Carbondale area. Just got in this morning, and was hoping to stay in town for a long while."

Smitty absently stroked the graying hair of his close-cropped beard. "Don't know many builders down that way," he said. "What do you do? I'm on a deadline, an I've got no time to train a rook."

Sam smiled, hoping it would disarm the man. "No rook here," he replied. "I've been doing this for a couple of decades. Mostly detail work like trim, casings, moulding and the like. I'm good with a saw, have my own tools, and I don't make a lot of mistakes."

Smitty nodded in approval. "You legal to work in the States?"

"Born and raised in Massachusetts, so I'd hope so," he said.

"Mass, eh?" One of Smitty's eyebrows raised slightly. "Where abouts?"

"Hollesley," he replied. "Near Salem. It's been a long time since I've been there, though. No family or roots, if you know what I mean."

"Nice area out there," the older man replied. "Michelle and I—that's my wife—spent a week in Boston a couple of years ago. Loved the history of it all. And that federal architecture is just something you don't see much anymore."

"I hear you," Sam replied. "Next time you're there, take a spin through Salem. Federal was practically born there. You'd love it."

Smitty nodded. Sam thought he could see a smile wanting to break free, but the man clearly knew how to run a business and keep himself distant from his crew.

"Cash at the end of each week," the man declared. "Show up on time, do your job, and don't let me down, and I think you'll do just find here. You can start Monday."

"Thank you, sir," he said, although it nearly burst out of his mouth as a laugh. "I really appreciate your willingness to take a chance on me."

"I can use the help," he replied. Then, as he turned back to the ladder and the man perched atop it, "Welcome to town. I'll see you Monday morning."

Sam showed himself out, making sure he didn't leave the front door open any longer than necessary, and then made his way down the street. Another car, a newer sedan with dark windows, had parked behind his truck, but he managed to extract his own without knocking over one of the porta-potties.

As he drove away, Sam felt a knot of anxiety untie itself and then melt into nothingness. Finding work was the most difficult part of this nomadic life of his. With no references and nobody on the inside to grease the hinges, he was often at the mercy of the people he approached. Fifty-percent of the time he had to visit a handful of job sites like this before he would land a position, but today certainly ranked up there with his easiest search.

Sam would prefer a more stable life, but that wasn't in the cards for someone with his issues. Random visions, miraculous warnings, and the occasional unexplainable event all added up to a lot of baggage that prevented him from settling down and having a normal life. But Holden showed promise.

If he could maintain a low profile, keep his mouth shut, and stay out of the damn paper, he had a good chance of spending months or even a year here before he had to move on. That sounded like heaven to him.

Whoever it was that was looking for him would find him, of course. They always did. But if he played his cards right, he could enjoy some much needed rest and freedom before that happened again.

CHAPTER FOUR

THE CARD THAT MR. OLMSTED had given Sam was one of those standard white business cards that anyone could get printed at a local office supply store. His name was displayed in large type across the top, and beneath it were two columns. The first contained his address and telephone number, while the second simply said CERTIFIED PUBLIC ACCOUNTANT, each word stacked on the next.

Sam could not help but wonder if the man, who was obviously well beyond retirement age, still worked, or if he simply used the cards because he had them. Perhaps, like many retired professionals, Henry still dabbled in accounting as a small job when people requested it. Whether the man was actively working or not, thinking of him as an accountant helped solidify his perception of Henry, who presented himself as a very put together man, where rules mattered and protocol was king.

Better than finding out he's a slobbish recluse who collects cats, he thought.

Sam turned his truck onto the final street and glanced around for house numbers. He found Mr. Olmsted's home about a block down the road on the right. It was a split-level ranch home with pale yellow siding and black shutters. Not a mansion, but it would certainly be a step up from sleeping on the seat of his truck.

The driveway was wide enough for two vehicles, and Sam pulled in beside a long, gleaming white Cadillac. It was spotless, which was amazing considering this was the season for snow and road salt, and judging by its age—at least ten years old, from what he could tell—it spoke to a disciplined, particular owner.

He locked the truck and climbed the steps to the front door, and then checked his watch before he pushed the white doorbell button. He was one minute early and that made him smile. First impressions always mattered, even with landlords.

A moment after pressing the glowing yellow button, the storm door shuttered slightly as the inner door was pulled open. Mr. Olmsted stood just inside, neatly pressed slacks and an Oxford shirt as spotless as his Cadillac, smiling warmly.

"Welcome, Mr. Hawthorne," he said as he opened the storm door. "Please, come in. And do take your shoes off, if you would be so kind."

Sam did as he was told, setting his shoes at the far edge of the door mat. He found himself standing on a landing, with stairs leading both up to their left and down to the right. The elderly man began to climb the steps, gripping the black wrought-iron banister as he did so.

"Lunch is ready in the kitchen," he pronounced. "Hot tea?"

"Please," Sam replied. "And thank you once again for the offer to rent your spare room. You've saved me a world of trouble tracking down a place to stay. I was afraid I'd be spending the night in my truck tonight."

Mr. Olmsted reached the top of the stairs and turned to look down at him. "I feel as though you are doing me a favor, young man. Considering what you did for me at the restaurant this morning, I almost feel guilty making you pay." Then, with a playful grin, "*Almost.*"

Both men laughed at the joke and continued walking. To the right of the top of the stairs was a living area, complete with a small sofa and a brick fireplace. The wall on either side of the mantle was covered with built-in bookshelves, each one holding a handful of books as well as an assortment of knickknacks.

Through the living room, by way of a large archway, was the dinning room. A small table sat against the right-side wall, neatly arranged with a long linen table runner, upon which sat two tea cups on matching saucers. It felt formal, but Sam knew that was mostly because of Henry's natural inclination toward order and presentation.

A counter to their left separated the dinning area from the kitchen, and Mr. Olmsted motioned toward the table.

"Take a seat," he offered. "I'll just retrieve our meal."

Sam sat with his back to the living room and glanced out the large glass patio doors that filled the wall on the back side of the dinning room. There was a small wooden deck on the back of the house, and he assumed the staircase was somewhere out of view. Beyond the wood rails and patio furniture he could see a large yard of mostly lawn, with the occasional pine along the edges.

"Soup and sandwiches," the elderly man announced as he set a plate down in front of Sam and then placed his own on the other side of the table. By the smell of it, the bowl contained a creamy tomato soup, but the sandwich was unidentifiable.

"Did you manage to find employment yet, Mr. Hawthorne?" his host asked as he lifted a spoonful of soup to his lips.

"Sam," he corrected, "and yes, as a matter of fact, I did. I'll be starting Monday morning with Smitty's Home Development. Do you know of them?"

He took a bite of the sandwich and discovered, much to his joy, that it was grilled cheese. He had fond memories of his mother serving tomato soup and grilled cheese sandwiches for special meals. It had been over twenty years since he had eaten them together, and the taste brought back memories. Perhaps too many, if he was honest with himself.

"Oh, indeed," Mr. Olmsted replied. "I processed Jim's taxes for a number of years before my retirement. He's a good, honest man."

"That's good to hear," Sam said. "I've worked with many contractors over the last two decades, and I know first hand that not all of them are good people."

"Decades?" the older man wondered aloud. "Sam, just how old *are* you?"

"I'll turn forty this year," he replied. "I left home when I was nineteen and moved here from New England. Since then, I've lived a pretty nomadic life across much of the Midwest."

"Sounds exhausting," his host replied. "And each new stop means finding work and shelter, is that correct?"

"Yes, Mr. Olmsted," he said. "Though, I only move two or three times each year, so it's not as bad as it sounds."

"Please," the elderly man petitioned, "call me Henry."

Sam nodded. "And you, Henry? Have you lived in Holden your whole life?"

"No, but for the vast majority of it," he replied. "I was born nearby in a small ghost town of a village named Long Point, but when I was very young my parents moved south to Holten. I grew up here, attended school here, and aside from a brief adventure at Eastern Illinois University down state for my accounting degree, I've never left. I met my wife here and together we raised our children here, although they've long since moved away."

"That's a wonderful thing to be able to stay in one place for a long time," Sam mused. "My family lived in the same town in Massachusetts for nearly three hundred years, so I can appreciate your accomplishment. What about your wife? Is she alright with you letting a complete stranger move into your home?"

Mr. Olmsted's eyes shimmered slightly but the welcoming smile never left his face. "Oh, Wendy passed on back in the summer of 2003," he said, his voice barely more than a whisper. "But I suspect she would be happy for me to have someone around again. Someone to talk with and share stories."

Sam felt as if he had inadvertently dropped a brick on the windshield of the man's spotless Cadillac. "I'm very sorry," he apologized. "I hope I didn't offend you with my comment. That wasn't my intention at all."

His host shook his head and waved the statement away with his hand. "Not at all," he replied. "At my age, it's hard to guess whether a stranger has been widowed or not. Besides, it's been over a decade. It will take more than a harmless question to set my mood off into the melancholy, I promise."

"Well, I'll do my best to be more sensitive in the future, regardless," Sam said. "So what can you tell me about the room? And will you be wanting a deposit?"

The older man set his spoon down and leaned forward, resting on one elbow. He appeared thoughtful, his brow furrowing slightly and his eyes becoming slightly distant. A second later he returned to the conversation with a shake of his head.

"No deposit," he said. "You don't start work until Monday, and Jim pays on Friday, if I remember correctly."

Sam nodded.

"Well then, your first month's rent can be due in two weeks. Why don't we say a nice even three-hundred dollars, due each month on the same date?"

Three-hundred dollars? Sam thought. *That's less than I payed in Muncie, and that was back in 1998.*

"That sounds like a deal to me, Henry. I'll want to help out around the house as well, though. Otherwise, I think I'll lose sleep worrying that I'm taking advantage of you."

"Nonsense," the old man replied. "I won't turn down the help, though. I have a door down the hall that refuses to hang straight, and I have a feeling you might be able to help. Do occasional requests like that sound reasonable?"

"Yes, sir," he said with a nod. "So, when can I move in? Not that moving in will be a major event; I only have two bags to my name, and they're both on the front seat of my truck."

Mr. Olmsted smiled. "Any time you wish," he said. "I'll get you a key before the end of the day, and we can discuss that door tomorrow. Now, let me show you to your room."

Moving into the room took Sam all of five minutes, most of which were taken up by the walk to and from his truck. He had managed to grab most of his possessions before leaving Benton in a hurry the day before. He had been rushed, though, and he knew unpacking would give him a chance to see what items he might have missed.

The entire room was furnished, a helpful feature for a tenant with nothing but a couple of bags of clothing and personal effects. A small bed was set against one wall, flanked by a nightstand and lamp. There was even a dresser against the wall just inside the door. It was into this that he emptied most of the first bag, filling the top three drawers and sorting out his pants and shirts as best as he could.

The first bag was almost entirely clothing, but jumbled at the bottom were an assortment of items he had picked up over the years and refused to throw away. A Red Sox cap, bent and faded, lay upside down at the bottom, and it was filled with a collection of smaller items. There were two pocket knives, a multitool, some keys, and a pair of dice. Nothing that warranted dying for, but each of them told a story, and Sam wanted to remember those tales.

The second bag was more of the same. Sam dug through it and found homes for almost everything. He didn't spread the items out around the room, however, because he knew how things here in Holten would end. Eventually, his stalkers—whoever they might be—would find him again, and he would need to leave.

More than likely, his exit would be swift. It usually was, so he had learned to keep his possessions clustered together in as few places as possible. It made running around the room and pushing the piles into an open duffle bag a manageable process. It was far from ideal, but it was a habit he had settled into.

At the bottom of the second bag was an object slightly larger than a cigar box. It was old and worn by many years of being handled, over which time the surface had taken on the polished, glossy appearance that one might expect from hardwood flooring or a wooden knife handle. Sam ran a thumb over the brass keyhole and latch, and soaked in the tactile experience. The characteristic that resonated with him the most was the color of the wood, similar to a coffee stain, although in places it was darker.

That was because of the fire.

Holding it in his hands brought back a flood of memories that he wasn't ready to deal with just yet. He ran his fingertips over one edge, feeling the places where splinters had broken off years before, and noted how the patina of age camouflaged each blemish. Sam knew where all the scratches and nicks were. He could find them in the dark with his eyes closed. He knew this box better than anything else he owned.

Which was why he kept it in the duffle bag, even after moving into a new place. If he was ever told he could only rescue one possession from a burning building, this small wooden box would be his first choice. Because of that, it stayed in the bag, ready for his next escape and guaranteed not to be left behind.

Sam was the first to admit that he had issues. Most of those were completely natural for someone who lived out of his luggage while moving from town to town. He hated the life he had been forced to live, but he didn't see another option. He occasionally entertained the dream of settling down in one location and spending the rest of his life there, but he did not see how it was possible.

Glancing at his watch, he saw that it was nearly 3:00 PM. The light that filtered through the large window on the other side of the room had begun to fade and yellow, casting a sickly glow across the walls. Sam approached it and glanced outside.

His room was above the garage, and looking down he could see his truck in the driveway. Henry's spot was empty, having yet to return from a trip to the hardware store to get his key copied. Sam made a mental note to ask Henry if the garage had room for his truck, or if he would need to keep it in the drive.

A garage would be amazing, he thought. It had been years since he had been able to park his truck indoors during the winter. *I'll feel like a regular suburbanite if that happens, complete with a garage door opener fastened to the sun visor.*

The neighborhood was quaint, each large yard containing at least one tall oak and a ranch-style home similar to Henry's. Some of them had been expanded over the years, while one or two had been neglected to the point of disrepair. Sam was glad that Henry took an interest in keeping his home in order, and he looked forward to helping improve it.

He turned to return to his bags when something caught his eye. A sedan was parked perhaps a dozen yards down the street. Part of the car was obscured by the branch of a neighbor's tree, but Sam was fairly certain that the windows were tinted.

It could be nothing; other neighbors had chosen to park their cars on the side of the street, so this one was not alone. But it might also be something to keep an eye on. Sam favored the latter explanation and decided to be on watch for anything unusual. After another glance, he pulled the curtains together, cutting off his view of the road—and the road's view of him.

Observant, quiet, and forgettable, Sam mentally recited. *This is how we stay alive. This is how we live our life.*

He stuffed both of the bags—one empty and the other containing only the wooden box—under his bed and then glanced around the room. This would be his new home. He did not know how long that might be true, but he was certain that he would enjoy it while he could.

Sam left the room and was about to head to the kitchen when he remembered Henry's request to look at the crooked door. In addition to the entrance to his own room, there were three other doorways off the hall. One led to the bathroom, while another opened into Henry's bedroom. The third, though, stood open directly across the hall from his own.

He opened and closed the door a few times and felt it catch on the carpet about halfway through the swing. There was enough friction in that area that a small patch of the carpet fibers had begun to wear slightly. He knelt down and felt at the bottom hinge.

Loose, he thought. *Just needs tightened.*

He stood and looked around the room. Henry had set it up as an office, and Sam guessed that this was where he did all of his freelance tax preparation. An aluminum Apple iMac sat on an old wooden desk, their individual styles complimenting each other perfectly. The few papers that were visible sat in a tray that was set off to the side. Henry loved order, that much was clear; everything had its place.

A filing cabinet flanked the right side of the desk, where a number of picture frames had been arranged in front of a small potted cactus plant. Sam stepped closer and studied the photo placed prominently in front of all the others. It showed a cleft of dark rock, water cascading gently down in the background where it gathered into a small stream before running toward the camera.

A slightly younger version of Henry stood on the wet rocks of the riverbed, his arm around a woman who Sam assumed to be Wendy, his now-deceased wife. Sam was struck by the joy that was clearly visible on Henry's face.

Sam sighed. He understood how loss could affect a person; he had carried his across thousands of miles and many years. He felt deep sadness for Henry, a man much closer to the end of his life than the beginning, for having to carry such a weight. It seemed unfair.

Can I keep the same thing from happening to me? Sam wondered. *I want to set this burden down. God, I wish I knew how.*

61

CHAPTER FIVE

SPRING HAD BEGUN TO pry the weather loose from the steely grip of winter and the first bits of color were slowly bleeding back into the world. Sam was glad to see it, too, as the winter had been exceptionally harsh, even by Illinois standards. He heard many people grumble about a "lake effect" and he stifled the urge to argue with them. Everyone thinks they are a meteorologist when the weather turns bad, but they're usually wrong.

Sam could see the sun rising in the east as he turned his truck onto Jackson Street. His morning routine for the last three and a half months had been the same: get out of bed earlier than any sane person would willingly agree to without the promise of payment, warm up his truck, shower and dress, and then head to the job site. When the day was done and he was back in bed, it all repeated the next day.

His first task on the nearly completed house nearly four months ago had been to install all of the trim for the downstairs doorways. Simple work, admittedly, but Sam knew Smitty's goal was to test him—a wise choice, given that Sam essentially rolled into town without a resumé or reference—and to see what his weaknesses might be.

Fortunately for Sam, and for Smitty as well, he didn't *have* any weaknesses—not on the job site, that was—and he made quick work of the assignment. That success earned him a trip upstairs, where he was partnered with another carpenter to work on the trim and casing in the master bedroom.

And that was how he met Cesar.

Cesar was a Hispanic-American superman. Sam had worked with hundreds of skilled carpenters across the Midwest and he had never met anyone as gifted as Cesar. Most of the doors that the man framed were flawless, and those that weren't were still closer to perfect than Sam could ever hope to get. He didn't know how or why Cesar was so good, but he accepted it as Gospel and told anyone who would listen.

They quickly became friends, passing their days by competing to see who could install the trim around a window faster and then inspecting each other's work. Their conversations started off in the safe territory of work and woodworking, but over the weeks that followed, Sam opened up more and more. They joked and laughed, shared meals during breaks, and even grabbed the occasional beer at a local bar — occasional, because Cesar was a family man to the core.

Sam eventually met the man's wife and daughter, both of whom were beyond gorgeous, and found them to be just as friendly as Cesar himself. Olivia, their daughter of ten, called him Sammy, and even asked him to attend her birthday party in late March. Cesar's wife, Sabrina, was equally warm and welcoming toward him.

Over time, a friendship bloomed that was unlike anything Sam had allowed for himself in years. He picked Cesar up for work each day and they worked like dogs, but it was that friendship that made the long hours and hard labor tolerable. Sam was not so sure that it was a good idea to grow so close to a person—let alone an entire family—who he would have to abandon someday without warning. But he trusted his new friend, and it felt good to have that kind of foundation. It felt *normal*.

He pulled into the driveway and gave the horn a quick honk, just as he always did. A moment later, the front door opened and Cesar stepped out, lunch pail in hand. Sam glanced up at one of the second story windows and waited to see if Olivia would make her daily appearance. Almost like clockwork, she slipped between the curtains and waved. He saw her mouth a greeting to him, and he waved back and grinned wide.

He could get used to normal life.

The job site had moved across town in late February when that first home was wrapped up and handed over to the owners. Their current project was a new McMansion on the north side of town. A spell of warm weather had allowed the foundation to be poured, and framing had commenced shortly after. It wasn't the indoor work that Sam preferred, but it was work nonetheless, and he was glad for it.

Now that May had finally rolled around, they had more good days than bad. More often than not, there was abundant sunshine and a cool breeze. Today, however, it had turned cloudy by the afternoon, and forceful winds had begun to move the budding trees above.

Sam could smell the rain in the air as he and Cesar began helping the others tarp off sections of the house and get supplies under cover. They worked quickly, strapping large pieces of plastic over the exposed frames of the new walls, and were just finishing up as the first drops began to fall.

When the mad dash to protect everything was finally over, Sam headed off toward the edge of the property to wait out the rain. He sat on the grass beneath a large oak tree which, despite its lack of leaves, had enough of a tangle of branches to provide adequate shelter.

That was when the vision hit him, like a bolt of lightning out of the stormy sky.

This one was preceded by a thunderclap of pain, as if a screw driver had been pushed through the soft tissue of his temple, right beside the eye. He slapped a hand to his head and bent over, closing his eyes. His mind flashed white before going completely black.

Empty. Like the vacuum of space. And then an image faded into view.

Sam saw a shape falling toward him slowly. It was pale against the stark blackness of the space, and a fuzzy halo of hair was waving in slow-motion around the figure's head. The closer it came, the more detail he could make out.

A woman? he wondered. *A girl?*

The pain pulsed and he squeezed his hand tighter against the side of his skull. It was as if someone or something were pushing the image into his mind through the smallest of holes, and the pressure was tearing him apart. But he watched. He had no choice but to watch. And the figure kept falling.

It came closer still, and Sam could now see that it was indeed a girl. She was falling with her body facing away from him, but there was a slow rotation to her descent. Her body was toppling over and over, spinning as she fell, all while drawing closer to the eye of his mind. As she did so, the blackness behind her began to soften, transitioning first to a deep gray and then continuing to grow steadily lighter.

Lines appeared in the background, darker than the fading color, like scratches on the surface of his mind. Sam could not make sense of them, but they felt familiar and natural, rather than intentionally carved by a human hand.

The figure continued to fall.

Whoever she was, she was now nearly head-down, her feet out of sight somewhere behind her torso. The long, straight hair was dark, but it shone in the growing light and drifted around her in hypnotic waves.

Sam groaned as the pain increased. He could not stop the vision, nor could he control it. It was happening *to* him, not *through* him, and it was ripping his mind apart. Still she fell, and still he watched.

When the figure finally rotated with slow, steady motion, her features began to come into view. As they did, the vision sped up, as if someone had doubled the play-back speed of a video. The closer she came to him, the faster she moved.

The lines behind the girl's form began to come into focus, and Sam could now see that they were the leafless branches of a tree, and the gray expanse behind them was sky. Dark, cloudy sky. Sky much like his own, in fact.

I'm looking up toward a tree, he thought. *She's falling out of a tree!*

But who? That was the question he needed to answer. He watched as the girl fell faster and closer, her body rotating through the air until eventually her entire face came into view.

"Olivia!" he shouted. Suddenly, he was out of the vision, out of his mind's viewfinder and staring at the skeletal frame of a new house, plastic sheets flapping in the wet wind.

Cesar had been walking toward him—no doubt concerned for the expression on Sam's face and the hand he was holding to his head—and his eyes opened wide at the sound of his daughter's name. He ran to Sam's side.

"What is it, man?" he asked. His voice was tight with concern. "Did someone call you?"

Cesar glanced at the hand Sam was still holding to his face, looking for a cell phone. There was none, of course. Sam had never owned a mobile phone. Cesar knew that, too, but maybe the surprise had confused him.

"Tell me, Sam," he begged. "What about Olivia?"

Sam looked up at his friend and knew he was about to make a decision he would regret.

"Where is she, Cesar?" he asked. "I know it's going to sound crazy, but you have to trust me. Is she home from school today?"

Cesar nodded. "She had a cold all weekend. Her school doesn't like parents sending kids to school sick, so we kept her home. Sabrina had to work, but Olivia's ten. It's not ideal, I know, but she can take care of herself fine. Why?"

Sam shook his head as he stood. "We need to go. I can't explain it, but she's fallen—out of a tree, I think—and she's hurt. And she needs our help."

Cesar didn't need to be told twice, and he was already off running toward Sam's truck. The pain was fading, but it still hurt, and Sam had a difficult time getting up to full-speed. When he reached the truck, his friend was already buckled in and waiting.

"Man, I hope you're just loco," he said. The look of fear in the man's face told a different story, however.

He believed Sam. Somehow, he believed him.

Sam drove fast, but not at an illegal speed. Auto insurance, much like mobile phone plans, required a bank account and an address, and those were luxuries that he had never been able to allow for himself. He drove with urgency, but safely, doing his best to avoid any chance that he might get pulled over by a police officer.

It frustrated Cesar, though. Sam didn't have to be telepathic to know the man was beyond worried. It was clearly evident by the copious amounts of swearing and slapping of the dashboard that the man engaged in during the drive. Sam was more than sympathetic, though; he was worried as well.

He cared for Olivia, just as he cared for Cesar and his wife. They were good friends, and now one of them was in trouble. He wanted nothing more than to speed through town and race to that little girl's side. Doing so would put himself in danger, though, and he had to navigate that fine line between being helpful and not drawing attention to himself.

When they finally pulled into Cesar's driveway, the man was already unbuckled and ready to bolt from the truck. Sam shifted into PARK, shut the engine down, and pulled the parking break as quickly as he could manage, but Cesar was already out and running.

Sam followed quickly. Cesar ran around the far side of the house. Sam glanced up and could see the spidering branches of a tall tree reaching up from behind the slope of the roof and knew that was where she was.

He arrived to find Cesar kneeling beside her in the wet grass. She was crying but otherwise laying perfectly still. Her father had reached down and was brushing hair out of her face while he murmured to her.

He glanced over his shoulder as Sam approached. "She's hurt, Sam." His voice shook with fear and emotion. "There's bleeding. God, Sam, what do we do?"

"Don't move her," he said firmly, hoping to maintain composure for everyone. Olivia whimpered from her spot in the grass, and Sam placed a hand on her shoulder. "Cesar, go call for an ambulance. I'll watch her. She's going to be ok, but I think we need to get her to a hospital.

Olivia watched her father disappear out of the corner of her eye but didn't move her head. Tears ran down the side of her face. There was blood in the grass.

"You're going to be alright, Olivia," he soothed. "Your dad's gone to call for help. I think you broke something, but you're going to be alright, I promise."

"My head hurts, Sammy," she said through pain. Her eyes looked past him toward the branches of the tree above. "I fell."

"I know," he replied. *I watched it happen,* he almost added.

He still had his hand on her shoulder but suddenly felt the urge to place it on her forehead. As he did, he felt something pulse through the palm of his hand. Her pulse, perhaps, but that didn't seem right. He closed his eyes but opened them quickly, shocked by what he saw behind his eyelids.

For a moment it seemed as if he had been looking up at the tree, and a pain was raging at the back of his skull. When he opened his eyes it all vanished, but for that brief instance it had been real and vivid and so very tactile. Somehow—Sam had no idea how and it had never happened to him before—he could *feel* her pain through his touch.

He glanced down at Olivia, and she was looking directly at him, her eyes locked with his.

"How did you do that?" she asked him.

"Do—do what?" he replied, knowing full well what she meant.

"You made the hurting stop," she said. "Just for a second, it stopped. I know you did it."

Sam shook his head. That wasn't possible. He understood that something unusual had just happened, but he wasn't ready to jump to such a wild conclusion.

"No, sweetie, I think you're just calming down," he tried to convince her.

"I saw you," she replied. "My eyes were closed, and I could see your face. The pain went away when you were there. Please, can you do it again?"

He opened his mouth to speak but instead let out a long breath. She was right, of course. With the wonder and faith of a child, she believed something could be true that defied all logic and explanation. Sam experienced it as well, and yet he was having a hard time accepting it. But Olivia wasn't fooled.

"Please," she whispered, her voice wavering with emotion.

Sam closed his eyes again. At first there was nothing, but when he thought of her injury—her pain and her fear —it all rushed back. He could see through her eyes. He could feel her agony.

He heard her sigh. It was the sort of sound someone makes when they receive something they desperately wanted: a gift, a hug, a comforting word. Her pain was gone.

But it wasn't. It was inside Sam. *He* felt it now. *He* was the one struggling to contain it. So he pushed back at it. He forced it to diminish and retreat and become less of what it was. For a few heartbeats he struggled in vain, and it felt useless to try. Gradually, though, it began to fade like the slow-motion descent of the figure in his vision.

"They're coming, Sam," Cesar shouted from behind him, breaking Sam's concentration. He opened his eyes and turned to see his friend jogging toward them. "She alright?"

Sam glanced down at Olivia. Her eyes were still closed and her breathing was deeper and more relaxed. Her face was no longer twisted into knots by the pain, and a sudden revelation occurred to him.

She's better, he thought. *Maybe not completely, but she's not feeling the pain anymore. But…how?*

"Yeah," he finally replied. "I think she's going to be alright."

Olivia made it to the hospital in neighboring Flanagan and the doctors took care of her minor injuries. They couldn't find a source of the bleeding that Cesar swore he saw, but the rain had washed away any evidence of it that might have lingered in the grass, so he slowly convinced himself that he had imagined it.

Sam stayed at the hospital until Sabrina arrived to join her family. Before he left, though, Sam pulled Cesar aside and spoke with him briefly.

"I know this is going to sound crazy," he began, "but can you keep what happened at work between you and me?"

"What do you mean?" the man asked.

"My...um...premonition," Sam replied. "The fact that I *knew* something had happened to Olivia."

"Man, if you hadn't said anything, she would have been all alone out there," Cesar replied. "She could have *died*, man. You saved my girl."

Sam nodded. "I know," he sighed. "But I'm not looking for attention or praise. I just want to keep this as quiet as we can. She's safe and doing well, and that's all that matters. My premonition needs to be forgotten, though. Alright?"

Cesar glanced back into the room where his wife was sitting with Olivia. The girl was smiling and playing with one of the cloth dolls that her mother had brought, not a sign of her tragic fall from the tree.

"If you say so, Sam," he finally agreed. "I'll keep it between us. But Sabrina is going to want to know what happened. It's hard to explain how we knew to drive across town and find her out back, you know?"

"I know," he replied. "Tell her as little as you need to. But this story doesn't leave the family, alright?"

"Understood."

CHAPTER SIX

THE WEEKEND THAT FOLLOWED the accident was a tense one for Sam. He had managed to successfully avoid any sort of incident that might draw attention to himself for many months, but Olivia's accident had erased all of that. He began to look over his shoulder more, to worry constantly, and take extra care with all of his interpersonal interactions.

He spoke less with Cesar during their Saturday shift, hoping that if there were fewer opportunities for the topic to come up in conversation that the man would forget about it. This distance made their lunch break awkward, with Sam breaking months of routine to run errands for Smitty before volunteering to help out in another part of the house. Cesar noticed it, but he did not press the matter.

Even Henry noticed a change in Sam. Before the accident, Sam would spend a few evenings each week sitting and talking with the elderly man. Mostly it was Henry who did the talking, filling Sam in on his family's history in Livingston County or stories about his wife and children.

The old man seemed to come alive when he spoke of her, as if a part of him was with her in the grave.

Now, however, Sam was more focused on the weight he felt upon his shoulders. He still sat with Henry in the evening, but as he listened he was also looking through the newspaper from earlier that day, scanning for anything that might hint at the story of Olivia's accident getting out. If it did, that would signal the lighting of a fuse that would burn hot and fast. He would need to leave quickly, and even then, he feared for the consequences.

Sam had never done anything as unusual and potentially attention-grabbing before, and whoever it was that was following him and leaving threatening messages might be driven to more severe attempts. He tried to imagine what could be worse than a blood-smeared wall and a crucified cat, and the prospects were frightening. All of this speculation led to Sam carrying a figurative sack of guilt and fear as he went about his routine each day.

Henry sensed this weight, and the evening of the incident had been quiet and awkward. The old man did not seem to like unresolved tension—perhaps an outward expression of his neat, orderly personality—and he asked probing questions to find the source of Sam's melancholy. He assured Henry that all was well, but it was clear his landlord did not buy the lie.

That had been Friday, and Sam endured the man's inquisition throughout the weekend while finding temporary escape in repairs and improvements around the house. He spent five hours replacing the steps on the back deck, mostly because the noise of the circular saw made talking impossible. But the dance was exhausting.

Work on Monday came as a refreshing change from spending all day with the old man, but it brought challenges of its own. Cesar seemed to want to talk, but Sam avoided each attempt and instead found areas of the job site that needed his attention more. The following day, however, Cesar won, trapping Sam as he was exiting one of the portable toilets on the edge of the street.

"Sam, we need to talk," he insisted, not moving from his spot just two feet from the door.

Sam's shoulders slumped. "Cesar, I told you I didn't want to discuss it any more."

His friend didn't move. "Sabrina told a friend," he announced flatly.

Silence. Sam slowly felt the grip of panic start to wrap its tentacles around him, beginning with a prickly tightness in his neck and shoulders. His eyes squinted in a grimace.

"Oh, God," he groaned. "Who did she tell?"

"She has a friend who works at the hospital. Maggie. She was asking about Olivia, and said the entire medical staff was amazed at her recovery. Sabrina was so caught up in the conversation that she let it slip that someone had helped Olivia before the ambulance arrived."

"Someone," Sam repeated. "Did she name me?"

Cesar winced at the question.

Sam sighed. "When did she tell Maggie this?"

"Saturday, I think," Cesar replied. "I know it was a few days ago."

"Great," Sam spat. "Just fucking great."

"Maggie said that one of the doctors wants to meet you," his friend continued. "He wants to know more about the condition you found her in, and what you might have done to help her before the EMT crew arrived."

"And what did you tell her?" Sam asked.

"That you aren't interested in talking," he replied. "Man, I've been trying to keep you out of it, but they won't let up."

"I don't get it," Sam said. "Why is it so unusual that I helped a girl who fell out of a tree? That doesn't mean I'm special or anything. I just helped out."

"I know that, man," Cesar replied. "But that was a long fall. I know that tree; Sabrina knows it, too. Olivia is always asking us if she can climb it. The lowest branch that she could possibly have fallen off of is at least twenty feet off the ground."

Sam didn't respond. How could he, when the evidence was so strongly in favor of the unusual. A drop like that should have hurt her more, of course. And it did, for a while at least. But Sam had done something to her, something that he was not entirely sure even *he* understood, and it had changed things for her.

"This isn't what I needed, Cesar," he furrowed his brow and frowned at the man. "I wanted to avoid attention. This isn't avoiding anything. They're going to find out about my premonition next, I just know it."

"She didn't mention anything about you seeing it happen before it we got there. No one knows about that except you and me, man."

"But they think I helped Olivia's injuries in some way," he replied. "Don't they?"

"Yeah, I guess they do," Cesar replied. "Sabrina is convinced you saved our little girl's life. And Olivia has mentioned that you made it hurt less, but she doesn't know how."

Sam's head was spinning. An entire medical staff had been handed his name in connection with a miraculous healing. He didn't even know how he managed to *do* it, and yet here he was, about to be punished for the action nonetheless. It was hopeless.

"Cesar...buddy...I need to go," he stepped past his friend, placing a hand on his should as he did. "Tell Sabrina and Olivia good-bye for me."

"Good-bye?" Cesar's face wrinkled in confusion. "What the hell does that mean? Where are you going?"

"Away," Sam replied, but he didn't turn around. He knew that if he did, he would be tempted to stay, to ride it out and see what would happen next. That would be the easiest choice, but it would be the wrong one and he knew it. Instead, he made the hard choice to keep walking to his truck.

He had to move fast.

—⁂—

Sam brought the truck to a quick stop on the front edge of the lawn. There was no time to spare for maneuvering in and out of the driveway. Henry's Cadillac was in the drive, and it would be more of an obstacle than he wanted to deal with. Instead, he pulled the parking break and bolted from his seat, dashing quickly across the lawn toward the front door.

He mounted the two front steps in one leap and gripped the nob of the door, twisting it as he leaned forward. The door swung inward and slammed into the wall. A framed photo popped off the wall and crashed to the floor. Sam didn't stop, though. He quickly mounted the stairs and ran down the hall to his room.

Inside, he dropped to his knees and skidded to a stop at the side of the bed. He found both of his duffle bags waiting for him underneath the frame and pulled them free. Looping the short handles of one bag over his right arm, he rushed to the dresser and pulled the top drawer open. He scooped with his left hand and dumped everything into the bag, no care for folding or order.

When the drawer was empty, he slammed it shut and opened the next. He did this until the dresser's contents all rested inside the bag, zipped it, and then tossed it onto the bed. The next bag was heavier, and he realized that he had left the wooden box inside.

We're making one more trip, you and I, he thought. *Two decades of running.*

The rest of his belongings were scattered around the room in small groups. He ran from place to place grabbing everything he could remember and tossing it into the bag. When he had packed all the items he could see, he began to quickly open other drawers and check beneath the nightstand. He had missed a pair of socks that he had tossed errantly off the far side of the bed, and a notebook that he hadn't been able to find for a couple of weeks. The latter he stuffed into the back pocket of his jeans and then he zipped up the duffle and walked back to the bed.

With both bags slung over his shoulder, he looked around the room one final time and then exited into the hall. He leaned into Henry's office and glanced at the desk, but the old man was not there. He wanted to say good-bye. He owed Henry that much.

"Henry?" he called out. The elderly man's hearing was not perfect, but Sam knew how loud to talk to be heard in the kitchen. Still, there was no reply.

He must have gone out without the car. A walk perhaps?

Sam sighed. Henry had been a good landlord, and his first roommate in years. He briefly considered leaving a note, but that would have done two things he did not want. First, it would have taken time, and time was something he simply did not have. It would also leave a trail, and if his unknown stalker did finally find him here, the note would only give them more confidence that they were on the right track.

No, he needed to leave, and now.

Sam quickly stepped down the stairs to the front door, and glanced back over his shoulder at the interior of the house. It had been his home for nearly four months, and he was sorry to leave it.

Damn Sabrina and her big mouth, he thought. *She didn't know any better, but dammit she spoiled everything.*

He shifted the bags and turned to leave, but as he did something caught his eye. He glanced down the stairs to the basement and saw that a light was on.

"Henry?" he called out, quieter this time.

Henry rarely spent time downstairs. It had been his wife's sewing room, and Sam was sure the memories inside that place hurt the old man too much. He could not help but wonder what reason Henry would have for spending time down there now.

"Henry, are you down there?"

Still no answer.

Sam set his bags on the landing in front of the door and stepped onto the first step toward the lower level. A knot formed in the pit of his stomach as a fear of the unknown reached up from the depths and gripped his heart. He slid his hand down the black iron railing as he descended the steps. The room below was silent.

"Henry, we need to talk," he called out, putting one foot in front of the other. "Something's come up."

He was now convinced that Henry was not in the basement. The man's hearing was poor, but not bad enough to explain how Sam's voice could go unheard from this distance. The light must have been left on earlier, before the old man left for his walk.

Sam reached the bottom of the steps and turned to the right. The room was directly beneath the living room, spanning the full length of its first-floor counterpart above. There was no light switch near the door, though. He was going to have to walk all the way to the back of the room and flick off the small lamp that would be sitting on the unused sewing table.

When he turned the corner and stepped toward the room, though, his blood froze instantly. The scene before him was unlike anything he had ever set eyes on. The feeling of horror and violation that he had felt upon finding his apartment in Benton vandalized, complete with the bloody message and the dead cat, were nothing in comparison to this new wave of fear.

Blood covered the carpet of the room in large irregular patches, staining the once pale taupe a deep crimson. The air closer to the room reeked of death and blood, but where it had come from was still unknown. Sam knew, though. Somehow, deep inside his gut he understood what had happened. He needed his eyes to tell him he was wrong. There had to be another explanation.

Oh God, he muttered under his breath. *It's worse than Benton. There's so much blood here. So much...*

He moved another step closer, his right foot almost touching the carpet at the threshold of the room, and then stopped. The door opened inward to the left, obscuring his view of the sewing desk and the lamp that would need to be turned off. That seemed oddly important to him now.

Henry wouldn't have left the lamp on. He'd want me to turn it off. It's a waste of electricity.

To the right, the room opened up before him. The blood that had pooled on the carpet was smeared in that direction, long dark ribbons of gore that led the eye in deeper. The stains were dark, but flecks of lighter material were scattered in them.

Bone? he wondered. *Skin? No, it's just a trick of the light. That can't be skin. Oh God, please don't be skin…*

The trail led his eyes to the body of Henry, who lay broken and torn apart against the front wall of the house. Like the cat in Benton, the old man had been gutted. A deep, vicious line ran up his torso from below the belt all the way to his neck. There, the killer had turned the blade and cut across the man's throat.

Or maybe they started there. Slashed first, then cut down. The thought chilled him to the bone. *God, it doesn't matter, does it? You need to get out of here, Sam.*

He knew it was true. His clock was ticking, the hands quickly approaching the end of his chance to escape. Whoever it was that had done this—*monster* might be the best term for them—would be back for him. That's why it had happened, after all. They had come for him and found Henry instead. It was Sam's fault, as far as he was concerned.

He glanced again at the elderly man who had given him a home so willingly. Henry's knuckles were torn and bloody, and Sam could not help but assume the man put up a fight. He thought back to the morning they first met at the Sunny Side and how defiant and courageous the man had been. In the face of an invader in his own home, Sam could envision Henry raising his cane and charging into battle. That was how things were done in his world.

Sam stepped into the room, careful to avoid the blood-stained patches that stared up at him like dead eyes, and moved closer to the body of Henry. One of his eyes was swelled shut from a blow to the face, the marks from which were still visible around it. The other, however, was still wide open. So wide, in fact, that it looked as if he were staring into a frightening scene.

He's the frightening scene, Sam thought. *Who would do this to another person? And why, in the name of all that is holy? Why?*

He knew why, though. This was a warning. He had been followed for years, and each time brought them closer to his trail. The warnings had become more violent, more bold and violating. But until Benton, it had never involved death and blood. This was new, though. Horrible and new.

He stepped close to Henry and squatted down. He knew the man could not be alive. Wounds as horrific as these were not something you survived, and the blood loss was too great. A man of Henry's age would barely survive a fall down the basement steps let alone injuries like these. Still, Sam wanted to be closer, just in case.

"I saved your life once," he said to the old man's body. "I saved you, and you rewarded me by bringing me home. I should have said no, Henry. When you brought me home, I brought your own death with me."

Sam sighed and forced himself to stand, scanning the floor for anything else that might tell him about what had happened here. A chair that once sat in the corner had been knocked over and he could see a smear of blood on the pale fabric of the seat. The bookshelf on the wall opposite the door had been knocked askew, and dozens of hardcover books lay scattered on the floor at its feet.

As he swept along the wall, his eyes were drawn toward the lamp. It was the only source of light in the room and the only reason he had come down in the first place. When he finally located it, though, he was shocked to find that it had been moved.

The long, curved metal adjustable neck had been bent upward to point the light at the wall behind the sewing desk. It was as if a spotlight had been trained on the most important clue of the entire scene. After Benton, he should have known to look for it sooner.

Another message.

Large, bloody letters had been painted across the wall, just as before. Three words, one over the other two, that spelled out the phrase SUSPECTA ET FORTIS. Sam had no idea what it meant, but he knew now was not the time to try and figure that out. He read it over and over, letting the words resonate inside his head, before remembering the notebook in his back pocket.

He found the page containing the message from his Benton apartment, drew a line beneath them, and then scribbled out a copy of this new phrase. Then, stowing the book back into his pocket, he turned to leave. It was more difficult than he had thought.

Seeing Henry across the room again, his body surrounded by bloody carpet and trails of gore, gave him one more kick to the stomach. He had been aware of the smell before stepping into the room, but the surprise of what he had found had pushed any thought of it from his mind. Now, with the scene fully taken in, the gruesome horror of what had happened here had fully set in.

He had never stayed long after finding clues that his stalker had found him. Even before they had resorted to violence he instinctively knew that it would not be good to stay. Finding out if they really were going to return for him was not something he wanted to do. So, each and every time, he had run.

This situation was no different, and the urgency to run washed over him like a tidal wave. He needed to leave this room—the house, even this very town—as soon as humanly possible. His truck was parked on the edge of the street and his bags were packed, ready to roll.

A minute later he was behind the wheel, putting distance between himself and Holden. Even though he held on to a dwindling hope that running would make a difference this time, if even for only a little while, Sam knew in his gut that this time was different. There was no escape for him now.

After twenty years, however, running was all he knew, and he was damn good at it.

CHAPTER SEVEN

SAM HAD DRIVEN EAST. At first he had nothing resembling a plan. About an hour from Holden he passed through the small city of Kankakee and stopped for gas and supplies. All he had managed to leave town with had been tossed into his two bags, but that had included a bundle of cash that he had been setting aside during his time working for Smitty.

The cash allowed him to move across the state without a trace. It was simple and easy and no one ever had to know his name. He did worry about keeping all of the cash he possessed in one place, though, so when he stopped he used the opportunity to split it up, keeping a portion in the bag, but also moving some to the glovebox and another bit in his wallet. He reminded himself to put some of it into his shoe when he stopped for the night.

That's if *I stop for the night,* he corrected himself. *It might be better to just drive and never stop.*

He was sitting in his idling truck with a flashlight in hand, looking over a map that he had pulled from a tourism display. He didn't know why, but every fiber of his being cried out to drive east. Beyond Illinois would be Indiana, then Ohio, and Pennsylvania. There would be plenty of small towns in that enormous area to find a place to live and start over. But that wasn't what Sam wanted to do this time.

Sam wanted to stop the cycle. He had moved from town to town for nearly twenty years now. The first few stays were long, multi-year stops. Each time he would make friends and grow roots. Eventually, though, he got used to the order of everything being interrupted, and learned to root more shallowly. But while that made it easy to relocate himself periodically, it also made it harder to grow and live.

There weren't violent threats or stalkers in the beginning. For a long time the only thing that drove him away from a town was the rare slip in judgment. His ability to see into the future at random times, or to know something about a total stranger, equipped him to be helpful if he managed it well. Mishandled, though, those action could brand him a pariah and signal the time for him to move on.

The advent of the internet caused his average time spent in one place to drop significantly. People communicated more quickly. Word spread faster. A simple, humble miracle that might have never gone noticed by anyone other than the person he helped soon became the grain of sand in the oyster of internet gossip.

The threats only began about five years before the events in Benton, Illinois. In the early day they took the form of letters that made it clear he—she? they? *it*?—knew something about Sam's abilities, and that he needed to stop using them. What he did for these people was *bad*, and should never happen again.

Sam ignored the messages, and over the years they had grown more and more angry and aggressive. The cat in Benton, however, was a line that had not been crossed until that night. Of course, Henry was worse. It was escalating, that much was clear, and Sam knew that the only thing worse than the death of a friend was his own. The game had changed, and now his very life was at stake.

It took that heightened level of risk to push Sam to consider his only remaining option. He had avoided home for decades. Not since the fire had he considered returning to Hollesley—the fire that had destroyed his home and claimed the lives of his parents as well as his younger brother. Not since the morning of the memorial service had Sam set foot in the town his family had lived in for nearly three centuries. That day twenty years ago had been dark and wet, and he allowed his emotions to drive him away from the source of his pain. He simply packed his bags and left, no word of warning or letter of good-bye to his few friends. Just flight.

If he was honest with himself, he would admit that he had been running ever since that day. He never thought of it in those terms, of course, but it had been escapism nonetheless. Only now, in retrospect, did he truly see it for what it was.

Even still, returning home wasn't an option he felt completely comfortable with. It was a destination loaded with deep pain and too many dark memories. Even after decades away, he knew returning would feel like jabbing a finger into a row of fresh stitches. He had avoided that pain as long as he could.

Time, it seems, had caught up with him, and now the road literally pointed toward home. Even now he could not help but think of it as that—*home*. There wasn't really anything left there for him to return to, but that didn't mean it wasn't the place he grew up and lived without a care in the world. And so, while he might find it easy and rote to believe that he no longer had friends, the truth was that there might still be someone back home who could help him.

So Sam drove east. From Kankakee he connected with Interstate 57 and took that north to Bremen where he joined I-80. It had been years since he had travelled along that major highway, but he found the frequent rest stops and added traffic comforting. He could blend in, vanish into the crowd, and focus on the drive.

That did not mean he had eluded his pursuers. He was confident that they were most likely already on the highway somewhere behind him. He believed that as thoroughly as he believed in his need to drive to Massachusetts. They would follow him there, of course, but he hoped that his destination offered more hope than the middle of nowhere.

Sam did not feel safe, but he doubted he would any time soon. He had just left the home of a friend who had been disemboweled by an attacker that really wanted to find *him*. That was reason enough to be afraid. For now, though, he would be able to set aside that fear and focus on something more therapeutic: a never-ending series of fuel stops, food breaks, and hundreds of miles of black pavement that would lead him ever closer to home.

The exit ramp south of Mercer was barren as Sam guided his truck off the highway. In the dark, the long stretch of pavement felt like like a runway, and he hoped it would lead him to a gas station. He had refueled back near Youngstown, but soon after crossing the border into Pennsylvania his bladder warned him that it was nearly full. He had been drinking far too much coffee for his own good in order to stay awake, and it had taken its toll on him.

Like it or not, he was stopping here.

He turned onto the north-bound road from the exit ramp and began to lean forward in his seat, straining to locate the glowing sign of a gas station. He didn't expect much, but he was hoping for a reasonably clean bathroom. Finally, after rounding a curve, he saw light ahead bleeding through a line of trees.

There, he thought. *Big red sign with glowing numbers. That's the ticket.*

Sam spilled into the parking lot and slowly circled the small brick building. He found the bathroom on the far side and parked in the dark near the door. He switched off the truck, climbed out, locked up, and then stretched. He had spent a long time in that seat and his back was angry at him for it. Considering how much farther he had to travel, he was sure it would only get worse.

Sam reached for the long, curved metal door handle, turned it sideways, and pushed. He expected the door to be locked, requiring a key that would most likely be chained to a small brick or some other oddly-shaped object. Instead, it swung inward easily, revealing his worst road trip nightmare: a flickering fluorescent bulb buzzing high above a filthy toilet and small sink.

Sam sighed and stepped in, closing the door behind himself. The mirror over the faucet had been shattered long ago, and there were enough words scrawled with black ink on the painted brick walls to fill a small book. The fixture above him sounded like a bug light, humming and buzzing with each pulse of artificial light. He could hear his breathing echo off the walls, giving the small room a cavernous feeling. Deep within his heart he wanted to leave the room as quickly as he could manage.

Across the bathroom from the entrance was another metal door, painted the same color as the wall. There was no knob that Sam could see, but he assumed it was used by staff when they needed to clean the room. How often they did that, though, was a mystery. Sam eyed the door for a moment before walking over to the toilet and standing over it to empty his bladder.

When he was finished, he flushed the toilet by tapping the metal lever with one foot, and then stepped over to the sink. He pulled a piece of toilet paper free and used it to turn the handles on the faucet, but the water that came out was brown and sputtering and so he decided to skip that step. He was far from a germaphobe, but he was not about to take any chances inside this bathroom.

Outside the air was cool and crisp. Sam checked his watch and decided he needed to restock his supply of food and coffee if he hoped to make it to sunrise alive. He wasn't hungry now, but he remembered from his move to the Midwest long ago that Pennsylvania had a tendency to feel like it was a thousand miles across from east to west.

Something crunchy might help him stay awake through the endless miles of forest.

He walked around the corner and headed toward the front of the gas station. Like most along the interstate, this one had a small convenience store inside, and a register where you could pay for your gas and snacks. It didn't look huge, but it would have to do.

"Evening," the clerk at the counter mumbled as he stepped through the door. The woman, who appeared to be about seventy-five pounds over weight and completely unhappy to be there, never even looked up from her magazine. Sam ignored her and headed toward the small cooler at the back of the shop to find something cold and filled with caffeine.

He saw the headlights in the reflection of the glass door of the drink cooler and squinted through the glare to find a suitable beverage. Only after he opened the door and pulled out three bottles—something with a green label that was covered in lightning bolts—did he turn around and notice the car.

It had parked directly in front of the store, headlights pointed into the building through the windows. No one had exited the car, though, and so Sam studied if for a moment from where he stood behind the tall rack of snack foods. That was when recognition coursed through his body like electricity.

A new sedan with tinted windows. That's the car from outside Henry's house!

He ducked instinctively, dropping the bottles on the floor where they scattered and rolled away. They had found him. Somehow, against the odds, his stalker had managed to not only follow him but also catch up. Sam was cornered, and as all of these realizations struck him, he panicked.

He couldn't stand still, though. That was how people got caught. Movement would buy him some options, and possibly raise the odds. Right now, though, those odds were looking pretty slim.

He swallowed hard, fighting the nervousness and panic that threatened to rise up and take control of his mind, and then began to crawl away from the end of the aisle, putting distance between himself and the front of the store.

But then what? he asked himself. *Where am I going to go? I'm cornered. Shit!*

Sam looked around at the interior of the store again, taking in every little detail, all the pieces he missed when he strolled in moments before. His mind had been exhausted and stretched, but now that adrenaline was coursing through his body, everything was popping out at him.

The low rumble of the car's motor outside the glass door.

The high ceiling and their bright fluorescent lights.

The dark corridor between the two drink coolers.

Where does that go? he wondered. *That might be my only option.*

He crawled to the end of the aisle closest to the center of the store and carefully peeked around the corner. The car was still there, idling in its parking spot with the headlights illuminating the front of the building. Sam glanced up at the corners of the ceiling, and then over to the fat woman absorbed in her magazine.

No video cameras, he decided. *Good.*

He glanced one more time toward the front of the store and what he saw froze his heart. Both doors had opened and two pairs of feet were swinging out onto the pavement. They were coming after him.

Run, fool! he thought, crawling backwards as quietly as he could before turning to bolt down the hall.

"Evening," Sam heard the fat woman mumble.

He was almost out of time. He stood up from his crouched position and ran down the short hallway. Five strides brought him to a small room lined on two sides by tall stacks of cardboard boxes. Brand names were stamped on most of them, but Sam skipped over then, scanning the room for a hiding place or some tool that might help him.

Then he saw it.

The sound of a voice brought him out of his thoughts, along with the sound of footsteps. He knew at least one of the strangers was headed his way, but he had no idea if both of the occupants of the car had actually entered the front of the store. For all he knew, one of them had circled around to the back to cut off his only means of escape. It would be the smart thing to do, at least.

Of course they did, he thought. *How many exits are there in this place. I'm probably heading exactly where they expected.*

Sam no longer had time to think. He bolted as fast as he could toward the back of the room. There was a door there, as well as a second one near it on the side wall. In the corner between both of them was a yellow plastic bucket on casters, the wooden handle of a mop jutting out of it and leaning against the brick wall. Sam grabbed the long shaft of the mop and turned to fight.

That's when his internal compass finally did the math. Ahead of him was the hallway, which pointed directly at the front of the store. To his left was the door on the side wall —the same side of the building where the bathroom had been located. Only this side of the door had a handle.

Sam saw shadows—more than one, he was certain this time—in the hall and knew he needed to act. As quietly as he could, he gripped the door handle and pulled. The familiar buzzing sound of the bathroom fluorescents greeted him, and he slipped in as fast is he was able. Without hesitation he crossed the room, pulled open the exterior door, and rushed out into the dark parking lot.

The night air felt exhilarating in his lungs. He could hear shouting somewhere behind him, echoing off brick and tile. Glancing down at the mop still clutched in his hands, he knew what he needed to do.

Sam turned and slid the long wooden shaft of the mop through the curved door handle. There was nothing on the exterior wall to rest the stick on, but it hung at an angle that still allowed it to catch against the frame of the door. Almost immediately after he let go, the door shook and clattered. Someone on the other side shouted angrily and pounded against it, but the mop handle held firm.

He didn't know who they were, but for the moment, they were trapped between the outer door he had barred, and the inner door which no handle. It would only be a matter of time before the fat cashier caught up to them and opened the inner door, but until then, Sam had the advantage.

He dashed to his truck, pulled the keys free from his pocket, and struggled to unlock the door. He managed to drop the keys almost at once, and then fumble in the dark for a few more heartbeats while he tried to get the right one into the lock. All the while, the pounding and shouting continued.

Finally, he unlocked the door and climbed it. Food and drink would have to wait. He keyed the ignition and shifted into reverse. A moment later, he was back on the road.

He drove the mile south to the entrance ramp to I-80 as fast as he could, but his intuition screamed at him just before he made the turn to get on the highway. They would expect him to continue his present course. He had spent hours on this highway, and he had stopped in the middle of nowhere. His most likely choice would obviously be to get back onto the familiar route.

Sam was not about to give them the advantage. Not after such a narrow escape, and not after so many years of staying one step ahead of them. No, he needed to think his way to safety, and turning east now was not going to do that.

Instead, he stayed on the road. He would take it south until he hit another large highway, no matter how long it took, and only then would he head east. It meant more time behind the wheel, sure, but it also meant taking a path that his pursuers would have a difficult time guessing. It would buy him precious distance, and distance was the same thing as time when you were on the run.

CHAPTER EIGHT

TWELVE HOURS LATER, SAM found himself north of Boston, curving eastward along Route 128. He had driven all night with only three stops for fuel and food, and had managed to avoid his pursuers successfully. In fact, there was no evidence that they discovered his alternate route at all. No dark sedan with tinted windows in his rear-view mirror, and certainly no further encounters at small town gas stations.

Sam took in the familiar scenery, along with all that was different. The last time he had driven this route had been the spring of 1994, and while parts of it remained unchanged, much of it was vastly altered by decades of growth. More traffic, more buildings, and more to think about and avoid.

For most of the morning, Sam had been contemplating what his destination should be. When he left Holden the day before, all he knew was that he needed to go home. Something about the place he grew up, the area that his family had called home for three centuries, beckoned him, like a lover waving from across a grassy field. He did not yet know why, but something in his gut told him that it was more than just a notion. It was an imperative delivered from the same mysterious source that generated his visions of the future.

The visions. It had all started with the visions two decades before, right here in New England. That was the first time a vision urged him to go home, only what he found was vastly different than anything he could see today. All because of the fire.

Sam passed the exit for Danvers and began to watch for the sign with Hollesley listed. A lump had formed in his stomach, giving off equal feelings of anticipation and fear. He was going home, and he knew even before getting there that it would not all be good. So much had changed. It always did. No one was ever really able to go home.

The exit appeared on the horizon just as it always had. Even after decades, the familiarity of it was shocking. As a whole, New England had changed over the years, but parts of it—and this included the North Shore—were more resistant to that change. Some towns refused to allow chain restaurants to set up business, especially in neighborhoods where the average age of the homes was at least as old as the United States, if not older.

Sam's view down the highway toward the exit that would take him home was equally unchanged. The shape of the tree line, the enormous granite outcroppings along the highway, and the flashes of white birch among the dark pines; seeing it all was like hearing a song he once loved but had forgotten about.

The only difference so far that he could see was that the old Clements mill, usually visible through a gap in the trees that separated the highway from the town of Hollesley, was missing. Sam was not surprised; the mill had been unsafe for decades. The year before he left New England, a teenage boy had died in an accident there. It was sad to not see the familiar bulk of the building off in the distance, but he understood why it might be gone.

Sam took the exit and turned left, following the road into town. The trees were thick here, in some places within just a few feet of the pavement. Long, ancient stone walls lined other portions of the drive, and he passed a good number of first-period homes, some of which dated to the mid-1600's. They each sat at an angle to the road, and his eyes soaked in their weathered clapboard siding and austere architecture like a thirsty man. It had been too long.

Crossing the Hollesley River answered any question he might have had about the mill. What had once been a tall, red-brick structure resting along the edge of the water like a sentinel was now a pile of rubble accented with yellow safety tape. From the bridge he could see three or four small sections of exterior wall that had refused to fall, but the rest was nothing more than a ruin of stone and wood.

More than I can expect to find at my home, though.

Home for Sam was on the west side. It was the oldest part of the town, dating back to the tail end of the Seventeenth Century when it was settled by a small group of people from Salem. It had been ancestors on both sides of his family, maternal as well as fraternal, that had been part of the group of colonists who moved north and broke ground on the community that would eventually become Hollesley. If he was to believe some of the stories his father told him, they had been on the run too.

Always running, he mused.

Sam turned at the first traffic light and headed west. The portion of downtown that he passed through was both familiar and alien. The images he had in his mind of Hollesley seemed more vivid and alive. Everything seemed to have diminished, becoming a lesser version of the town he had grown up in. To be back after all these years, to see what had become of the town he once loved, was painfully romantic. It was still here, but it was less of itself. Faded and tired.

He wondered if it seemed that way to those who still lived here. Or did the high school seniors down the road still think of this place as the pinnacle of New England life, full of hope and opportunity? It was all a matter of perspective, of course, but Sam knew that it wasn't just his memories that had drifted from the town he knew in 1994. It was truly, painfully different.

Salem Road was one of the intersections along Main Street, and Sam felt as if he could make the turn with his eyes closed. He had driven it in the heat of summer and in the bitter cold of winter. He had memories of taking the turn too quickly in the middle of the night, and lazily rounding the corner with his parents after a long, fun day in Boston.

It was a road that led straight into his past, into the memories that he still clung to after all these years. Driving down it now caused the knot in his gut to twist and sharpen, knowing full well that in less than a minute he would be standing outside what was once his family's home. Land they had owned for generations.

Sam rounded the last curve and looked to his left. The trees were the same as they had always been, towering and broad along the edge of the property. The old wall that separated the road from the rest of the yard remained mostly intact, save for the occasional fallen stone that lay in the long grass. Beyond the wall, though, there was a hole in Sam's memories.

The lot was empty. No one had rebuilt on the land. He didn't even know who owned the property now. The vast majority of the debris from the fire had been hauled off and disposed of long ago. Pulling through the space in the stone wall that had once been the driveway, Sam knew that it was all gone, all changed.

He parked and exited the truck, but left it running. There was no point in staying long, what with nothing here to greet him but overgrown grass and a few weathered pieces of stone from the foundation. His heart was not about to let him leave without walking across that grass one last time, however. This is where he had been raised; this is where his life seemingly ended so many years before.

Sam stepped away from the truck and walked toward what would have been the old gravel path to the house. Decades of weeds and the elements had all but erased the walkway, but to his experienced eyes it was still there, guiding him toward the house porch.

The faded trail ended at a long, flat piece of concrete that had once been the sole step leading up to a low wooden porch. The step had settled into the soil over the years, and now sat like a capsizing ship, tilting hard to port. He set his foot on it for a moment, feeling the firmness of that stone beneath his foot.

It wasn't magical, but he certainly never thought he would set foot on any part of his old home ever again. He did it for the same reason an elderly man might kiss a photo of his deceased spouse. They had once been close, but now that was gone.

Stepping over the concrete block, Sam walked into what would have been the house. The old fieldstone foundation had been filled in over the years by debris and rain-washed silt, and now it existed only as a sunken depression in a field of weeds and wild flowers. He could picture it all, though, and closed his eyes to see it again. The kitchen, the stairs leading up to his room, the living room where his family gathered and spent time after dinner. Even the hallway, filled with the light from the setting sun through a small stained glass window.

He sighed and circled the foundation, heading toward the road and moving in a counter-clockwise direction. On what would have been the front yard, he stopped, remembering the original door that opened into the dining room. The ground was bare here, as if someone had walked across it hundreds of times, and Sam stared at it.

Then the vision came.

Not a vision of the future, but of the past. It had been during his sophomore year of college, away at Keene State in southern New Hampshire. His spring semester was full of courses in the American History degree path, and though the classes were challenging, he had been managing to keep his head above water.

Sam had always been the sort of student who chose late-night study sessions over parties with friends, and as a result, he made frequent trips to the convenience store across from the southern corner of campus to buy snacks and caffeinated beverages. That's where he was when he had his very first vision.

He could still remember the cashier's face. Tall and skinny with long blonde hair, the man was a student, although Sam had never shared a classroom with him. He had one of those small patches of facial hair just below the bottom lip, the kind of thing a guy did when he was too timid to get his lip pierced. And, of course, he always smelled of pot, like a cloud that followed him from place to place.

"Dude," the cashier had intoned from across the counter that night, "did you hear about Cobain?"

Sam remembered shaking his head as he set his purchase on the counter. "I'm more of a Pearl Jam fan, myself. More refined. What did he do this time?"

"Blew his fucking face off," the man replied while he keyed each item into the register. "It's all over the news, dude. Just fucking *offed* himself. Who the hell does that? Five-seventy, please."

Sam had shrugged, pulling his wallet out to find the cash he needed. "Must have had issues, man," he replied. "You know how fame can get to people. Everybody wants to make it big, but I don't think everyone can handle it."

"Dude," the cashier said with the kind of wide-eyed stare that only a recent toke on a joint could produce, "that's profound."

Sam remembered picking up his things, smiling at the cashier, and then leaving. Outside, the only light came from a tall street lamp at the corner, and he passed beneath it on his way to the crosswalk that led back to campus. The air was crisp for a spring evening, and the sky was clear.

The moment Sam stepped off the sidewalk and into the grass at the edge of the streetlight, his head exploded with pain. The bag in his hands fell to the lawn and he quickly followed, landing on his knees with his hands on either side of his head. He remembered that it felt less intense with his eyes closed, but the throbbing never truly let up.

Hands pressed to his temples and eyes closed, Sam was thrown into world of fire. The vision was beyond real. It wasn't a hallucination or a dream; this was a full-blown vision, as if a projectionist were beaming a feature film directly into his brain. Surrounding everything he could see were walls of flame, complete with crackling sounds and waves of unbearable heat.

Sam could not remember how long he knelt there in the grass on the edge of campus that night, but when the vision finally released him he was trembling with fear. The flames were wrapped around the image of a home, *his* home. And hidden in among the cacophony of sounds were the voices of his own family, crying out in agony.

He ran back to his dorm. He only knew that because he could remember trying to call home from the phone on his desk. If he thought back to that moment, he could still feel his heart thumping in his chest, even after two decades. The fact that no one answered didn't help him, either.

The drive from Keene to Hollesley normally took Sam two and a half hours, but that night he had managed it in just under two. His truck had been brand new back then, and panic had pushed caution out the window, making for a fast journey.

Not fast enough for Sam, though. No speed could have been, honestly. He needed to get home as fast as possible, and the wait had been maddening to endure. Sometimes, though, he wished he had never driven home that night, that he had simply ignored the vision and gone on with his life.

Hindsight is always a dangerous portal to view life through. However much he would like to change the past, it would never be possible. Reliving it was all he could do, even though that also meant regretting it and second guessing himself.

Sam had arrived, much as he did today, but driving down the driveway to his childhood home. Then, though, he was greeted by a massive fire that had engulfed the house. All of the windows that he could see from the driveway had already blown out, and tentacles of flame were lashing out, grasping at the sides of the building.

He had arrived too late.

He remembered screaming. He remembered running as close as he could get to the burning house until waves of dry heat slapped at his face. And he remembered seeing no one else by the light of the fire.

No one, that is, except for his father.

The man who had raised him, who had taken him to little league games and coached his soccer team for years during grade school, was crawling out of the wreckage of the house. His hair was on fire, and the skin of his arms and neck were already blackened when Sam found him, but regardless of his injuries he was crawling. He had somehow managed to open the front door and was moving, inch by inch, across the grass just beyond the flames.

Sam remembered standing over his father for a long, horrible moment before the dying man looked up and recognized him. His hands were red with burns, but he held something up between them.

"Sammy," he had said, though it was more of a rasp than anything else. It was as if life was literally leaking out of him as he spoke. "Saved this…you…take it…please… Roger."

It had been a wooden box. *The* wooden box.

Sam could remember seeing it on a shelf in his father's study. It had never been opened in his presence as far as he remembered, but it sat in a place of importance. There were other small objects on display on those shelves —a couple of old photographs, an antique Bible, a handful of family heirlooms—but none of them had ever seemed as important to his father as the box.

He would not have been able to tell anyone why he felt that way about it. Even today, decades later and with a lifetime of memories and pain behind him, it was still a mystery. But that night, by the light of his burning home, his father had managed to save the box and pass it to him with his final, dying breath.

Sam kicked a foot at the patch of dirt and grass where his father died and fought the urge to scream. He still had the box. It had moved with him from town to town all across the Midwest for years. Not because he wanted it, or even because he knew what was inside it, but because his father asked him to take it.

He didn't say good-bye, or tell Sam he loved him. No, his father had simply lifted up a box and told him to take it. Now Sam had no one left. No father, no mother, and no brother. Everyone had been taken by the fire. All he had left was the box.

His shoulders slumped and he exhaled deeply with resignation. He knew it wouldn't help to dwell on it, that his current troubles were much more urgent and pressing. Still, it wasn't a simple matter to just box up his memories. He had to try, but it would not be easy.

It had been years since he had relived it, but thinking back now, he was amazed that he had forgotten the mention of Roger. As he walked back to his truck, Sam began to think through the list of family friends he had known before the fire. He had no extended family to speak of, and at this point he assumed all of his childhood friends had grown up and moved away. But Roger had always been there.

Roger Sandbrook had been a friend of his family for many years. Sam could still remember photographs of holidays during his early childhood, and it had been common for Roger to be in many of them. Though he'd really been a friend of his father's, Roger had done an admirable job of playing the role of surrogate uncle to Sam and his brother Jason, who had been two years younger.

It was Roger who had offered to help him after the fire, but Sam hadn't been in a place to listen, let alone accept it. He said things that, in retrospect, he deeply regretted, but it became nearly impossible to make things right after he put a thousand miles between himself and Hollesley.

In his pain and anguish he had driven Roger away, and with him one final chance to make it through the tragedy intact. Instead of leaning on that friendship, he had thrown it away. Now, twenty years later, he couldn't help but wonder if Roger might still be around.

Sam knew what he needed to do. He had to apologize. He needed to reconnect. Most importantly, however, Sam needed help. Roger Sandbrook might very well be his only hope.

CHAPTER NINE

SALEM WAS ALIVE WITH traffic and springtime colors. As Sam approached from the Beverly side of the Ayube Bridge, he could see the North River cutting into the green landscape to his right, and a sea of white sails to his left just off Tuck Point. After a brief pass between a residential neighborhood and the river, the road curved inland and became Bridge Street. It was along that street that old Salem began to show itself.

Sam knew Salem nearly as well as he did Hollesley. To grow up on the North Shore of Boston was to grow up in the shadow of Salem, no matter where you lived. With a past more nuanced and rich than most cities in the nation, it held an attraction for a myriad of people. Some traveled there daily for work, while others for tourism, but what kept people there was the atmosphere.

Salem was beautiful, all dressed in old red brick, black shutters, and weathered copper. Sam turned his truck off Bridge onto Washington and was instantly reminded of the buzz of activity that swarmed within the maze of centuries-old buildings. Pedestrians crossed the street at every intersection and cars pulled in and out of parking places along the street.

Although he had long ago forgotten what address Roger Sandbrook lived at in Salem, he knew the street, and that would be enough. Sam took Essex westward, passing the Salem Public Library, before taking a quick left onto Flint and another quick left onto Chestnut. It was here, somewhere along this short stretch of historic real estate, that he remembered Roger owning a home.

Chestnut was breathtakingly beautiful. Sam remembered reading once that it was the most photographed street in America. He didn't know how true that was, but one drive down it was enough to sell most people on the notion. Nearly every home was a masterpiece of federal architecture, with flat red-brick walls and white columns and trim. Black shutters flanked every window, and it was easy to see how a walk down those brick sidewalks might transport a person back in time.

What Sam *did* remember was that Roger had moved to the area already wealthy at a young age, and had managed to find a home on the right side of the street, about halfway down. To live on Chestnut was a dream for many people, but only those with perfect timing and the finances to back it up managed to achieve that goal. Roger somehow arrived at the right time with a bank account large enough to unlock the door.

Sam pulled off to the side of the street and parked in an open space—a rarity anywhere in Salem, even here—and looked around at the homes. A dozen or so yards ahead, between one residence that had been painted entirely white and another with classic New England wood siding, he saw it. The large home was set far back from the street, its stately white columns flanking a glossy charcoal gray door beneath the portico. Even the granite steps looked familiar to him.

Of course, Sam wasn't even sure Roger still lived in Salem. If he didn't, then Sam was out of luck. He literally had no one else to whom he could turn. And if there was anything he needed at this very moment it was someone to help him. He was not yet certain just how much of his own story he was willing to share with his old friend, but he knew that before anything else, he needed to make sure the man was still here.

Sam locked the truck and headed down the sidewalk toward the house. It was three stories tall and every bit impressive as a court house or library. The yard was separated from the walk by a tall iron fence, the decorative points managing to appear both menacing and classical, and beyond it the lawn was well cared for and vividly green. There was no name on the mailbox, but that did not surprise him at all. Most residents of the street chose not to advertise their identity. Adding a name to a wealthy owner was akin to placing a target on him or her.

Sam mounted the steps quickly and approached the door. It was just as he remembered it, with its rectangular panels and ancient iron handle that had recently been painted a glossy black. There was no doorbell that he could find, but the old wood of the door looked to be well-used, so he settled for rapping on it twice with his knuckles.

He felt certain that no one would be home. It was nearly 1:00 PM on a Thursday afternoon after all, a time when most people would be at work. Nevertheless, he waited expectantly.

He decided to count to thirty, and if no one answered the door before then, he would leave and rethink his plans. At the twenty-eight mark he saw movement in one of the windows off to his left, and something inside his chest tightened.

What if Roger doesn't live here anymore? he worried. *What if he* does, *and he doesn't remember me? I'm about to impose on someone I haven't seen in two decades...is this even appropriate?*

He had no answers for his own questions, but the door opened before he could slip farther into self-doubt. The man who stood holding it open was tall and slim, his salt-and-pepper hair swept off to the side above a pair of black-framed glasses. He was smartly dressed in nice slacks, with a maroon sweater over his gingham dress shirt. And he was smiling.

"Samuel Hawthorne," he quietly announced. "My God, Sam, is it really you?"

Relief washed over him. "Hi, Roger," he managed to say in reply. "Yeah, it's me."

———— ∞∞∞ ————

Roger had set out tea and they were seated at a small table in one corner of his kitchen. Afternoon light was pouring in through a window nearby and classical music was emanating from some other part of the house. The two men had talked for over two hours, catching up on as much as they could. Roger was the one with the most questions, though.

Sam spread his hands apart, palms up, and shrugged. "I guess I never really thought about coming home until now," he replied.

The older man smiled warmly at him. He still looked slightly amazed at Sam's appearance, and his eyes had yet to lose their wide, open appearance. The man was shocked, and clearly happy.

"So, tell me what you've been up to, Sam," he asked. "It's been, what, twenty years?"

Sam nodded. "Yep, twenty years since—" but he broke off before he could finish it, choosing instead to look down at his cup of hot tea.

Roger's smile remained intact, but it seemed less genuine now, like the smile of someone trying to be encouraging in the face of bad news.

"I know," he said. "Those were hard times, for both of us."

Sam waited to let the moment pass before going back to Roger's question. "I traveled around," he replied. "Mostly through the Midwest. Learned a few skills, put them to use, and moved around a lot."

"What sort of work were you doing?"

"Carpentry," he said. "It was usually new constructions, but I occasionally found myself doing odd repairs and handyman work."

Sam was reminded of Henry and the door that he repaired just a few months ago, and that brought in a fresh wave of sadness. Roger didn't seem to notice it this time, something Sam was thankful for.

"No girlfriend or wife or family to speak of, though?"

"Nope," Sam replied. "I'm not sure I could handle the commitment. Besides, I moved around too often to really take root in any one place."

"Why is that?" Roger asked.

Why indeed, Sam thought. *That's a question I'm not sure I can answer completely.*

"It was hard to...fit in," he replied. "I have issues, I guess you could say."

"Issues?" Roger echoed back. "What, are you an alcoholic? On drugs? Trouble with the law? What could possibly prevent you from settling down for two whole decades, Sam?"

"It's complicated," he replied dismissively. "Give me some time to sort things out and I'll tell you what I can."

"Fair enough," Roger replied. "But you're well, right? Healthy and happy?"

Sam nodded. "No complaints," he lied. "But I recently started to miss home, you know? I needed a change of pace, and coming back here sounded like a good idea. I think it was time."

"Well you certainly took your own sweet time getting back for a visit," Roger said with a smile. "But I'm glad you did, Sam. Really, I'm very pleased to see you again. I've never felt as if you and I parted ways in the right frame of mind. Grief can twist our minds and our actions. I know it did mine."

Sam shifted the conversation away from himself, trying to buy some time for him to figure out exactly what he wanted to share with his old friend.

"What about you?" he asked. "What have you been up to for the last twenty years?"

Roger leaned back in his chair. "Well, when I moved here from California thirty-some years ago, I was fresh out of grad school and looking for a college to teach at."

"Grad school," Sam interrupted. "How the heck did you afford this house, then?"

"I inherited young," Roger replied with a smile. "It's more complicated than that, but needless to say I had a wealthy father who didn't want his hard work eaten up by inheritance taxes, and he got creative. But that didn't change the fact that I really, truly wanted to teach. With a graduate degree in American History, nothing made more sense than to move out here.

"Boston is essentially one massive college town, when you get right down to it. I looked there for a while, but finally settled here in Salem. The historical significance of this city was too tempting of a prospect to miss out on."

"So how did you meet my parents?" Sam asked.

"It was a genealogy club of sorts," the older man replied. "I met Matthew—sorry, your *father*—the first year I was here. He and your mother were very welcoming people, and they must have recognized how out of place and alone I was at the time because they took me under their wing and gave me a family."

"Other than my family, though, you've not started one of your own? Even after all this time?"

"No," Roger replied wistfully. "I think that ship has sailed, I'm afraid. I'm married to my work now. What began as an internship back then has led to me becoming the chair of the History department at Salem State. I stay incredibly busy with my work there, as well as side projects and personal research."

"That's fantastic," Sam said. "I'm surprised I even found you at home, then. Sounds like you spend a lot of time on campus."

"Not at all," Roger chuckled. "I've managed to build a schedule that's incredibly flexible. I do most of my office work from here, and only go to campus to teach two courses each week and attend a handful of meetings. The school pays me to research and grow the field of American History. Don't ask me why, but they apparently think I'm smart or something."

Sam couldn't help but grin back at his old friend. It felt good to be reunited, and he hoped that it would lead to many changes. First on his list, however, was his present situation, if he could decide how to bring it up.

"Sam, what really brought you home?"

He felt his stomach knot up at the sound of the question. It was insightful and cut to the chase. Roger's face didn't show signs of anger or disapproval, but his brow was bent in a concerned, sympathetic manner. Sam felt his resolve melt.

"It's complicated, Roger," he said, burying his face in his hands with a sigh. "There's a lot I don't know, or understand, but what I *do* know is confusing and frightening."

"God, Sam, what could possibly be that bad?" Roger's question was innocent enough.

"I have a stalker," Sam replied. "Someone has been following me for a few years. I move, they find me. It's a game they play, and I've grown tired of it so I've moved back home."

"Well, that's certainly creepy, but I'm not sure how it could be frightening."

"I get death threats," Sam replied.

"For what?" Roger asked. "Did you hurt someone, or break a social rule or something subversive?"

Sam shook his head. "No, nothing like that." He paused. *How much should I say? Most people don't claim to be clairvoyant.* "I have a bad habit of trying to help people, and that typically leads to too much attention, attention that seems to draw the eye of this stalker."

Roger tilted his head to the side slightly. "You're being awfully cryptic, Sam. I'm not sure I understand."

"I know," he replied. "It's all I can say for right now. But I'm being honest when I say that I've broken no laws.

I'm simply the target of a hate crime, someone angry enough about something that they're trying to find me and kill me."

"*Kill* you?" Roger was visibly shocked. "Sam, that's big. Have you gone to the police?"

"With what? Stories of dark sedans following me? Break-ins where nothing was taken? No, I've got nothing to show for it."

Almost nothing, he thought. *There was Henry, of course.*

Roger forced a smile and opened his hands. "How can I help?"

"Can I stay here for a while, at least until I find a place of my own and get my feet on the ground?"

"Absolutely," Roger replied. "Given the circumstances, I'm not sure I want you moving out any time soon, though. There's safety in numbers, after all." He offered a warm grin.

"Thanks, Roger," he replied. "And do you have a garage? It might be good to get my truck off the street for a few days. Just in case."

"Wow, you think they followed you all the way out here from...where were you last at?"

"Holden, a small town in central Illinois," Sam replied. He wondered almost immediately if he should have done it, but he needed to trust someone. If he couldn't trust Roger, he was up the proverbial creek without a paddle.

"That's a long way to follow someone, no matter how angry they might be at you."

"Yeah, but I'm positive they're looking for me," Sam replied. "I had a run-in with them in Pennsylvania last night on the way out here. I literally had to lock them in a gas station bathroom and make a run for it."

Roger's eyes opened wide.

"Long story," Sam said, holding up a hand to stop his friend from asking more questions. "I'm fine, but it's only a matter of time before they find me. They always do."

Roger stood up and looked at his watch. "Alright," he said. "Dinner is in an hour. Let's go move your truck and get your things. Do you have bags?"

"Just a couple," Sam said with a nod. "I can handle them."

"Fair enough," the older man smiled. "Well, I can't say you've arrived under the most clear circumstances, but I look forward to learning more and helping out in any way I can."

Sam nodded and followed his friend outside. After some automobile shuffling, they managed to get Roger's BMW out and onto the street so that the truck could be pulled into the safety of the garage. Once his own car was back in the drive, they both took a bag and headed inside.

Roger led Sam to a large bedroom on the second floor, across the hall from a bathroom. It was warm and inviting, with a high ceiling and beautiful craftsmanship in every detail. He couldn't help but think even Cesar would be impressed.

"Can you think of anything else you might need?" Roger asked before he left to manage dinner.

Sam shook his head. "No," he said with a smile. "This is absolutely perfect. Again, thank you Roger. You're being very generous with your time and home. I really appreciate this."

"Just to have you back is reason enough, Sam," the man replied, flashing his white teeth. "I'll see you in a bit."

———— ∞∞∞ ————

That night, long after dinner and more conversation, Sam dreamed again of fire.

He didn't know where he was, but the air was wet and dark, save for the glow of a fire somewhere in his periphery. He could smell damp earth, there was a bitting sensation in his wrists, and his senses were telling him that he was positioned on his side.

Fire burned somewhere beyond the top of his head, but the orange glow shimmered on the wet grass and dirt. There were trees, far too many to count, but looking toward the sky revealed a field of stars.

A clearing?

There were voices, too, but they were nothing more than murmurs, seemingly miles away. Sam tried to stand up, but it felt as if the world were pressing down on him. He twisted and rolled and craned his neck for a view of the fire. The pain that cut at his wrists and feet was blinding as he moved.

He finally saw it, though; a tall beacon of orange light a dozen or so yards away. Dark shapes moved around in the background beyond the reach of the fire's light, and as he watched it flicker and waver in the night air, another shape approached from the side.

Not a figure, no. It was many. At least three, and they dragged something long and writhing behind them with great effort. Sam could feel his mouth stretching to scream, but no sound came out. He strained against his numb, unresponsive body and cried out at the figures approaching the fire, but nothing worked like it should.

Whoever they were, they reached the edge of the light and stopped before turning around to grab hold of the thing that twisted and thrashed on the ground. Then, as the object was lifted up and the figures tipped on one end toward the fire, Sam screamed one final time before everything went black.

A moment later he was sitting up, and something cold and wet was pressed against his bare chest. His heart thumped rapidly, driven by primal fear, while his eyes scoured the darkness for some sign of the fire or mysterious figures.

A moment later, he realized where he was: the guest room in Roger's house.

He ran a hand through his hair before closing his eyes and forcing himself to calm down. His wrists still burned, and he could almost smell the wet soil and woodland decay in the air. In some ways, it was as if the dream were still there, draped over his shoulders like a cloak.

"So," he asked aloud to no one, "was that just a nightmare, or something more?"

The darkness did not answer him.

CHAPTER TEN

WHEN SAM AWOKE FOR the second time, the late morning sunshine was flooding one end of his room with golden light. If he had dreamt a second time, he could not remember it, and that was a good thing as far as he was concerned. Sleep without dreams was freedom.

The overnight drive the previous day had taken its toll on him, and he was not surprised in the least to learn that he had slept until almost noon. His Ford Ranger was not known for its creature comforts, but it had certainly been a reliable vehicle. Still, it felt good to rest in a bed after the loud, confining interior of his little truck. His low back was most likely going to punish him for the next week, but he had arrived safely enough.

He swung his legs out of the bed and rubbed at his eyes. A fresh change of clothes would be another small victory, but only after a shower. Sam gathered up something to wear, found his small bag of toiletries, and stumbled out of the room. He found the bathroom across the hall, and when he stepped inside it he found a large walk-in shower as well as a stack of fresh towels waiting for him.

The decor was mid-century modern, with white subway tiles and a checkered floor of black and white, and though the colors were cold and harsh, the air felt warm and comforting. An old cast iron radiator stood against the wall below the room's lone window, and he could feel the heat that drifted away from it.

The shower felt like a religious experience after the trials of the last two days. Once dried off and dressed, Sam wandered downstairs and looked for Roger, but his friend appeared to be gone. In the kitchen, he found a note on the table where they had shared tea the afternoon before. The message was short and simple, spelled out in Roger's tight, precise printing: *HOME FOR DINNER, FOOD IN FRIDGE*. Resting atop the note was a key which Sam took to be for the front door. He pocketed it and moved toward the refrigerator.

The mention of food had kicked off an audible rumble in his stomach, reminding him of how empty it was, and he was desperate to fill it. Sam opened the door and found a ham sandwich on the main shelf, which he liberated eagerly. There was little time to decide whether he liked it or not; within a few moments it was completely gone. He was certain he could eat another, or perhaps two more, but Roger had only left one and that would have to be enough.

Sam took the opportunity to wander the first floor of the house. From the kitchen on the west side, he walked out into the central hall. From there, the main staircase rose up into the vaulted hallway ceiling. Farther down the hall was a door that led to a small room filled with shelving and a counter for preparing drinks. Wine glasses and tumblers lined the shelves like soldiers, and an assortment of alcoholic beverages were gathered at the back of the counter.

A butler's pantry, he decided. *Must be nice.*

Across the hall was a quaint sitting room furnished in large, comfortable armchairs and a long leather sofa, all arranged to face a fireplace nearly as wide as Sam was tall. Two doors flanked it, one on each side, and he checked both. The first, nearest to the hallway, opened on a nondescript closet where a pair of winter coats hung over a tidy row of assorted footwear. The other door, however, led into a new space.

Upon entering, Sam was struck with wonder. It was an enormous library, each wall covered in bookcases that extended upward to the ceiling at least a dozen feet above the floor. The fireplace that had been in the sitting room had a duplicate in this space, just to the right of the door as he entered. Like the sitting room, this one too had a small cluster of chairs that had been arranged in front of it. Large area rugs filled the open spaces of the room, covering wood floors that Sam assumed to be nearly two centuries old.

Sam approached the fireplace and examined the objects on the mantle. A large antique clock sat in the center, complete with a winding key that protruded from the polished wood body. A framed photograph was propped up against the wall with a picture of Roger and his parents from his college days. Various other tokens of sentiment filled the mantle, but nothing that seemed familiar or important to him.

What *did* catch Sam's eye, however, was the enormous table at the center of the room. It resembled a large farmhouse dinning table, but the dimensions were outside anything he had seen before, stretching nearly a dozen feet in one direction, and at least four feet wide. On the table were half a dozen small piles of books, scattered papers, and a silver laptop that had been closed.

Sam decided that this was the office Roger had spoken of, but it was unlike any office he had ever been inside. The vast majority of the books on the surrounding shelves appeared ancient and well-used, and if the workspace was any indication, his old friend spent quite a bit of time here. It was almost overwhelming.

The sight of all the books reminded Sam of something he had wanted to do for months. Instinctively, he reached around to his back pocket and found the notebook that he kept there. He opened it to the page where he had scribbled the two messages his stalker had left for him. He much preferred the versions he had written in ink to the original bloody phrases left for him.

He didn't know what the words meant, but at least he knew how he could find out. Unfortunately, his Latin was beyond rusty; it had disappeared entirely over the years, leaving nothing but a shadow in his mind where the knowledge used to sit.

Not that he had ever been good with the language anyway. His historical studies had been limited to American history, a field where Latin was hardly a major player. But he knew where he might find some answers.

Sam left the room and closed the door behind himself. He briefly considered running upstairs to get his keys, but decided that he could walk. It would probably be better to leave his truck hidden in the garage for as long as possible anyway. After a quick check in his pocket to make sure he still had the house key, Sam headed out the front door and locked up.

He needed to make a trip to the library.

Salem Public Library was a short walk from Roger's home, just around the corner and to the northwest. Sam could see the red brick and square shape as he approached from a distance. The lawn, like many of the homes in the area, was bright green and fenced in with black iron bars. The stone portico above the entrance bore the name of the facility in gilded letters, adding to the classical feel of the structure.

Sam pushed through the glass door and stepped into the sort of silence only a library can produce. There was activity, with a pair of mothers and their small children off to the left in the children's area, but his eye was drawn to the long counter directly ahead, a mid-century addition of clean lines and golden coloring. A young man sat behind it, working his way through a tall stack of hardcovers, stamping and closing each one in quiet sequence.

Libraries were, for the most part, the same all across the country. Sam had been in his fair share of them over the years, usually to find free reading material, but also for the occasional public internet access. He had so far avoided the things that most people would take for grated, such as a Facebook account or even an email address, but he knew enough about computers to find his way around a search engine. That would fit his needs nicely today.

To his right was a large reading area complete with long oak tables. The walls were lined with tall shelves filled from top to bottom with colorful spines, some more weathered and faded with age and use than others. The bookshelves along the wall farthest from the entrance had a gap in them for a large fireplace, part of which was obscured by an enormous card catalog. Beside it, though, he found what he was looking for.

He took a seat in front of an old desktop monitor the size of a compact car and moved the mouse to wake up the computer. He found himself on the library website by default, and replaced the text in the address bar with the address for his favorite internet search site. Once there, the large white space and lone search field beckoned to him. It was time to get answers.

What worried him was that he might not find anything at all. Words could just be words. There was a chance, however slim, that his stalkers had left messages of their own creation in a language they felt was more comfortable or safe or threatening, rather than quoting something he could find online. Sam didn't quite know how to approach it, but he knew he should begin by simply searching for the text.

He pulled out his notebook and opened it to the page where the messages had been written. Then, Sam clicked into the search field and typed the phrase from his apartment in Benton, LUX SUSPICIONE, and pressed ENTER. The internet churned at its task for a heartbeat before returning the results.

A translation box appeared at the top of the search results, declaring the phrase to mean LIGHT SUSPICION.

What the hell does that mean? Sam thought. *There's no context. And everyone knows that if you take the text out of context, all you're left with is a con. There's got to be more to it that this.*

He scanned the other searches, all of which were results from foreign language webpages. What he did know, however, was that the phrase was in Latin. That was a start, but considering it was nothing more than a translation from the original language, it was a piss-poor one.

Starting over, he looked back down at the page and entered the second phrase, SUSPECTA ET FORTIS. Again the search engine did the job it was created to do and returned another handful of results. All of these new entries, however, were like the first: quotes in Latin from random websites. The translation was the only part that caught his eye this time around.

This time, the translator returned a new, but similar, phrase: STRONG SUSPICION.

Light suspicion and strong suspicion, he pondered. *They could certainly be related. They're both about suspicion. It's almost like they're a progression.*

Each of the attacks had certainly been a progression from the previous encounter. The first message had appeared along side a dead cat, and though it had not been the first message they had sent him, it *had* been the first one written in blood. The most recent one followed the same style, but rather than a cat, poor Henry had been murdered. Progression indeed.

It occurred to Sam to try searching for both phrases together. Perhaps that would add enough context to help narrow down the original source material. He refreshed the search tool and this time typed both phrases into the text field. After pressing ENTER, the search engine generated a shorter set of results, and he scanned them all for the complete phrases.

One entry, halfway down the page caught his attention. It was a transcription of a table of contents for a book. Sam clicked through and found himself on another library's website. The book in question appeared to be entitled *Malleus Malificarum*, though he couldn't find a description on the page . Promisingly, though, the scan of the book's title page was also in Latin.

He paused and stared at the screen for a moment. The book in question was located in a library, just as he himself was at the moment. Perhaps this library had a copy, or access to a copy through the library network. He opened a new tab in the browser and allowed the default page to load, bringing him back to the Salem Public Library's own search page.

His hands felt sweaty and unsteady as he copied the name of the book and pasted it into the library's search field. The odds were slim, if he wanted to be completely honest with himself. But the risk was high enough that he had to try. He hovered the mouse pointer over the SEARCH button, closed his eyes and said a cursory prayer, and then clicked.

The library catalog site returned its results. The page was a vast expanse of white space, with one single result listed at the top. Against all odds, the library—*this* library, the one he was currently seated in—had a copy of the book in question. Sam closed his eyes and reopened them, waiting for the vision to evaporate and leave him empty-handed, but nothing changed. The book was real, and it was actually here.

He wrote its name on the same page in the notebook where the messages were listed, then glanced back at the monitor. Beneath the title of the book was a call number, and he quickly copied it down before clearing his search results and exiting out of the library system.

Armed with the number and title, Sam set off into the depth of shelves to find his prize. He wondered if finding one's way around a library was still a skill that was taught today, or if he represented a dying breed. In his middle- and high-school days, every single student had been trained in the process of finding books in the catalog and then locating them on the shelf. Countless research papers were assigned to reinforce and test that skill, and Sam discovered that he was actually very good at it.

Those skills were rusty now, but he wanted to try on his own before asking for help. After locating what he was sure to be the correct portion of the library, he began to follow the numbers written on the sides of the metal shelving units. A few minutes after starting, he found the aisle he needed, and stepped inside to find the right shelf. That was when his run of success dried up.

The book wasn't there. He started by trusting the numbers and only looking where he was supposed to, but when that turned nothing up, he began systematically going through each shelf one by one. Still nothing. He could point to the place on the shelf where the book *should* be, but it just wasn't there. There wasn't even a space for it, and that struck Sam as odd.

Giving up, he decided to ask for help, but that meant approaching someone at the front desk. A brief wave of fear swept over him at the thought of the librarian being curious about what he was looking for. He couldn't exactly tell the truth and explain that he was looking for source material behind a series of bloody messages left by men who killed a cat and his landlord in an attempt to frighten him. He would need a much less alarming story than that.

Sam thought it through on the way to the desk, and when he approached the man there he felt secure in his false story if it needed to be shared. The man smiled cordially when he looked up and saw Sam headed toward him.

"How can I help you?" the man whispered.

"I'm looking for a book and can't seem to find it on the shelf," he replied. Sam picked up a slip of paper and copied the call number onto it. Handing the slip to the librarian, he added: "I was hoping it was just on a cart somewhere waiting to be put back."

The man took the paper and rolled his chair over to a computer near him. After pressing a few keys and frowning at the display for what felt like an eternity, he returned to the counter.

"It looks like this book is actually part of our Fine Books collection," the man quietly explained. "It's absolutely something you can look at, but it would need to be by appointment, I'm afraid. Would you care to set up a time after the weekend when you can returns and work with one of our volunteer archivists to see the book?"

Great, he thought. *Sign up, wait, be supervised. All of that sounds about as exciting as a chaperoned date.*

Finally, Sam nodded. "If that's my only option, I guess that will have to do. I'm in a hurry, but I can understand if you have procedures to follow."

The librarian smiled back. "I appreciate that, sir. Just pick a time on the chart and print your name in the box provided. I'll make sure one of our volunteers is available to assist you."

Sam was handed a clipboard with a schedule for the Fine Books room, and put his name in the box for Monday at 1:00 PM. It would be difficult to wait, certainly, but he couldn't bend the rules however much he wanted to.

"Just show back up on Monday, then?" he asked, handing the clipboard back.

"That would be just fine," the man nodded. "Ask for me if I'm not at the desk. I'm James."

The librarian extended his hand and Sam shook it. "Alright then, James," he said. "I'll see you Monday."

Sam turned and left the desk, but before he exited the library he decided he would do some more research on his own. He headed back over to the computer but found a middle-aged woman using it, and so he sat at a nearby table to wait for her to finish. She appeared to be a student, and spent a few minutes scribbling down words from a search results page before packing up and moving toward the card catalog.

Sam smiled at her as he took her spot, and then settled into the seat. He pulled out the notebook, typed the name of the book into the search engine, and was about to click the SEARCH button when James, the librarian, approached him.

"Sir?" he began. "I'm glad you're still here. I just spoke to one of our volunteers and they seem to be willing to help you now. If you are still interested, I can escort you to the Fine Books room where they can assist you in your research."

"That would be fantastic," Sam replied, his voice a bit louder than necessary. This was just the lucky break he needed.

He cleared out his search field and grabbed the notebook before following the librarian. James led him through a small door at the back of the main reference area and into a smaller room that appeared to be a new addition. A darkly colored wooden door was set into each of the two side walls, and the librarian motioned for Sam to approach the one to their right.

"Here you are," he said cheerfully. "They'll be expecting you. Just knock and wait for someone to let you in. And if you need anything else, you know where to find me."

"Thanks," Sam replied. "I really appreciate this."

The man nodded and then quickly exited the room to return to his post. Sam glanced at the door and firmly rapped it twice, the sound of his knuckles echoing in the small space. A few short moments later, he heard someone turning a lock, and then the door swung inward.

The man inside was Roger.

"Hello Sam," he said with a grin. "Looks like you and I have a bit more to talk about."

CHAPTER ELEVEN

"I DON'T UNDERSTAND," Sam said as he entered the room. "What are you doing here?"

Roger led him to a large work table, similar to the one he had seen in the library back at the house. This one was covered with antique books, some of which were still inside locked polystyrene boxes. Lining three of the four walls around them were tall shelves that contained hundreds of other volumes.

"I volunteer here," Roger replied, handing Sam a pair of white gloves. "There are few locations in the United States as historic as the city of Salem, and the library of documents here is a treasury of historical wealth and information. I helped create this department, and have helped the collection grow over the years."

"To what end?" Sam asked, taking the gloves and tugging them on. "And what are these for?"

"All titles in this room must be handled with protective gloves. It aids in the archival process and protects them from the natural oils in our skin. Plus," Roger added with a grin, "some of them are pretty filthy."

"But why?" Sam continued. "What's your goal here?"

Roger stepped over to one of the shelves and removed a large book wrapped in black cloth. He carried it back to the work table with care, and then placed it gently in front of Sam.

"This city has been the focal point of an international interest in witchcraft for centuries. The tragedy of 1692, what the rest of the country refers to as the Salem Witch Trials, was simply the manifestation of the symptoms of a larger paranoia. Salem had the horrible honor of playing host to centuries of superstition through a modern interpretation of the Inquisition.

"Because of this, one of my tasks has been to gather as much material as I can to study and preserve the traditions that were behind the hysteria, and to examine all of the Salem records of the time through the lens that this collection provides. I'm studying the trials of 1692, but I'm doing it in reverse."

Sam nodded with understanding. "So you're not looking back and following the records to the trials; you've chosen to start centuries prior to 1692 and walk toward it, looking for new insights and information. Does that sum it up well enough?'

"Absolutely," Roger said with a grin. "It's a shame you never finished college, Sam. You'd have been a fine historical researcher."

"Well, I might have walked into a project unintentionally," he replied. "But having your help would be invaluable."

Roger tilted his head to the side and gave him a knowing glance before his eyes drifted toward the dark shape on the table.

"What's your interest in this book, Sam?" Roger patted the covered tome that sat on the table. "I'll be honest with you and say that I'm more than a little baffled. What on earth brought you to the library today to see if you could look at a copy of such an obscure title?"

Sam shrugged. "Honestly, I didn't come here to find it. I was just looking for answers. There are some things I need to know, and my search led me here."

"This is about your troubles in the Midwest, isn't it?"

"Yeah," he replied. "I guess you could say that."

"Tell me about them," Roger said calmly. "I want to help you, Sam, but I'm going to need to be invited into your world to do that. Can you trust me enough to open up about this?"

I don't know if I can trust anyone, he thought. *But I also know I can't do this on my own. I'm in over my head, and I need help.*

Sam nodded, closing his eyes as if it hurt to agree. "Alright," he replied. "But you need to promise you aren't going to judge me. This isn't my fault, Roger. Just keep that in the back of your mind."

Roger nodded. "Agreed."

"A few years ago," Sam began with a sigh, "I started to receive messages from someone. I don't know the identity the person or persons sending them, but the messages have always been threatening in tone. They began as simple notes, letters dropped into my mailbox or beneath my door. But they escalated over time."

"What did they say, these notes?"

"It was typically the same message: 'We know. Stop while you can.' But I honestly had no idea what they were referring to, so I ignored them. Only later did they start to do other things, like breaking into my apartment while I was out. They never stole anything, but the place would be trashed and the message behind it was pretty clear."

"They were telling you that they had power over you," Roger suggested. "That you were not safe."

"I think so, yes," Sam replied. "And that's pretty much the main reason I moved from place to place so frequently. Coming home from work to find my home violated was always a sign that it was time to move on.

"I think I was hoping that moving might help me get away, you know? Vanishing into the night to throw them off my trail, as it were. That never happened, though, and each new message from them sounded more menacing than the last. Then, at the beginning of this year, things got bad."

Roger tilted his head to the side. "How so?"

Sam pulled his notebook out. "I came home one night to find the usual signs of a break-in. What was written on the wall, however, was new."

"On the wall?"

"Yeah," Sam replied. "Whoever they are, they used blood to write their message on the wall of my apartment. This is what it said."

Sam pointed at the first phrase on the page, covering the second deliberately. Roger leaned over and read it.

"Light suspicion," he translated. "Well that's not as helpful as I would have thought."

"Exactly," Sam agreed. "Hell, I didn't even know what it said, so I've spent months completely ignorant of what they were trying to tell me. This one, and the new message I received just two days ago."

Again, Sam held the page out and let Roger read it. He expected the same confusion as before, but this time the man's eyes opened wide.

"Strong suspicion," he whispered and then looked Sam in the face with wide eyes. "Good God, Sam, I think I know what those phrases mean."

"Good," Sam replied. "I hope so, because all I was able to find online was that both phrases are mentioned in this book. And as I mentioned, I don't speak Latin. So what the hell is this thing?" He patted the large bundle.

"That," Roger intoned, "is the *Malleus Malificarum*. You've really never heard of it?"

"Nope," Sam replied, shaking his head. "I had hoped looking through it would give me some context, but again, old Latin isn't exactly helping the matter. But I have a feeling you could do a much better job explaining this than I ever could."

"Indeed," the older man replied. He took a deep breath and then settled into a posture that reminded Sam of a university lecturer.

"Let's start back further in time than you might expect. In the early 10th-century, the Catholic Church issued a set of church rules, known then as a *penitential*. Within that book is something referred to by scholars today as the *capitulum Episcopi*. It urges bishops and church leaders to expel anyone from their ranks who practices witchcraft.

"The reason, according to this document, was that the Devil himself had seduced those people, and they needed to be removed from the Church as quickly as possible. In essence, it was one of the first occurrences of a order from the Church to find and punish witches."

"So is that what kicked off witch hunts all across Europe, then?" Sam asked.

"No, not exactly," Roger replied. "For some reason, it took centuries before people began to accuse their neighbors of being witches. Most scholars think it's because most people didn't actually believe witches were real. That changed over time, though, and by the the middle of the 15th-century attitudes were different. Suddenly, anyone could be a witch, and almost everything unexplainable that happened was blamed on them.

"One of the first attempts to take legal action against an alleged witch took place in 1484 by a German man named Heinrich Kramer, but it was a failure. The Church refused to support him, and he left town in disgrace. After the dust settled, however, he wrote a book. He wanted to create a manual for finding witches and bringing them to trial, something very much on the mind of many people in his day. By combining false advertising about his co-author Jacob Sprenger's support with some creative editing of a papal bull called the *Summis desiderantes affectibus*, he managed to pass himself off as an official Church-endorsed witch hunter."

"Witch hunter?" Sam repeated. *Why would quotes from a book about witches be written on* my *walls as a threat?* "Did it catch on?"

"Salem owes a large portion of its historical legacy to the very fact that it did," Roger replied. "His book, the book responsible for fanning the flames of paranoia, was published in 1486. He called it the *Malleus Malificarum* — 'the hammer of the witches' — and you, my friend, are standing in front of a very early edition from 1520."

"The hammer of the witches," Sam repeated quietly.

Roger nodded. "The Catholic Church condemned it almost immediately, but that didn't stop it from spreading. It was reprinted dozens of times over the subsequent centuries, each time giving the book a little boost in accessibility and moving it back into the public mind.

"One of those reprint dates was 1669. It was said by some that Cotton Mather, the famous Puritan minister, possessed a copy of the book, and that he used it extensively during his involvement with the Salem trials of 1692."

"Alright," Sam said, reaching up to his head with one hand and rubbing his temple. "So this was a handbook for hunting witches, first throughout Europe and later in New England. But what's the significance of the two phrases that were left for me?"

"Ah," Roger replied, holding up a finger. "That's easy enough to answer."

He turned to the large bundle and carefully unfolded the black fabric. The leather cover of the antique book had been worn bare in a few places, and Sam could see through gaps in the spine that the binding had begun to crack. Despite having clearly seen use, however, it had remained remarkably intact.

Roger opened the book to reveal pages that were in immaculate condition. He carefully turned the pages, skillfully navigating toward a portion near the end. Moving from page to page, he scanned the text with his experienced eyes until he found what he had been looking for.

"This book," he began again, "is broken into three sections. The first pertains to the existence of witches, and makes the case that they are indeed real. The second part focuses on their powers, going through a variety of conditions or phenomenon that can be attributed to them. The last section, though, is the most important. That's where Kramer walks his readers through the act of accusing a witch and bringing them to trial, as well as how to punish them."

"Okay," Sam said, nodding.

"The two phrases that were left for you as warnings were pulled from this latter portion of the book." Roger pointed to the page and Sam followed his finger. "It's organized into sections that progress as they go, and each section is titled as a numbered question. Question twenty-three right here deals with declaring what it calls a 'light suspicion' toward the accused."

Roger turned the page a handful of times to go deeper into the book, "Here we find the next question, this one explaining when to declare 'strong suspicion' towards someone. After that is one final level of accusation. It's a progression, Sam. Like moving from a misdemeanor to a felony charge; every time they move up another notch, it gets more and more serious."

"Alright," Sam said. "So the phrases come from the book. But what does it *mean* for me, Roger?"

"It means," his friend replied. "That someone is accusing you, and they've been slowly turning the dial over time. Your last message was the fifth of six levels of accusation."

Sam was suddenly very uncomfortable. He sensed the next question before it was even asked, his stomach cramping into a ball at the thought of exposing more of himself, putting more of himself on the line.

"For some reason," Roger continued, "quotes from this book are being used as threats against you. Now, I don't know what's been going on, but the only logical reason that something like this would happen is if the people behind these threats really, truly believed that you deserved it. So tell me, Sam: why would they think that?"

Sam did not know how to respond. He didn't like either choice that he had been presented with. On one hand, he could deny it all and play dumb. The trouble with that was that Roger was a very smart man, and he would see through the lie. If he was to have any help at all during his time in Salem, never mind a place to stay and some semblance of safety, then he needed to keep Roger on his side.

The other choice, though, involved exposing something he had never shared with anyone else before. The closest he had ever come was admitting to Cesar that something happened involving a vision, but as far as he knew, the man never really believed Sam ever had anything more than a hunch about Olivia's accident. Telling Roger everything would be frightening and revealing, and it was hard to gauge what the man's reaction might be.

Sam found it difficult to even believe himself most of the time. The things he had done were beyond his understanding, and that was possibly the most frightening aspect of it all. He didn't feel as if he could control what he didn't understand. And yet...

"Sam?" Roger was waiting patiently for an answer, but the man clearly wanted him to hurry. His mouth was twisted into a frown, and the look of disapproval shook Sam to the bone.

"You won't believe me," Sam finally replied. "I know that sounds cliche, but I mean it. You're going to think I've lost my mind."

"Try me," the older man suggested. "You'll be surprised by what I'm willing to accept."

Sam sighed and pulled a stool out from beneath the work table. He took a seat and struggled to gather his words.

"I can do things," he began cautiously. "For a few years, in fact. Things that people aren't supposed to be able to do."

"Such as?"

"No," Sam said, shaking his head. "You'll think I've lost my mind."

"Sam," Roger said in a firm voice. "What sort of things?"

"I see things from time to time. Visions. Almost like a movie playing in my head."

"And these visions," Roger coaxed, "they come true, I suppose?"

"Look, I know how it sounds—" but Roger cut him off.

"Do they come true, Sam?"

He nodded.

"So you have premonitions." His friend didn't appear shaken yet, and he pressed for more. "Do you control them, or do they simply happen?"

"They happen randomly," Sam replied. "Usually in my sleep, but sometimes during the day. Those types hit me like

I've been shocked by a live wire, and they're a lot more clear and understandable than the ones I see while I'm sleeping."

Roger seemed to relax, a smile returning to his face. "I have a feeling I know the rest of the story, then. Your visions give you clues to help people sometimes, don't they? And when word gets out that you saved a life or delivered important news, your stalkers find you, right?"

Sam nodded again. "I try to keep them to myself, but sometimes I just can't. Sometimes, like last week, ignoring them could mean someone gets hurt. So I act on them. Some people are appreciative, but others haven't been to happy to hear the truth. Either way, I rarely come out on top when it's all said and done."

"No, I doubt you would," Roger said. "Probably because most people are wired to pull away from the unexplainable. It can't be compartmentalized or categorized by their minds, and so they lash out. Some strike out physically, and others do it in more subtle ways. And even though you just want to help, the dice are loaded."

"Wait," Sam said timidly, "you're not upset and frightened about this? No desire to run away?"

Roger smiled and shook his head. "Not at all." Then, glancing at his watch, "I'm not sure I have time to explain why at the moment, but rest assured, you haven't shocked me at all."

"Good," Sam sighed. "What a relief. I have more to share with you as well, but I think I'm holding you up. We can chat more tonight."

"The Fine Books room is only open for another forty-five minutes or so, and I think I have one last appointment before closing up shop. But yes, let's continue our conversation tonight. I have more questions, but I also think I might have some answers for you. If you're ready for them, that is."

"Absolutely," Sam replied.

Roger wrapped the large antique book back up in the black cloth and slid it farther across the table before escorting Sam to the exit. He held out a hand as they paused in the threshold, and Sam shook it.

"I really appreciate your honesty, Sam," the man told him. "We've cleared the air—for the most part, that is—and I really think you and I are going to be able to figure this one out. Together, right?"

He nodded. "Together."

Back in the main area, Sam noticed that the library had become more crowded during his time with Roger. A dozen or more people slowly moving in and out of the aisles. The computer station was occupied again, and James the Librarian had a line of people needing assistance. The young man was picking up the phone as Sam passed by, and he nodded politely. Sam returned the gesture.

Outside, the air had taken on a chill. The sun was completing its journey into the western horizon and dusk had fallen over the city of Salem like a veil. Sam walked slowly down the steps and turned to begin his short walk back to Roger's house.

He was too preoccupied by his thoughts to notice the car parked across the street at the end of the block. In the fading light, its dark windows resembled the dead eyes of a corpse.

CHAPTER TWELVE

SAM ALWAYS THOUGHT OF Spring in New England as the red-headed step-child of the four seasons. Fall was the one that everyone talked about, with its vibrant colors and refreshing chill. In addition, the autumn holidays of Halloween and Thanksgiving, though nationally celebrated, had deep roots in the local area, and that only added to the hype.

Winter usually took second billing, mostly because of the heavy snowfall and beautiful landscapes. It seemed as if everyone owned a ski cottage in Vermont. And while summer was vehemently loathed by many during July and August, it added a lot of life and energy to the area. Beaches exploded with tourists, and port towns like Rockport and Ogunquit saw most of their annual economy rush in like high tide.

Spring, though, didn't have that quintessential New England spirit. It was a time of renewal, certainly, but aside from some of the local manor house gardens, it lacked a formal celebration. Sam felt that was a crime, though;

Spring had the potential to be just as vibrant and refreshing as autumn. The trouble, as he saw it, was that people were still too busy complaining about the winter that was winding down to even notice that spring had sprung. Before they knew it, summer was knocking at the door.

Nights like this reminded Sam of why he loved New England so much. The air was cool—cold enough to cause him to regret leaving his coat at Roger's house, at least—and the sky was clear of clouds. The few stars that cut through the glow of the city below seemed to wink and sparkle like diamonds. Combined with the cobblestone sidewalks of the neighborhood and the stately, classic architecture, it put him in a nostalgic mood.

Sam took his time walking home. At the corner of Hamilton Street, he turned right and walked past a large antique federal-style house. Without the white trim and black shutters it would have resembled a large brick box, but the few elements that had been added to it were beautiful in their simplicity. The granite steps beneath the small portico led to a back door set in a few feet from the front of the building.

A white plaque near the doorway, something that was very common to find on most historic homes and buildings in the area, informed him of the year it had been built and by whom.

Benjamin Brown, 1844. Apothecary.

He passed the building and walked across the entrance to their driveway. As he did, Sam thought he heard a sound, and turned to look for the source. The driveway ended in a small yard and a vine-covered fence, but he could see nothing that might have made the noise.

Cats, he thought. *Enjoying the death of winter just like me.*

Past the large brick building was a series of beautiful victorians, their wood siding painted with the same conservatism that drove the Puritans to find a home in the New World, and fenced off with white pickets and their ornamental tops. Each was a masterpiece and historical bookmark all in one.

With the light fading, Sam was able to partake in one of his guilty pleasures: window-watching. Wherever he saw an open window leading into a well-lit room, he could not help but glance inside. The furniture, wallpaper, and artwork that hung on the walls all spoke to the personality of the people inside. Yes, it was voyeuristic of him to look, but there was something refreshing about seeing the side of a stranger that few ever had a chance to witness.

Another noise interrupted his thoughts, and he glanced back down the quiet street. There was no one else on the cobblestone sidewalks. Not even a car to be seen. He assumed it was someone inside one of the homes, perhaps with a window open to let in the cool night air, and quickly returned to his walk.

Hamilton was a short stretch of road that spanned just one block between Essex Street, where the library was located, and Chestnut. While Chestnut was not a very busy street—probably due to the fact that it was a one-way road —Sam felt it was safe to assume that he would see more cars and foot traffic once he turned onto it. For some reason, that was something he wanted to do as quickly as possible. He wasn't sure why, but he knew it to be true.

The last two houses stood like sentries on either side of the end of Hamilton. Sam hurried down the sidewalk, moving his feet just fast enough to satisfy his growing urgency without breaking into an all-out run. He had nearly reached the end when a dark figure stepped out of the shadows behind a shrub and walked straight into his path.

"Going somewhere, Mr. Hawthorne?" a voice asked. It was deep but otherwise unremarkable. The figure, though, was far more intimidating.

The man stood a good four inches taller than Sam, and judging by the width of his shoulders he was powerfully built. There was a street lamp directly behind the figure, casting a glow around him and obscuring his features, and that anonymity frightened Sam more than anything else.

Friend or foe, he asked himself.

"Who are you?" Sam asked, stopping a dozen or so feet from the figure.

"We've been following you for a very long time, Sam Hawthorne," the man declared. "We've gone to great lengths to watch you. You have travelled far these past twenty years, and we have been there the entire time, watching and waiting. But now, I think, the wait is over."

The figure took a step forward, and Sam instinctively backed up.

"Look, I don't know who you are, but I think you've got the wrong guy."

"Oh, I seriously doubt that," the man replied, his voice heavy with amusement. "I'm amazed that you think I could be mistaken. After all we've done to make you aware of our presence. To help you see the error of your ways."

"Who are you?" Sam spat. "And what do you want?"

The man took another step toward him, and Sam backpedalled an equal distance. They had moved far enough from the street lamp to reveal more of the man's face, however. Sam attempted to memorize the features but they were unremarkable. The man's jaw was square and firm, his nose was of average length and flat along the bridge, and his eyes were set into the shadows below a short hat.

"We are Purga Immundus," he replied as if it should already have been guessed. "We are the keepers of the guard. We watch and we wait. We purge the unclean."

Purge the unclean? Sam thought. *What the hell is that supposed to mean?*

"Again, I think you're mistaken, buddy," he replied. "I might be a bit of an odd duck, but I'm nothing worth this kind of trouble."

The man reached up and adjusted his hat. The scalp beneath was smooth and absent of any sign of hair. His thin lips parted in a grin that reminded Sam of a predatory reptile, right down to the flash of white teeth.

The man suddenly exploded forward, moving with the speed of a cat. Sam flinched instinctively, and tried to take a step backwards. His right foot planted on the cobblestone sidewalk just fine, but it was his left that gave him problems, slipping off the curb. His ankle thankfully did not twist, but the sudden move to the side pushed him completely off balance. The street began to rush up to meet him.

The stranger had not expected Sam to trip, and rather than grasping at Sam's arms he continued forward, catching his own foot on Sam's outstretched leg. The man did not stumble, but his momentum had clearly been disrupted. As Sam collided with the pavement, he tried his best to use that small window of time.

"Stand still and accept your sentence, Sam," the man hissed from behind him.

Sam rolled and found his feet. He was far from out of shape. Living on the run and working on construction sites had helped him stay active and fit over the years. Other than

Repo, who was a physical anomaly, Sam had usually been able to hold his own in a fight.

He straightened up and reached for his keys, but his pockets were empty.

Dammit, he thought. *I didn't bring them with me. Fan-fucking-tastic.*

It would have been nice to have some semblance of a weapon, but at least the other man did not seem to be armed either. He was angry, though, and anger could be weapon enough when wielded by someone with skill.

"Either you come with me peacefully," he said through gritted teeth, "or I drag your corpse behind me when I leave. That decision rests entirely in your hands."

"Bite me," Sam spat.

The stranger lunged again, but Sam saw it coming. It was just a flash, and only a second or two ahead of time, but he watched the man swing his clinched fist directly at the side of his head a moment before it actually happened.

That's new, Sam thought as he ducked and stepped to the side. *I'm not trying to do that. Or am I?*

"Gar!" the man grunted as his hand punched through the empty air above Sam's head. "I will assume you have made your decision then?"

Sam stepped away, backing toward the intersection where Hamilton joined Chestnut. There were no cars. He did not know how, but they were completely alone on the street. Families in their homes around them were probably just finishing their evening meals, and here he was, trying not to get himself killed in the middle of the road.

"I told you," Sam said. "I don't know who you are or what you want, but you've got the wrong guy."

The man laughed, tipping his head back slightly. "Really?" he asked bitterly. "There is another Samuel Hawthorne out there, informing people of their future, interfering in their lives, and meddling where he isn't wanted? I find that highly unlikely."

"Hey, I helped those people," Sam spat back. "It's not my fault they sometimes took it too far, or got the wrong message. I just wanted to help them."

"You are a freak, Sam, and we hunt people like you." The stranger seemed more calm now, perhaps because Sam had admitted to doing some of the things he was being accused of. "You willfully continue to engage in actions that are unlawful and unnatural."

It clicked. Somewhere in Sam's head he could hear Roger's voice, covering the main ideas behind the book they had looked at. People had used it as a handbook for witch hunting. People like this man.

He thinks I'm a witch!

The stranger moved his powerful body quickly toward him again. Sam was given another glimpse of what was about to happen, and rather than duck this time, he stepped to the side and kicked upward. His foot connected with the man's stomach, dropping him to the ground.

Sam was not interested in fighting. He simply wanted to escape. A voice in his head told him that he should finish the fight while his attacker was still down, but instead he turned to run. That's when the man reached out and grabbed his foot.

No vision aided him this time. There had been no forewarning or premonition. One moment he was lurching toward Chestnut Street, and the next he was toppling to the pavement. He did, however, manage to tug his foot free of the man's grip and scrambled out of reach.

"I think I am done giving you the grace you so obviously do not deserve," the stranger growled. "You are certainly not the first I have killed, and I doubt you will be the last. I have no qualms about using this."

He reached into his coat, and Sam fully expected to see the hand pull out a handgun. Instead, the man held a long knife. Lamplight reflected off the curved blade as he held it up for Sam to see.

"You're insane," Sam panted. "I've done nothing wrong. Why can't you just stop following me and leave me alone?"

"Because that is not our calling," the stranger replied. "We are keepers of the guard. We watch and we wait. We purge the unclean. There is no grace, no second chance, and certainly no looking the other way. You are marked, Sam Hawthorne, and I will end your life."

"Try me," Sam spat at him, clenching his hands into tight fists.

His attacker did not waste a moment, lunging forward with the knife. Sam's head throbbed with another vision, and he jumped back, swatting at the man's wrist in an attempt to knock the blade free.

The other man was faster, though, and he swung out with the knife, connecting with Sam's shirt. The blade passed through the fabric and scrapped across his skin. It felt like a cat scratch, thin and hot, but he didn't think it was any deeper than that. The shock of it distracted him, though, and the man stopped and turned to face him.

Sam knew that something needed to change. The attacker was armed and he wasn't. The man was fast and powerful, and obviously had the advantage of being armed. He was certain that, given enough time, he would lose this fight and find himself on the receiving end of that long blade. No, if he was to survive, he needed to get far away from this stranger.

Sam turned and bolted for Chestnut.

Running wasn't something he enjoyed, but at this moment in time it felt like freedom. He could hear the sound of his attacker following close behind, the footsteps echoing off the houses around them in quick claps, and their rhythm drove him forward. He didn't want to find out how sharp that knife was, but the stranger was closing the gap.

"You can't escape," the man shouted at him between breaths.

The corner was only a few paces away, and Sam was sure he would make it out into the main road. Hopefully traffic would be heavier there, allowing someone to see his struggle and come help him. At the very least someone might call for the police, though Sam was convinced he needed to avoid law enforcement as much as possible right now.

The footsteps behind him did not relent, but he ran as fast as he could into Chestnut Street. Just as he was about to step onto the far curb, headlights turned onto the street.

Thank God! he cheered to himself. *Finally, someone to help.*

He could heard the roar of the car's engine as it sped toward him. Had they already seen that he was being attacked? Could they really know that much already? Something about the approaching vehicle did not sit well with him.

He stopped cold on the side of the street and spun around to meet his attacker. The man lunged at him, but missed as Sam dove to the side. The knife shimmered by the light of the headlights as they drew closer, but the man was not frightened off.

And then Sam's heart sank.

The car came fully into view and from where he stood he could see the dark tinted windows. He instantly recognized it as the car he had seen many times outside of Henry's house, and again at the gas station in Pennsylvania. Whoever this man was, and the organization he worked for, they had wisely sent backup. He was outnumbered and trapped.

The car sped faster as it approached, but at the last moment the driver engaged the breaks and turned the wheel. The back end of the sedan swung sideways with a screech, and both Sam and his attacker dove out of the way to avoid being struck.

Sam landed on the side of Chestnut opposite Hamilton Street, while his assailant went the other direction. He heard the distinct sound of metal skittering across stone, and looked to see the long knife a few yards from where the stranger had landed.

This is my chance, he coached himself. *Run while you still can!*

For a moment, Sam could do nothing. He was frozen by indecision. Roger's house was just down the street, but he was afraid that running there would only drag his friend into this conflict. The car no longer blocked the street from the other direction, and because it was a one-way road, it made more sense to Sam to run that way.

Just do it. Do something!

Sam sprung forward, ready to run, when both car doors swung open. Two men in dark suits stepped out, handguns drawn, and Sam watched as the one on the far side of the car moved toward the stranger who was retrieving his knife.

"Stay back!" the man in the suit shouted at Sam's attacker. "Back off now, buddy."

The bald man returned the knife to his coat and glared at the men in suits. His face was twisted in rage and frustration like a cornered animal. Just before he turned and ran, disappearing into one of the neighborhood yards, Sam saw him turn his eyes toward him. What he saw was pure hatred. Anger seemed to pour from those eyes, and it chilled Sam to the bone.

"Get in the car, Sam," the man closest to him said urgently. "Before he comes back. Get in."

Sam did not know what to think, but he was unwilling to trust the man unconditionally.

"Who are you?" he asked, glancing over at the other side of the car.

"FBI," the man replied, holding up a leather wallet with federal identification affixed inside. "If you want to live, you'll want to get into the car. That man will be back, and I doubt you want to be here when he returns with help."

"FBI?" Confusion washed over him. "But I thought —"

"Sam, I'm serious," the man said firmly. "We're here to help you, but you need to get in the car. Get in or I'll push you in."

Sam forced his intuition into the back of his mind and reluctantly nodded. These men had saved him from the man with the knife. That should be enough to earn his trust. He hurried over to the side of the car and pulled the back door open. The moment his feet left the pavement, the car roared to life.

The door closed on its own as the car lurched forward, and within seconds they were out of sight.

CHAPTER THIRTEEN

SAM WATCHED FROM THE back seat as the highway quickly slipped by.

After ten minutes of quick driving they had escaped the urban center and approached the smaller town of Danvers, where the car pulled onto Route 128 and headed south. All of it was familiar scenery to Sam, and all of it passed by in a numb daze.

"I'm Agent Clifton," the man in the driver's seat said as he urged the car to full speed. "My partner here is Agent Sharp."

"FBI, eh?" Sam asked.

"That's correct," Clifton replied. "We've been watching you for a while, Mr. Hawthorne. We're here to help."

"So you say," Sam replied. "I guess that means it was you guys I locked in that gas station bathroom a couple of days ago. Sorry about that."

"I can still smell that place," Sharp spat. His voice was tight and bitter. "I don't like small rooms, and I can't stand public toilets. Disgusting." He spoke the last word with the urgency of a man leaning over a toilet, ready to vomit.

Sam wanted to chuckle but managed to keep his enjoyment private. It was not that he had intended to do that to them, but at the time, he found he had little choice. There was one way out, and the situation presented itself. He had simply taken advantage of the circumstances in an effort to save his own life.

Or so he thought. Now, it seems that he had been mistaken. The men he had thought of as his stalkers, responsible not only for the messages but also the dead cat and Henry's murder, had turned out to be government agents tasked with watching him.

The natural question, then, was why? Why would the FBI be keeping an eye on him? Were his visions and interactions with the people around him that unusual that it warranted surveillance from the government? How did they even know to look for him, and to what end? These where mysteries he hoped could be cleared up soon.

Now that he knew the true identity of the people who had been watching him, he was left with the nagging question about who his stalkers really were. The messages and vandalism, the blood, and eventually the killing all pointed to a group of individuals who were angry and dangerous. Until today he had no idea who they might be.

The man with the knife said he was part of a group of people called the Purga Immundus, but Sam had never heard of them before. The language the man used, however —references to accusation, unclean people, and purging— all seemed to connect with the themes within that mysterious book, the *Malleus Malificarum*. He didn't like that connection one bit.

It was unsettling enough to learn that the book had been used as a guide for the slaughter of hundreds, perhaps thousands, of innocent people across Europe and the New World. To even suggest that there might still be people alive today who were equally misguided was akin to being told that, yes Mary Jane, monsters are real and one lives under your bed.

Only in this story, I'd be the monster, wouldn't I?

Agent Clifton guided the car onto the exit for Route 1 and slowed for the long, winding loop of ramp that led south. Once they were back on the highway and moving at a steady pace, the agent spoke up.

"Mr. Hawthorne, do you have any idea why that man might want to harm you?"

Agent Sharp glanced over his shoulder at Sam as his partner asked the question. Sam did not like the look in the man's eye, though. It was hungry and full of a seething anger. He didn't strike Sam as a friendly man. At least Clifton had presented himself as more personable so far.

"I don't know," he lied. "But I get the feeling from what happened back there that you know more about him than I do. So what, are you trying to figure out how much I know before you say something you shouldn't? Some kind of government clearance thing?"

"He asked you a question," Sharp growled at him.

"Hey," Agent Clifton said calmly, holding a hand up toward his partner. "No need to play 'bad cop' here, Sharp. We're all on the same side."

The men exchanged tense glances, and then Sharp turned back toward the highway ahead, watching the shops and restaurants of Route 1 pass quickly by.

"So you don't know much about him, then?" Clifton asked again.

Sam shook his head. "That was the first time I've seen him. I got a good look at him, though. I could pick him out of a lineup, easy. But I'd be lying if I said I didn't want to know more."

"Well, maybe we can answer some of your questions," Clifton replied.

"When you first got there, and you were getting out of the car, you mentioned that the guy might return with others. So there's more of them?"

"We aren't actually certain about their exact number," Clifton said, "but yes, there are more where that guy came from."

"If you don't know who they are, how do you know there's more than just that one crazy guy?"

"Because we've seen them," Sharp interrupted. "While you've been living your carefree, happy-go-lucky life all over the Midwest, we've been keeping an eye on you, and we've seen people like him drift in and out of the picture."

Clifton glanced at his partner with a furrowed brow. "We've witnessed at least a dozen unique individuals who have all participated in what seems to be a long-term tracking operation. They're very interested in you, Mr. Hawthorne. Are you sure the man you met this evening didn't explain why?"

Sam did not know if he wanted to answer that question yet. If he said yes, then the agents would be curious about whether or not the stranger's suspicions were true. It was still unclear if the agents had been watching him because they knew about his abilities. There was a good chance they had simply been tasked with watching this mysterious group, and Sam's involvement had only been happenstance.

It was not as if Sam had been raised to dislike the government. His parents had been model citizens, and he had never been led to believe he should act any different.

Of course, living off the grid for two decades was not exactly the life he had hoped for himself, but he did his best to avoid willful lawbreaking. He never used his gifts to blackmail people, and he certainly didn't ever intentionally set out to commit a crime.

Still, something about these two government suits did not sit right with him. He decided, at least for the time being, that he would prefer keeping what he knew to himself. He had no problems sharing things with Roger, but his friend wasn't here now, and Sam had a nagging feeling that he might not see him anytime soon.

He glanced out his window and realized they had already made it all the way to the Tobin Bridge. Ahead, the lights of Boston's skyline covered the horizon, the water beneath them sparking in the light. Sudden panic rushed over him.

"Where are we going?" he asked, trying to sound calm. "Am I going to get to go home night?"

"The field office," Sharp replied tersely.

"We have a few questions for you, that's all," Clifton replied. His tone was friendly, but Sam could sense a finality behind them. "If we're going to keep you out of harms way, we might as well do it in style. We'll just head over to the Boston field office and use the time to see if the three of us can find any answers that might help you out."

Sam leaned his head against the window, staring out at the city all around them.

"I don't suppose I have a choice in this, do I?" he asked hopefully.

"No," replied Sharp. "No choice at all."

The first sign that things were not going to be as friendly as Sam had expected was the room they escorted him to upon arriving. It looked to be pulled right out of the script of a television network crime drama, complete with the square table and metal chairs. There were no windows, only one door, and the horribly outdated fluorescent light fixture over head seemed to flicker and hum with the most indeterminate rhythm.

Looking around, Sam was positive he could see signs of the intended use of a space like this. The arms of the chair that he was seated in had small metal fixtures that he was positive were meant for connecting to restraints. And while the agents who escorted him to the room did not cuff him, they *did* close the door behind them. Sam had a feeling that if he got up and checked, the door would be locked. It was becoming clear that he was less of a guest and more of a prisoner here.

Agent Clifton claimed that he and his partner were looking for food that they could bring back to Sam, but they had been gone for nearly fifteen minutes when the lock finally turned and the door reopened. Agent Sharp tossed him a cellophane-wrapped sandwich that looked to have been purchased at a local convenience store, and his partner set a bottle of water down on the table.

Sam had forgotten how hungry he was until the food appeared. His stomach rumbled at the sight of it, and it was all he could do to keep himself from tearing the wrapping off violently before taking the first bite. He had eaten little in the last twenty-four hours, and between the excitement of the evening and his road trip the day before, Sam was ready for a four-course meal. Instead, he got dry turkey on whole wheat. It wasn't perfect, but it would have to do.

Agent Sharp set a thick manila folder down on the table and took a seat in one of the metal chairs. He stared at Sam for a long moment before turning his gaze to the file. After slowly opening it and looking over the first couple of pages, he pulled out a pen and notebook and then returned his cold eyes to Sam.

"You did a lot of traveling across the Midwest, Mr. Hawthorne," he began. His voice was thick with condescension and distaste. "It seems like everywhere you went, you left a trail of weirdness in your wake. Care to explain that to me?"

Sam took another bite of his sandwich. He could not help but wonder what these agents used to qualify something as 'weird'. If he tried to explain his visions, only to discover that they simply meant something more benign, then he would have given away too much. Better to play dumb for as long as possible.

"What reports?" he asked, trying to look as confused as he could.

Agent Sharp turned over the first page and then selected the next, holding it up to get a better look at it.

"June of 2000," Sharp replied. "A woman named Rachel McGinnis reported to authorities that a man fitting your description—a man who called himself 'Sam', coincidentally—stopped her from stepping off the curb, only to watch a police car speed past second later. Parked cars had obstructed her view of oncoming traffic, according to her report. I guess I would just want to know how you managed to see the car coming if she couldn't."

"Lucky guess," Sam offered, a slight grin on his face.

"Davenport, Iowa," Sharp continued, ignoring Sam's comment. "Alfredo Herrera claims you walked into his pawn shop on the evening of Friday, October 12, 2001 and warned him that a man would be in later to rob him. You recommended that he request a police officer in street clothes be there between 7:50 PM and 8:15 PM. He took your oddly specific advice and the robbery was stopped by the authorities."

This time Sam did not offer a reply. He took another bite of his sandwich without taking his eyes off of Sharp.

The agent continued. "Another report, this one from July of 2003. Jack Hannover of Table Rock, Nebraska claims that you walked onto his property while he was cutting his lawn so that you could tell him his son Max had fallen into a well. Turns out he had—over two hours earlier. Yet witnesses say you had only arrived in town less than ten minutes prior to speaking with Mr. Hannover."

Sam was silent. The agent set the sheet of paper back down on the pile inside the folder and closed it.

"Do I need to continue, Mr. Hawthorne," he growled. "This is what I meant by 'weird' reports. These are things that have no logical explanation. And you were there for all three of them, and dozens more just like them." He jabbed his index finger firmly down on the folder.

"What do you want me to say?" Sam asked. "That I sometimes have visions of the future? That for some unknown reason, my brain tunes into the world around me like a radio and tells me if something bad is happening?"

"For starters, Sam, yes," Clifton said from where he sat beside his partner. "That interests us greatly."

"I bet it does," Sam replied. "But there's nothing more I can tell you. I don't know how it works any more than you do."

"I have a feeling that's not true, Mr. Hawthorne," Sharp said. "I would be willing to guess that you could spend the next hour telling us all about how it works, what it feels like, and how often you've been right. Care to elaborate for me?"

"No," Sam replied. "I don't. You've given me no reason to trust you. And to be perfectly honest, it's none of your business."

Clifton leaned forward, resting his elbows on the table. "I beg to differ, Sam," he said calmly. "You see, it's our job to keep this country safe. We are tasked with preventing and investigating terrorist activity, foreign espionage, cyber crimes, fraud, and violent crimes. It's a messy, never-ending job that leaves us worn out and frustrated that we can't do more."

"That must be so very difficult for you," Sam replied sarcastically. "Not. My. Problem."

"Listen, you little shit," Sharp growled, leaning forward across the table.

Agent Clifton extended a hand to hold his partner back, but never took his eyes off of Sam.

"We have at our disposal some of the most advanced technology on the planet. Many of our field agents are highly trained experts in a vast assortment of fields, from forensics and criminal psychology to nanotechnology and advanced computer sciences. We're the best of the best. Yet every day, criminals slip past us. There are simply too many of them and not enough of us, and we can't be everywhere at the same time.

"You, though, offer us hope. Your gift exists on a whole new level, Sam. You can see the future, allowing you to influence how it plays out. The things you've done, however small and insignificant you might think they've been, are things we would never have been able to do. Agent Sharp and I have spent our careers reacting to the present, Sam. *You*, though, have the chance to react to the *future*. The difference between those two paths is more than a matter of mere semantics; it's a matter of life and death."

"I don't follow," Sam replied. He understood perfectly well what Clifton was suggesting, but he needed to hear it for himself before he believed it. "Connect the dots for me, Agent Clifton."

"Think about the worst tragedies of the last two decades," the agent replied. "Imagine a world where the events of September 11, 2001 could have been prevented, Sam. Imagine knowing ahead of time about how ill-prepared New Orleans was for hurricane Katrina. Less than three years ago, one phone call from you could have stopped an insane man from walking into an elementary school and killing nearly two-dozen children and teachers."

"It doesn't work like that," Sam said. "I don't control it; it controls me. Do you think I want tragic things to happen? God, no. But I can't force my mind to show me things it doesn't want to."

The room fell silent for a moment. Sam's heart was pounding, and a thousand other reasons why their request was insane kept streaming through his mind. He tried to calm himself by closing his eyes and taking a deep breath. What he really wanted was to go home, but he had a feeling that was not going to happen tonight.

I'd love to know what they're thinking right now, he thought. *Any edge to help me get out of here would be nice.*

For a moment, he imagined the agents sitting across from him, waiting impatiently for him to speak again. As he did, eyes still closed, he began to see a faint glow of light ahead of him. It was barely noticeable at first, but steadily grew as he focused on it.

With the light came sounds. At first they were indecipherable, but as the brightness of the light increased, so did the noise. In a matter of seconds it was clear that they were not just sounds but actual human voices. And one of them sounded like Sharp's.

Gotta keep him afraid, the voice seemed to say. *Drive him to panic, keep him from thinking straight. Don't want him going home before we have a chance to put the screws to him. Too much at stake here.*

Sam's eyes shot open, and he looked directly at Agent Sharp. For a brief moment he was tempted to call the man out and tell him he knew what their plans were, but he stopped himself after opening his mouth. They had a limited view of his abilities at the moment, and Sam had a strong hunch that he would only become more valuable to them if he revealed other abilities.

"No, I'm done talking," Sam finally said. "We're done, and I'm out of here."

Sam pushed his chair back and stood. Both agents hopped to their feet so quickly that Sharp's chair toppled over backwards. The loud metallic clang echoed off the small room's hard walls and tile floor.

"Sit down, Mr. Hawthorne," Sharp growled. "We're not done asking our questions. There's a lot more to discuss."

"Fuck off," Sam told the man.

He moved toward the door, but this time Clifton was there, hand held out to stop him.

"Sam, listen," he began. His voice was much more calm than Sharp's, and he was visibly less aggressive. "Just a few more questions. I promise it will be worth your time."

"You've had me here long enough," Sam replied. He glanced at the door, and then back to Clifton. "Unless you plan to bring in an attorney for me, I think this interview is over."

Sam approached the door and had just wrapped his fingers around the smooth metal handle when Sharp spoke up from behind him.

"You don't want to do that, Mr. Hawthorne," he said with a cold, insidious tone. "If you leave, we'll have no choice but to implicate you in the death of Henry Olmsted."

Sam stopped and turned slowly toward the older agent, locking eyes with him. Every muscle in his body seemed to be surging with a bitter mixture of anger and fear.

"You'll do what?" he managed to say through his gritted teeth.

"The evidence is rather overwhelming," Clifton added. "Your prints are all over the house. It even appears you stepped in the man's blood. I'm sure a shoe print analysis would confirm it was you. It wouldn't take much to have you arrested for his murder before the sun was up tomorrow. You wouldn't want that, now, would you?"

Agent Sharp stepped closer to Sam and put his hand on the door.

"Sit down, Mr. Hawthorne," he snarled. "Before I'm forced to put you in the chair myself."

CHAPTER FOURTEEN

THE TWO AGENTS CONTINUED to question Sam for some time before giving up late in the evening. Sam managed to say little else after their initial threats, but the fear that they instilled in him kept him in his seat until they finally exited the room for good.

A few minutes after Clifton and Sharp left him in peace, a third agent arrived. He was in his early fifties, and his face the kindest Sam had seen since arriving. He introduced himself as Agent Cabot, and escorted Sam to a small room down the hall where he would be able to rest for the night.

As he walked alongside the new agent, he became acutely aware that his case had elevated him to someplace above the normal limits of the law. These FBI agents intended to hold him against his will for the greater good of their mission, whether or not he had the right to leave.

Sam found this to be unacceptable, although he had no idea how to change it. He could not leave the building of his own free will, and as far as he knew, no one in the world knew he had been brought here beside the agents themselves.

At least for the moment, there was nothing he could do. He gave up for the evening and settled down onto the room's small, uncomfortable cot and attempted to fall asleep. Compared to the bed he had been given at Roger's house, this one felt like an old barn wood plank, but he made the best that he could out of it.

In the morning, Agent Cabot returned and asked him to dress and ready himself. Fifteen minutes later he was silently escorted back to the interrogation room. Agent Cabot had been such a bright spot in an otherwise frustrating experience that Sam almost felt a pang of loss when the agent did not enter the room with him, but instead closed the door between them.

Waiting for Sam on their metal chairs at the table were agents Sharp and Clifton. The thick manila folder was back, and a small paper cup of steaming coffee waited for Sam on his side of the table.

"Good morning, Sam," Agent Clifton said as Sam took his seat. "Are you ready to continue last night's discussion?"

Sam looked at the pair of agents and tried again to push past their surface and read their thoughts, but for some reason he could not replicate what he had done the night before. Still, he was certain he knew their goal for today: break Sam and put his abilities to use in the service of their agenda. He wasn't going to allow that to happen, though.

"I think I said everything I needed to last night," replied Sam. He took a long sip of his coffee and winced at the bitter aftertaste. "There's nothing more to discuss."

"I think you better leave us to be the judge of that," said Sharp. His voice, despite the early hour, already had a harsh edge to it. "Let's talk about—"

A knock at the door interrupted Sharp. His partner stood and approached the door and opened it slightly to peek out into the hall, but as he did the it was pushed fully open from the other side.

An older, well groomed man stood in the hallway outside, and from where he sat, Sam could see Agent Cabot behind the man. The newcomer wore a well-tailored suit and carried a black leather briefcase with the same level of confidence one might expect from an agent and their sidearm. With the door open, the stranger stepped inside.

"Who are you?" Sharp demanded.

"I am Robert Atmore, Mr. Hawthorne's attorney," he announced with a solid, confident voice as he set his briefcase down on the table. He reached into the breast pocket of his suit coat and pulled out a pair of business cards. He handed one to Sam, and another to Agent Sharp.

"Unless there are pending criminal charges, I will assume my client is free to leave."

"Now see here—" Sharp began, throwing the card on the floor and standing up abruptly.

"Are you well, Sam?" the lawyer asked. Sam was not sure, but he could almost believe that the man was holding back a grin. If so, he was doing an admirable job of it. "I trust they haven't mishandled you."

"N-no," he managed to reply, still in shock. "Unless you consider bad coffee and an uncomfortable bed inhumane."

Robert smiled warmly. "No, Sam," he replied. "That's just the government trying its hardest to be hospitable, I'm sure. Gather your belongings, if you have any with you, and I will escort you out."

Clifton had a hand on Sharp's shoulder, but the older man was pulling away like an angry dog attempting to break free from his master.

"This isn't over, Hawthorne," he barked.

Sam stood and pushed his chair against the table. "No, Agent Sharp," he replied. "I believe it is." He stepped toward the door, following the attorney.

"You'll be back within the hour," the angry agent continued. "Henry Olmsted's death still needs settled, and I'll make sure you spend the rest of your life in prison for it."

Robert stepped away from the doorway and let Sam pass through. "Agent Sharp, correct?" he asked. "The Attorney General of Illinois is a good friend of mine, and he has already informed me that Mr. Hawthorne has been ruled out as a suspect in Mr. Olmsted's murder. They are currently investigating the reports of a new-model sedan with tinted windows that had been seen parked near the home by multiple witnesses."

The agent closed his mouth almost immediately and backed away from the attorney.

"Further," Robert continued, "I suggest that if you find that you have further questions for my client, you will direct your communication to my office. Good day."

The attorney nodded politely at the pair of agents, and then stepped out into the hall with Sam and Agent Cabot. Without a word, they were led through a series of long hallways until they arrived at an elevator. Cabot slid a keycard through a small metal box, and the elevator surged to life somewhere below. When it finally arrived, Sam and Robert stepped in alone, while Agent Cabot gave them both a friendly wave before returning down the hall.

Once the elevator doors closed, Robert turned to Sam with his hand extended.

"Good to meet you, Sam," he said with a warm smile. "Roger's told me a lot about you. It's a pleasure to finally meet you."

A lot? Sam thought. *Finally? I've only been here for a day.*

Sam shook the man's hand. "Thanks for the rescue back there," he offered. "I didn't know if I was ever going to get out."

"If they had it their way, no, you never would have. But thankfully, they don't always get what they want."

A bell chimed as the elevator car slowed to a stop, and the doors slid open to reveal a busy lobby. Robert led Sam out and through a security checkpoint before guiding him toward a row of benches along the lobby wall near the entrance.

"Sam!"

It was Roger's voice. Sam looked up to see his old friend rising from a seat, hand waving to catch his attention. As they approached, the two older men quickly shook hands.

"Thanks for your help, Robert," Roger said. "I hope I didn't pull you away from anything pressing at work."

"Na," Robert waved dismissively. "I'm a full partner; I barely work at all these days. But I do have a meeting to get to. I'll see you both soon, I hope. Good to meet you, Sam."

"You too," Sam replied as the man slipped out through the glass front doors. Then, to Roger, he said, "I'm speechless. How in the world did you manage this?"

"We can talk about that on the way home, Sam," he replied. "There's a lot we need to talk about, actually. I'll drive slow."

Roger nudged the accelerator and guided the car onto Storrow Drive, making his way back toward Route 1 and home. Sam was glad to see Boston again, and this time in the daylight. Before falling asleep the previous night, he had been unsure if he would ever see the light of day again, and that made the drive even more rewarding.

"Alright," he said to Roger, "you have some explaining to do. How the hell did you know where to find me?"

Roger chuckled. "I've got a lot of friends," he replied. "Well-connected friends, I mean."

"I mean it," Sam urged. "That must not have been an easy task, and I'd love to know how you managed it."

"Well," began Roger, "it started after I left the library. I assumed you would be at home, waiting for me and our dinner conversation. I left a little less than an hour after you did, and must have picked the same route to walk home. It was fully dark by then, of course, but I know the streets of this neighborhood well.

"Near the end of Hamilton Street under the light of the streetlamp, I noticed something laying at the edge of the road, where the cobblestone sidewalk touches the curb. I picked it up, only to discover that it was your notebook, the one you referenced during our chat earlier. I knew it was important to you, so finding it on the street hinted at only one of two possibilities: either you had dropped it, or something had happened to you that caused you to misplace it."

The older man reached into the pocket beside his seat and withdrew the familiar shape of Sam's notebook. Sam took it eagerly and tucked it into the back-left pocket of his jeans.

"Sadly," he said, "I hadn't even noticed it was gone. They had me so full of fear and frustration back there that I didn't even think to check for it."

"Maybe that was a good thing," Roger replied. "Who knows what kinds of questions your notes might have raised."

"So, you found my notebook," Sam summarized. "Then what?"

"Then I walked home," Roger replied. "I searched the house for a few minutes, but it was clear you weren't there. After your tale of these mysterious stalkers, and your fear that they might eventually find you here, I put two and two together and decided things hadn't gone well for you. So I called a friend."

"Robert Atmore?" Sam asked.

"No, not Robert. Not immediately, that is. No, I called my friend Lewis, who happens to work at the Boston field office for the FBI. I hoped that he could locate a report somewhere that might hint at your whereabouts. A police report, hospital admission, the county morgue; anything that might help. Turns out, he didn't have to search long, as you were being held down the hall from his office."

"Agent Cabot," Sam guessed through a grin.

"Correct," Roger said with a smile. "He couldn't intervene, but he did his best to manage the situation from the outside. I hope he was helpful."

"He was," Sam replied. "Considering how ruthless that Sharp was, Cabot was a breath of fresh air."

"Good. Lewis is a good man. He happens to be one of a few close friends that I meet regularly with. Another of those friends is Robert. Once we knew your location, Robert volunteered to step in and provide legal assistance."

Sam thought for a moment. "Those are some powerful, helpful friends," he said. "What's the nature of your connection to them? You said you meet regularly?"

Roger sighed. "Ah, see, this is where it gets tricky," he said hesitantly. "Sam, I'm not sure I've been entirely truthful with you. Perhaps I should spend a few moments bringing you up to speed on a few things. You were completely honest with me yesterday afternoon, and I owe you the same transparency and trust."

"I'm all ears," Sam replied.

"Alright," Roger began, "the first lie I told you was that I moved to New England to find a teaching position. That was not entirely true. I could have found a university of equal stature in California, or a handful of other locations across the country. What drew me here was a friendship I had formed with a small group of others who were about the same age as me. Our backgrounds were just as diverse then as they are today, but we were united around a common interest: genealogy.

"Specifically, we all share a passion for the genealogy of a very particular group of people. Sam, are you familiar with the concept of the Mitochondrial Eve?"

Sam shook his head. "Not a bit."

"It's a term used in the field of genetics to describe a specific path into the past. When two humans conceive a child, that child inherits a combination of the DNA from both parents. A part of the DNA passed down from parent to child is called mitochondrial DNA. It's the DNA information found within the mitochondria, a component of most cells in the human body.

"The difference between most DNA information and mitochondrial DNA is that the mitochondria information passes unchanged from mother to child, without altered or recombined with other DNA. It's a pure, unbroken chain that geneticists can use to trace human lineage backward in time, from mother to mother, nearly 200,000 years."

"So," Sam said, "it's kind of like breadcrumbs, then?"

"Yes, exactly," Roger replied. He sounded excited, and Sam could tell that this topic was something that interested him greatly. "So the concept of Mitochondrial Eve is that at the end of that chain, far into our past, we all share a common 'mother' who started it all. Eve, of course, because of the Judeo-Christian teachings about Adam and Eve.

"It's fascinating, actually, because geneticists can use that information to study the movements of our species across the globe over time. It's as if we left a trail behind us, and only recently have we learned to follow it. But my colleagues and I believe that Eve was not alone."

Sam tilted his head slightly as his tried to understand Roger. "What do you mean? That there are other Eves?"

"In a sense," Roger replied. "There is an unpopular theory that *some* people—a very small handful of the general population—can trace their mitochondrial DNA to a different source, one that is not Eve. There are ancient Jewish stories about Eve being Adam's second wife, not his first. That honor, according to the Babylonian Talmud, belongs to a woman named Lilith. Some historical documents say she was a monster, or a demon. But what is clear is that she and Eve were set up in Jewish mythology as peers. They were both mothers.

"So, to lend a name to this alternative mitochondrial strand that can be traced back to a different source, some refer to it as the Mitochondrial Lilith. It's not an acknowledgment of the existence of a real woman named Lilith any more than geneticists are claiming Eve really existed. It's just a way of naming a secondary source of DNA information that, though rare, is out there."

"So, studying this Mitochondrial Lilith had been a group project for you and your friends over the years?"

"Yep. Nearly thirty years, to be exact. And we've learned a lot in that time. One of the interesting things we discovered was that up until the middle of the 14th-century, only an incredibly small percentage of the human population could claim descent from this Lilith figure. And then something changed. Any guess what that might have been?"

Sam thought for a moment but shrugged his shoulders. "No clue," he replied. "Remember, I've been building houses for the last two decades. My days in the history department are far behind me."

"Even still," Roger replied, "you'll have heard of this one: *Yersinia pestis.*"

"The Black Death?" Sam said with surprise. "You mean the plague that burned Europe to the ground?"

"The very one. Nearly half of the population of Europe died as a result of that plague, and in some places the number was closer to three-quarters. The pandemic was ruthless, and very few were immune. One group that was, however, were those who were descended from this mitochondrial Lilith."

"So as a result of the plague, their percentage within the population grew virtually over night," Sam mused, connecting the dots. "The survival of the fittest."

"Not just that," Roger said, "but as a result, their offspring had a head start on repopulating Europe. For a time, their numbers swelled."

"Wait," Sam interrupted. "Why is this lineage so important to you? What's so special about these descendants of your so-called Lilith?"

Roger was quiet for a moment, and Sam could tell he was choosing his words carefully. They had taken the exit off of Route 1 onto 128, and had begun the long curve that would soon lead then back to Salem.

"They were different," he replied. "They were gifted, much the same way you are, Sam."

"You mean they had...," Sam paused to find the right word. "They had powers like *mine*?"

Roger nodded. "Indeed they did. But their world was a much less tolerant one than ours. And with the publication of books like the *Malleus Malificarum*, the general population became increasingly hostile toward them. The hysteria surrounding witchcraft throughout the 15th and 16th-centuries was a direct response to these people."

"So you think the witch-hunts that ravaged Europe and eventually colonial America were really a prejudice against a small, gifted group of people born with special abilities? Roger, that's a really big stretch, don't you think?"

"Sam, do you know who Nostradamus was?"

"Sure, he was the guy who wrote down all those predictions through poetry, right?"

"Essentially, yes," Roger said. "He was a French physician who lived in the first half of the 16th-century. He also lived through a resurgence of the plague, which claimed the lives of his wife and children. But history remembers him for his special gift: his prescience."

"You think Nostradamus was a witch?" Sam was astonished. Roger seemed less and less like a conservative historian with every passing moment.

"I know it," Roger replied. "There were hundreds like him. My colleagues and I have spent our entire adult lives researching them, following their trail, looking for clues, and reconstructing the overarching narrative that the evidence is telling us. And you, Sam, are part of that story."

"How?" Sam asked.

"I told you that I met your father through a genealogy club, remember?" He gave Sam a knowing glance, a look that told him there was more to it than that.

Sam nodded. "Yes?"

"That was a half-truth," Roger continued. "My colleagues and I found your parents through the course of our research. You see, your father was a direct descendant from someone that we know conclusively to have carried the mitochondrial Lilith DNA. Your mother, too, for that matter."

"Both of my parents?" Sam let the information sink in, and the realization slowly dawned on him. "Wait," he said. "You think I'm part of that same genetic minority?"

Sam's head was spinning. The things that he had kept secret for so long, all the aspects of who he was that he viewed as a curse, were traits he inherited from his parents, along with his blue eyes and dark hair. Had they managed to live through the fire, he could only assume they would have told him at some point.

"I don't think it," Roger replied. "I know it. When you were younger, your father and I had you tested. One of our colleagues worked at a genetics research lab in Cambridge, and we had her test a sample of your blood. Everything lines up, Sam."

"You did what?" Sam was beyond shocked. "And no one was going to tell me about this?

"Your parents died before they could tell you, Sam." The older man kept his eyes on the road, but his voice was heavy with the weight of emotion and concern. "I would have told you myself, but you left town so quickly, and then never came back. The truth is, your body contains mitochondrial DNA with roots in the genetic Lilith."

Sam felt numb. "So what does it mean? What am I supposed to do with this?"

"That's what we need to decide," said Roger. "Your parents didn't die in a random house fire, Sam. They were killed because of who they were and what they knew. And that is why you're being hunted."

CHAPTER FIFTEEN

"SO WHAT YOU'RE TELLING me is that my parents were witches," Sam said from across the table.

They had finished their meal of take-out Chinese food and a couple of bottles of Leinenkugel, but those dishes had been pushed out of the way long ago. Sam was finding it difficult to put all of the pieces together that Roger had been detailing for him, but the hardest bit of news to believe was that his parents were gifted like him.

"I think the term 'witch' might be too loaded to use in this case, but yes, your parents had certain abilities. Theirs were subtly present, and they manifested randomly. Neither of them really had much control over them."

"And that's why they died?" Sam asked. "Because of some genetic fluke?"

Roger nodded. "Look Sam, history paints a very bleak picture when it comes to the descendants of the genetic Lilith. Once superstition mixed with religion in the Middle Ages, it got out of hand very quickly. Thousands of people lost their lives in witch-hunts all across Europe. And most of them were women. Coincidence?"

Sam took another drink from his beer and thought it over. "There have been people like me throughout history, then?"

"You bet," Roger nodded. "I mentioned Nostradamus earlier, but there were others you might recognize. Roger Bacon is one example. Imprisoned near the end of his life for what they called alchemy. Nicolas Flamel was another. And then there was John Dee, philosopher and advisor to Queen Elizabeth I."

"And they were all hunted and killed?"

"Not all," replied Roger. "We know from historical records that some lived long, healthy lives. Others, however, met an untimely death at the hands of others. Superstitions involving the occult and the supernatural have existed across Europe for at least a millennia, but as Christianity spread across the continent, so too did a fear of the heretical. Then things changed for the worse."

"How so?" Sam asked.

"Culture shifted," Roger replied. "The religious fanatics who spoke out against the supernatural saw these genetic differences as spiritual aberrations. It was the work of the devil, they said. Something that each person had willingly chosen to do. That moved it out of the realm of human nature and into one of willful disobedience.

"As I told you earlier, when the *Malleus Malificarum* was published, that fear exploded into panic. The general public became acutely aware of the existence of people who were different. I believe they instinctively knew that these people were *better* than them, a more evolved humanity. But as has always been the case throughout history, we prefer to fear what we don't understand, and fear gives way to all sorts of other compromises."

"But what about records of rituals and rites? The 'witches' sabbath' and things like that? And didn't John Dee have a book of spells? I don't use spells to do what I do, Roger. That just doesn't make sense to me."

Roger shrugged. "I would imagine that, for most, these so-called witches were something to be feared. But others would have found it to be fascinating, I'm sure. People emulated and exaggerated. They invented activities and artifacts that helped explain something that was otherwise unexplainable.

"Think of it this way, Sam: would you be likely to believe that someone just envisioned the future in their minds, or that they read a magical spell out of a book? Logic would favor the latter idea. Telekinesis, telepathy, clairvoyance…these are all abilities that are difficult to explain, even in the modern world we live in. I imagine it was even more challenging to do so three or four hundred years ago."

Sam nodded as the logic of it all took hold. "So what most people think of as witchcraft—the popularized things like spell books and broom sticks and pointy hats—those are all inventions that helped medieval people grasp what they saw?"

"Precisely." Roger grinned, and Sam felt a swell of pride, as if he were in school and had answered the teacher's question correctly.

"Some went to the other extreme, though, right?" Sam asked. "Is that where you were going with this?"

"Yes," the older man replied. "Some took it upon themselves to hunt and kill anyone who might have been different, who might have been *special*. There were trials and burnings and countless lives were ruined as a result. And sadly, as time went on, people began to abuse the system. Many people were accused of being witches purely so that others could claim their land or property when they were executed."

"Like Salem," Sam realized. "What happened here three hundred years ago was a horrific, brutal event that had been built on the lie that someone was performing magic."

"See, that's where you might be surprised to know that I disagree," Roger added cautiously.

"With what?" Sam asked. "That it was barbaric?"

"No, that it was all a lie."

"You mean you believe there was something real happening?"

Roger nodded. "Think about it from a different angle. Historians have been trying to explain why the hysteria happened at all. They've gone as far as to blame moldy bread and the resulting ergotism as the cause of the crazy behavior. I'm not saying that can't be true, but there are too many other odd reports. Witnesses claimed to see astral projections of the accused in their homes—they called them specters—and others said they felt physically struck when no one was near them. These sound like clues to me, Sam. They point toward someone with psychic abilities in old Salem Village."

Sam picked up his bottle to take another drink but found that it was empty. He pushed it away toward his empty plate. "You're suggesting that someone descended from this mitochondrial Lilith was alive in Salem, and they somehow managed to escape getting accused, is that it?"

"Exactly," Roger said. "All the while, the townsfolk around them began to have odd experiences, so they naturally went looking for a scapegoat. In other words, I think the events that kicked off the Salem witch hysteria were real, but the blame was placed on innocent people. The real witch got away."

Sam thought through the implications of that theory. It meant that the real Salem witch had brought the sentence of death down upon over two dozen innocent people. It might have been an accident. It most certainly had not been intentional. Regardless, nearly thirty people lost their lives as a result of someone else's carelessness.

"Man, Roger," he began. "That really rewrites things, doesn't it? I mean, the whole message people are taught is that religion killed innocent people because they believed in a fairy tale. Now you're saying the fairy tales are true."

"But most people don't believe that," Roger replied. "Most, but not all."

"What do you mean?" asked Sam.

"Sometime after the trials of 1692, a group was formed. Think of them as the colonial America version of the European witch hunters. They were founded by none other than Cotton Mather himself, and built their mission around the text of the *Malleus Malificarum*. Their purpose was simple: find and execute anyone who showed signs of witchcraft.

"They are the spiritual descendants of the religious fanatics of the 15th-century who slaughtered thousands. Like those who came before them, they don't understand *why* these people are different. They just assume it is heretical, and therefore all of them must die. And they've done their job very well over the centuries."

"This group," Sam asked. "You're talking about the Purga Immundus, right?"

Roger sighed. "The person you met last night identified himself, then?"

"Well, not completely," Sam replied. "He never told me his name. But he mentioned what group he represented. I could probably pick him out of a photo collection if I had to, but I'd rather not meet him again. Who are these people, Roger?"

"The Purga Immundus are old," he replied. "They've been around at least three hundred years. As I mentioned, one of the most vocal proponents of the witch trials here in Salem was Cotton Mather, a Puritan minister with a deeply fanatical interest in seeing criminals punished. He pushed for the trials to happen, and though he claims he was never there, witnesses place him at some of the executions."

"He liked to watch, eh?" Sam cracked a sarcastic grin.

"Evidently," Roger replied. "Some historians believe that without Mather, the trials never would have taken place. And after they were done, he became very vocal about their success and efficacy. He did it all in the name of God, of course, but under that puritanical veneer was a cold, vicious man who wanted others to suffer for simply being different.

"We don't know exactly when, but sometime between the trials in 1692 and his death in 1728, Mather founded what became the Purga Immundus. Their mission was, as their name suggests, to purge the unclean. They eradicate carriers of the mitochondrial Lilith DNA as if they were diseased. And though he did not fully understand the genetic complexity, I believe he had a suspicion that these gifted people passed their abilities on to their children. So he moved his efforts into biological warfare."

"Wait." Sam did a double-take. "Say what?"

"Inoculation," Roger declared. "Smallpox, to be precise. A number of small outbreaks happened during Mather's lifetime. Nothing on the grand scale of the Black Death, but upwards of 30-percent of the people who contracted it died. Mather owned a slave who claimed that he had been inoculated by the British before they took him from Africa. The idea fascinated Mather, and after a while he began a crusade to inoculate all of Boston."

"Did it work?" Sam asked.

"Sort of." Roger took a drink from his nearly empty bottle of beer and then set it aside. "He partnered with a doctor named Zabdiel Boylston, but less than three-hundred people were inoculated. When smallpox returned in 1721, hundreds died. Only eight were patients of Boylston, though. I've long wondered why they treated so few, when the risk was so high. My colleagues and I have a theory about that."

"It was a cover, wasn't it?" Sam suggested.

"Sam, you've got a sharp mind," Roger grinned. "I believe my group could use your intuition. Yes, I think it was a deception meant to give Mather the freedom to move about and attempt to eradicate carriers of the Lilith DNA. Unfortunately, as a result of the highly public Salem trials, as well as general hysteria surrounding witchcraft, we can't know for certain if he managed to kill any of these people. If I was forced to guess, though, I would say he succeeded."

"Why do you lean that way?"

Roger spread his hands apart and shrugged. "Mostly a hunch," he said, "but the overall population of gifted individuals, at least in the New England area, dropped significantly in the years before Mather's death. Seems too coincidental, to be honest."

Roger seemed to become wrapped up in his thoughts, and Sam chose not to interrupt his friend. This was a deep, nebulous topic, and he doubted if Roger could teach him everything over one meal. But he wanted to learn more.

If he started with the premise that his abilities were not in fact a curse as he'd viewed them for so long, but actually the product of inherited genetic characteristics, then he could accept a lot more of what he was hearing. If he was proof of a genetic offshoot of humanity that possessed supernatural powers, then that meant it existed in the past. The story seemed to be right there in the historical record, if one knew where to look for it.

"How many are left?" Sam asked. He had meant to think it, but his mouth took control and spat it out.

Roger was startled out of his thoughts. "Well," he said, eyes briefly glancing out the window, "we can't know for sure; we can only guess, really. My colleagues and I have a rough number of slightly more than one hundred that we know about."

"That's not a lot," Sam replied with a sigh. "This is the work of Purga Immundus, I assume?"

Roger nodded. "They have been systematically hunting witches for centuries. It started with Mather's inoculation ruse, but quickly moved to targeted assassination. I don't know of another group in all this time that's stood up to them, though. They've operated with complete freedom for longer than our country has been a nation, and their resources are limitless."

"How?" Sam asked with shock. "They can't be funded by an outside source, can they? There would be a paper trail, some kind of record of proof. We wouldn't have to expose the truth about witches, only implicate them in a series of murders. Why isn't that an option on the table for us?"

"*Us*, Sam?" Roger asked with a grin. "So you're joining up, are you?"

"I figure I have two choices," he replied. "I can continue running, or I can stand and fight. But I've done enough running and I'm tired of it. They're getting better at finding me every time I settle down. No, I think fighting is my best choice now, and that means finding partners."

"Fantastic," Roger said. "That's good to know. As to how they've stayed undetected, we have theories. One important thing to know is that Dr. Boylston, the man who helped Mather with his biological warfare, was the ancestor of many powerful men, including President John Adams. Mather was wildly influential as well. I think it's safe to assume these men were able to set up a group that could exist outside the law. They seem to still enjoy that privilege to this day."

Sam sighed. It was bad enough to be chased across the eastern half of the country by some unknown group who seemed hell-bent on scaring the living crap out of him. Now, though, that group had turned out to be a centuries-old secret society with a blank check for murder. He didn't like his chances.

Roger and his friends seemed to have done well over the years, though. They had learned a lot and possessed solid information regarding these people. There were questions that still lingered, though.

"So what's their end goal?" he asked finally.

"The Purga Immundus? They want every descendant of the genetic Lilith eradicated." He furrowed his brow and then shrugged. "I'm not sure what we can hope to do against them, to be honest. We've watched them for decades, though, much the same way they've been watching you."

"So why haven't they simply killed me already?" Sam asked.

Roger furrowed his brow. "It's more complicated than that," he replied. "As crazy as it sounds, they actually think they are doing the moral thing by hunting witches. Because of those morals, though, they can't just execute you; they need to give you a chance to repent, to stop using your gifts publicly."

"What, and if I do that, they'll leave me alone?" Sam asked. "Somehow I find that hard to believe."

"You'd be right," Roger replied. "They would most likely kidnap you, offer you a chance to give up your gifts, and then keep you behind bars the rest of your life. Killing an innocent, repentant man would be a sin, you see, so they might be trying to avoid that if possible."

"And these warnings, they've been their attempt to get me to do that?"

"Yep. And if the *Malleus Malificarum* is a good guide to their reasoning, you only have one chance left. In the mean time, they'll do whatever it takes rein you in."

Sam sighed. "Do you know how far back they learned about me?"

"Before the house fire," Roger replied. "Sam, these people have been watching your family for generations. Your self-imposed exile to the Midwest only slowed them down for a bit. It wasn't as if you were hard to watch from a distance, though."

Roger grinned, and Sam took a sharp breath.

"You?" he replied. "*You* were watching me too?"

"Sam, I had to," Roger said. "You were all that I had left. Your parents were like family to me. You and Jason were practically little brothers. After you left, all I could do was hope to stay aware of what you were doing. To know you were safe. To know they hadn't found you yet."

"How much did you know before I even showed up on your doorstep?" Sam asked. His throat felt tight. A part of him felt violated for having been watched from afar by so many people.

Roger looked apologetic, and he leaned forward toward Sam as he spoke. "Almost everything," he replied. "I think the extent of your powers and the most recent threats were the only parts that were new to me. Although, I did know about Henry."

Sam's stomach sunk at the mention of that old, dear man. He felt the weight of immeasurable guilt every time he allowed himself to remember him. The tightness in his throat was joined by heat behind his eyes. He fought to keep the tears at bay.

"Henry died because of me," he managed to whisper. "If I hadn't taken his offer for a place to stay, he would be alive today."

"Sam," Roger said. His voice took on a softer, more conciliatory tone. "You could second-guess every choice you've ever made if you allow yourself to. Henry made a choice to bring a stranger into his home. And you never invited the Purga Immundus inside. They did that on their own."

"That's what bothers me so much," Sam said. "How do you stop a group that is so invasive? They seem to be able to follow me anywhere. Worse, they know I'm here. Hell, they tried to attack me just a block from here. Roger, I don't even know if *you're* safe anymore."

Roger smiled. "Oh, I never assume I'm safe," he said. "But I agree that their reach and power can be overwhelming to think about."

"So now what?"

"Now," Roger replied. "I have an idea I want to run by you."

"I'm all ears."

"It's pretty clear that the Immundus have eyes on you," Roger said. "And they know when you do something, shall we say, supernatural. In fact, not only do they notice it, but it irritates them. They see it as flaunting something that is unclean and heretical."

"It's that pact with the devil I made when I was a child, you see," Sam said with a grin. "They just can't get over that."

Roger smiled. "You joke, but they truly believe that you and others like you can trace their lineage back to some otherworldly arrangement."

"The burden of proof rests squarely on their shoulders," Sam replied. "Until then, I'm just a victim of my genetics, and I can't help it."

"Anyway," Roger said dismissively. "They watch and wait for you to show signs of activity, and then they strike. Traditionally. I realize that yesterday's attack did not follow the use of your powers, but maybe the sight of you out and alone after dark was just too much for their operative to resist. My plan is to use this curiosity, this *trigger*, to our advantage."

"How so?" Sam asked.

"By luring them out in public," Roger answered. "Broad daylight. We can set out the bait and wait for them to make a move. Like you said before, we have no case against them if we approach them as hunters of the supernatural. But if we can present them as kidnappers and murderers, we might have a chance."

"And you think the authorities are going to give them equal treatment?" Sam asked. "Roger, they've been getting away with murder for centuries. How can you be sure that this will work?"

"Because before today, you were unaware of the big picture, and they like it better that way. The next time you step out in public, though, they will view it as blatant and aggressive. They'll need you to be taken care of, and that will cause them to get sloppy. Lewis—you know him as Agent Cabot—is ready to help when you want to move forward."

Sam thought about the proposition for a moment. It was clear that this group became more confrontational when he allowed his powers to manifest. It was also beyond obvious that they wanted to capture him. Still, it seemed to be a big risk.

"How confident do you feel that you can guarantee my safety?" Sam finally asked.

"Absolutely confident," Roger replied. "We'll be in public, in the light of day. These people aren't stupid enough to do something that might jeopardize their safety. Are you willing to try it?"

Sam was quiet for a moment before nodding solemnly. "Yeah, I'm in," he said. "So what's the next step? When do we start?"

"We shall start," Roger answered, "tonight."

CHAPTER SIXTEEN

SAM HAD MANAGED TO settle in and fall asleep rather quickly the night before. It had been a long day, one that had begun with harassment at the hands of the FBI and ended with an emotionally draining conversation. He had walked upstairs with too much on his mind and had expected that to keep him awake, but that ended up not being the case.

For the first time in as long as he could remember, he slept a full night that was absent of dreams or visions of any kind. Although the major ones were few and far between, Sam awoke most mornings with the nagging feeling that he had seen something he should be remembering, or fragments of pictures in his mind. All signs of those dreams would be gone within an hour of getting out of bed and starting his day, but it was hard to forget that even in his sleep, his abilities were working hard.

This morning, though, arrived with no such feelings. Sam opened his eyes to sunlight through one of the large windows in his room and felt truly refreshed. With no job to get ready for, he moved slowly, taking his time and walking that fine line between laziness and the lack of urgency. When he finally did walk downstairs, he was slightly hopeful he would still find breakfast waiting, but more than prepared to be disappointed.

Thankfully, Roger had thought of him, and he found a plate on the counter with a small stack of pancakes flanked by cold bacon. A minute in the microwave warmed the meal up sufficiently, and he sat at the table with a cup of hot coffee to refuel his body. Everything tasted great, although he suspected that was due to the horrible quality of food at the FBI field office in Boston the day before.

He was not entirely sure, but he thought that it was Sunday morning and therefore Roger should be home somewhere. Sam rinsed his plate and set it beside the sink, refilled his coffee cup, and then began his slow search of the downstairs of the house. The place was enormous, but he knew where to look thanks to his previous wanderings. Through the hall and into the sitting room, he found the door to the study, where he had a sense that Roger would be waiting for him.

He paused at the door, which was closed, and listened. He could hear Roger's voice from the other side, and his words stopped Sam from reaching out to grip the door knob.

"Yes, he'll be there," Roger said to someone else. There was a long pause, and the silence told Sam that it was most likely a phone conversation. "I understand that," Roger continued. "Look, he's agreed to do it, so I need you to have your team ready. I doubt we'll have another chance like this again."

Sam felt his shoulders tense and his stomach clench. He could not help but wonder who it was that Roger was speaking with. Walking into the room now might be awkward, though, so he waited a moment longer, listening with his breath held tight in his lungs.

"Ok, good," Roger continued. "Thanks for your help with this."

There was a faint BEEP sound that Sam knew to mean the call had been ended, and he took that as his signal to make his entrance. He gripped the knob, turned it slowly, and stepped into the study. Roger turned to greet him, a faint hint of surprise on his face.

"Good morning, Sam. Sleep well?" Roger asked.

Sam nodded curtly. "Much better than that tiny cell in Boston," he replied. "Were you just on the phone? I hope I didn't interrupt you."

Roger's expression changed. Sam was not sure but he thought the man's eyes darkened. For a moment his smile faded, but then returned as strong as before.

"Yes," he replied. "I had just finished when you walked in, though. I thought it would be a good idea to check in with Lewis to see if any news had come past his desk yet. Neither he nor Clifton and Sharp have had any success in finding the man who assaulted you down the street."

"Well," Sam said as he walked across one of the large, antique rugs toward Roger's work table, "at least they're trying. Thanks for that."

The men exchanged uneasy glances, and then Sam turned his attention to what his friend had assembled on the table in the center of the room. What he found there was out of the ordinary enough that it completely shifted his attention off of the mysterious phone call.

"What in the world is this?" he asked curiously.

Sam motioned to the center of the table where a number of strange devices and objects had been gathered. In the center sat a candelabra with four thin, tall candles mounted in the holders. A collection of small objects had been arranged around it like a miniature army. There was a stack of playing cards, a pair of old, well-worn spoons, and even a feather. Each item was innocuous on its own, but together, in the center of the vast, stately library here in Roger's home, the collection resembled something out of a vaudevillian performance.

AARON MAHNKE

"Ah," Roger said, turning to face the table. "You've stumbled upon my gymnasium. Well, not mine. This one is meant for you."

Sam tipped his head slightly to one side as he tried to decipher Roger's meaning. The man was clearly being metaphorical; nothing in the collection struck him as even remotely related to fitness. He could not see the purpose behind it all, and said as such to his friend.

"Your abilities," Roger replied. "They are very much like the muscles on your arms and legs. You can use them innately, but if they are pushed on a regular basis, they can grow stronger. This is that stereotypical moment where I kick sand in your face and tell you that you're a skinny wimp and it's time to start working out."

"Work out?" Sam replied with surprise. "Roger, I've barely used the powers I know I have. I wouldn't know the first thing—"

"I realize that," Roger interrupted, "but *I* do. Or do you actually think you are the first gifted person I've met in thirty years of research?"

The idea was not earth-shattering, but for some reason Sam had never even considered it. Of course there were others like him out there, and the chances that they had interacted with Roger were good. Not guaranteed, but he knew Roger and his colleagues were thorough researchers, so it stood to reason that they had reached out to some.

"I guess I never thought of it that way," Sam finally replied. "You'll have to tell me about the others you've met."

"I will," replied Roger. "But right now, you and I are going to work on your abilities. Because I firmly believe that you are capable of so much more than you are aware of. The question is whether or not you are interested in growing."

"I don't know if it's a matter of interest," he replied. "If anything, I'm frightened."

"Frightened?" Roger asked. "Why would that be?"

"Because I don't know what I'm capable of doing. It's like holding a handgun for the first time. The lethal potential is overwhelming."

"Thankfully," Roger said with a warm tone, "I know what I'm doing. Everything will be controlled, and you are in a safe place. Trust me."

"Alright then," Sam agreed. "What should we do first?"

"We'll start off easy," Roger said. He picked up one of the metal spoons and placed it on the edge of the work table near Sam. "Some psychic abilities require you to push through the human mind, and that can be a noisy, confusing, and often times complex effort. So why don't we start with inanimate objects. I don't want to put restrictions on you, Sam, but perhaps you can try moving or bending an object like this."

Sam nodded. He pulled one of the tall wooden stools closer and sat down facing the table. Then, not really knowing how he should approach the test, he closed his eyes and thought about the spoon. He pictured it where Roger had placed it, the curve of its edged and the shine of the morning sun off the polished surface, and he held that image steady in his mind.

He was not sure he was doing anything that another person could not do, but he kept the spoon in focus. Finally, after several heartbeats of waiting and thinking, Sam held his breath and imagined the spoon hovering above the table, rather than resting on it.

"It's moving, Sam," came Roger's voice. His friend sounded as if he were in another room, though. Sam tightened his attention on the spoon and visualized it moving higher, stopping it about ten inches off the surface of the table. Then he opened his eyes.

The first thing he saw was the spoon fall quickly to the table. It landed with a metallic *thwang* and bounced to the floor. For some reason, opening his eyes was enough to break his concentration. Either that, or he needed his eyes to be closed to even attempt something like that. That option, though, seemed impractical and did not offer much hope.

"Well done," Roger said cheerfully, giving him a congratulatory slap on the back. "That was most impressive, Sam."

"Thanks," he replied. "I lost it once I opened my eyes, though."

"Well," Roger suggested, reaching down to retrieve the spoon. He set it back on the table. "Try starting with your eyes open this time."

"I'll give it a shot," he said, and then focused on the spoon again, this time keeping his eyes open.

Nothing happened for a few seconds, and then Sam saw the spoon begin to rock slightly on its curved bottom. He strained and concentrated, but the spoon refused to do more than move back and forth, never leaving the surface of the work table. After a minute or two of painful concentration, Sam let go.

His head was throbbing, like a slow, steady pulse of fire behind his forehead. He closed his eyes and waited for the pain to fade. It had not worked as he had hoped, not nearly as effectively as the first attempt. He wondered if that was maybe just a matter of practice.

"Are you alright?" Roger asked.

Sam nodded. "Just a bit of a headache. Seems to happen when I try too hard."

"That's common," Roger replied. "Think of it like a muscular cramp. I think that the more you do this, though, the less it will hurt and the further you will be able to take it. Why don't we switch gears and try something less physical."

Roger picked up a stack of cards and showed the backs to Sam. They were normal, everyday playing cards, the kind he would expect to see at a poker game in the back corner of a Midwestern dive bar. Roger fanned them out so he could see that there were dozens of them, most likely the full deck.

"Pick one out but don't turn it over. Keep it facing me."

Sam did as he was instructed, plucking one of the cards from the center of the deck. He kept it held up and facing Roger, while his friend set down the remaining cards.

"What is it?" Roger asked him.

"What?" Sam was confused. "It's a card."

"No, I mean, what card is it?"

Sam understood, and frowned at the new question. Rather than fight it, though, he sighed and closed his eyes. He understood what Roger was aiming for, but he had no idea how he was going to deliver on it.

He pictured the card as he had seen it, positioned away from him with Roger's face in the background. He could not see through the card, however, no matter how hard he tried, and was about to give up when an idea struck him. It was beautiful in its simplicity.

What does Roger see? he thought. *That's the question I need to answer. Roger has a clear view of it. That was his point all along.*

This time, rather than focusing his attention on the back of the card, he tried to do what he had done to Agent Sharp in the FBI interrogation room. He listened with his mind, bending his senses to try and locate Roger's thoughts. Every step of it felt awkward and foreign, but he had a feeling that his intuition was the only guide he could count on.

He pushed and probed, and for a while it resulted in nothing, but after a few moments something seemed to snap into place. It was that feeling Sam got when he tried to push his truck key into the ignition without looking. He would sometimes fumble wildly with the key, but most days it was a simple, rote task. After a second or two of probing, the key would snap into place.

Sam held no key with his mind, but even so he could feel his own thoughts and awareness slip into his friend's. The moment of a *click* was accompanied by a flood of images and sounds, as if he had flipped on a television in the middle of a barrage of commercials. Everything flew by at a speed that was beyond his comprehension, nearly a blur of experiences.

And then he saw the card.

It was behind the confusion of sights and sounds, hovering in space with intense focus and stability. Sam could tell that it was still buried, but thought that perhaps Roger was aiding him by focusing intently on it himself. That might be why the image did not move, instead floating in space amidst the rest of the noise.

"Five of diamonds," Sam said confidently.

"Very good!" Roger exclaimed. "I expected that one to take you longer to manage."

"I think you were helping me," Sam suggested. "You were focused on the card, and that helped it stand out from the noise inside your mind."

Roger nodded. "I was concentrating on what I saw, yes," he replied. "But don't get lost among the trees and miss the fact that you've reached the forest, Sam. You just accomplished what is known as remote viewing. No small feat for a first attempt."

Sam grinned, but the blossoming pain in his temples kept him from beaming. He winced as the pressure grew slightly.

"Are you alright, Sam?"

Sam tipped forward slightly on his stool and barely caught the edge of the table with his hand. He felt as if he were close to passing out, and the pain pulsed like a heart beat inside his skull.

"Just a headache," he replied. "It'll pass."

"Maybe now is a good time to take a break," suggested Roger. "We can always try again later, when you've had a chance to recuperate."

"No," Sam said, shaking his head painfully from side to side. "One more test. I'll stop after that. Let's try one more."

Roger gazed at him, his eyes squinted with concern. Still, there was an excitement in the air, and it was clear that even a man of his age and education could not resist continuing down the path. He nodded once.

"Alright, then," he said, and then pointed at the candelabra in the center of the table. "Do you think you could light one of those candles?"

"That's possible?" Sam asked.

"You bet. It's called pyrokinesis." Roger paused. "Look, are you sure you're up to this?"

"I think so," Sam replied. "So what, I just imagine the wicks engulfed in flames?"

"Honestly?" Roger asked. "I'm not sure. It's not a skill I've ever seen demonstrated before. I've worked with a handful of people like you, and the overwhelming majority of them were low-level psychics. You've already tested outside of that bell-curve, so at this point, your guess is as good as mine."

"How can some of us be less powerful than others? I thought these powers were passed down through an unaltered maternal genetic strand?"

"They are indeed," Roger agreed. "But it seems that the expression of that genetic information is determined by other characteristics, many of which are passed through both parents in the same way eye color or height might be. You have a lot going for you, though, because both of your parents were carriers."

"Both?" Sam was shocked to hear this. "I didn't realize that she was as well. Sometimes I feel like I barely knew my parents."

Roger smiled, and the sight of it warmed Sam's heart. "They were both amazing people, Sam. In fact, each of them sat in that seat many long years ago and attempted to do some of the same things you are doing now. Surprisingly, your mom was much more adept at these things that your father was."

"Really?" Sam asked. He thought of his mother every day, but in this way, in this light, he couldn't help but think of her as a stranger. "What abilities did she have?"

"The ones I knew of," Roger replied, "were what you might expect: telekinesis, levitation, a bit of remote viewing. She even healed you once, after a nasty fall."

Sam took a sharp breath. "I've done that, too," he said.

"I know," Roger replied. "She even demonstrated psychometry for me once."

"Psychometry?" Sam asked.

"Learning things about an object just by touching it," Roger answered.

Sam grinned. "And did she ever light a candle?"

"No, I'm afraid not. In fact, no one has." The man paused and studied Sam intently, and then added, "Yet."

Sam turned and faced the center of the work table, picking the central candle to focus his thoughts on. Almost immediately, his head began to throb anew, as if someone were pumping it full of air, ever expanding the size of his skull and building up the pressure inside. It eased slightly when he closed his eyes, but he had to fight through the residual pain to find the image of the candle in his mind.

He slowed his breathing. It was difficult to relax with so much tension between his temples, but he pushed the sensation out of his conscious mind and focused steadily on the long, white wick. He pictured the orange glow of flames around the end of the waxy cord, the creeping blackness that would slowly descend down the wick toward the candle itself. He could see the air above the flame shimmer and flex as the heat distorted the light that passed around it.

He could very nearly smell the faint odor of charred wick and melting wax. It seemed real. It *felt* real. And for a moment he certainly thought that it was happening. All of this convinced him to open his eyes slightly, just to take a quick glance at the real candle. He hoped to see the yellow glow of a flame atop the central candle. Deeper inside he hoped to find them all aflame, that he had somehow blown away all expectations for the test and left his old friend in awe.

The candelabra was cold and dark, though. No flames burned atop any of the candles. For the briefest of moments, as Sam pointed the full force of his concentration at the long, pale wicks, he felt a feeling of hopelessness and failure. Then, finally, he felt pain as the throbbing in his head resurfaced with a vengeance.

It felt as if someone had pressed the razor-sharp tip of an awl against of the flesh of each temple. The pain was nearly blinding, and his view of the candelabra began to dim as blackness crept into his field of view. Then, in an instant, the unseen man with the invisible awls pushed them both in fast and deep.

Sam's head erupted with white, searing pain, before his mind caved in and he passed out. Then, only darkness.

CHAPTER SEVENTEEN

WHEN SAM OPENED HIS eyes, he was on his back. The sun had filled one of the nearby windows with warm, yellow light, and Roger was leaning over him. He was immediately struck by two observations that left him temporarily disoriented. First, whatever he was laying on was very soft, not like any hard wood floor he had ever reclined on. Secondly, Roger was wearing different clothing.

"How long was I out?" he managed to croak through dry lips.

Roger held a glass of water out for him, and Sam propped himself up on his elbows to take a drink. "Nearly twenty-four hours," his friend replied. "Had me worried for a while, but you pulled out of it."

"What happened?" Sam asked.

"You pushed yourself too hard. You did splendidly, and I think all the excitement drove you to do too much. Do you remember the headaches?"

Sam brought a hand up to the side of his head. There was no pain, but he could imagine it, and he did not like what he remembered. Splitting, searing pain that drove all other thought from his mind. Yes, he had pushed himself far beyond his limits, and he had paid for it.

"Headaches," Sam repeated. "God, yes. I've been out for a whole day?"

"Just about," Roger answered. "It's a bit past 8:00 AM right now. I was about to make myself breakfast. Care to join me?"

Sam's stomach rumbled at the thought of a hot meal, and he nodded enthusiastically.

"Good," Roger said. "I'll go get it started. Come down when you're ready. We've got a lot to do today."

Sam lay back on his pillow and felt the cool joy of relaxation wash over him. It felt good to relax and not think about doing anything. A part of him did not even want to get out of the bed.

Roger reached the door and pulled it open. He stopped in the threshold and looked back over his shoulder for a moment. Sam turned and caught the man's eye.

"By the way, Sam," he said. "You lit the candle."

After breakfast it was clear that Sam was feeling completely restored. Whatever bits of the headache that might have lingered after sleep had vanished along with the cup of coffee and scrambled eggs with bacon. He felt alive and invigorated, and was sure that he could conquer whatever task Roger laid out before him.

Roger was ready to meet the challenge. As they finished their breakfast, he informed Sam that he thought it was a good day to begin their experiment in public. He had called in to the university and informed them that he would be unavailable for the entire week, and then he and Sam began discussing their approach.

"We want to lure the group out into public," he reminded Sam. "We're not trying to land ourselves on the evening news. So, no, I won't allow you to light anything on fire while we're out today. Besides, that left you unconscious for nearly a day. I don't want to have to carry you home."

"So what am I supposed to do, then?" Sam asked impatiently as they were putting on their coats. "We're just going to sit around and wait for one of them to happen upon us?"

"Sam, they'll know we're out of the house the moment we leave," Roger said. "They've probably had the neighborhood under surveillance for days now. The moment we drive away, they'll be following us. I think all we'll be waiting for is for them to feel safe enough to make a move."

Sam remembered overhearing the phone conversation Roger was having in his study the morning before, and he could not help but wonder how his friend could be so sure of what these people would do. He wanted to run, to escape from this risky situation, but there was a nagging feeling in the back of his mind that told him he needed to trust his friend.

A friend I haven't seen in twenty years, Sam thought. *For all I know, he's part of the Purga Immundus and this has all been an elaborate cover.*

Doubt was not going to get him anywhere, and he knew it. He needed to trust *someone* at this point, and Roger was his only option. Still, the nagging would not cease, and he followed his friend out of his large, safe home with more than a little trepidation.

They picked a spot in downtown Salem with plenty of visibility and foot traffic. On the edge of a small square of grass and trees, between a pizza shop and a used book store, was a cafe with a perfect view of the road. Roger and Sam took their drinks out to a table on the sidewalk and began settling in.

It took a while for Sam to feel comfortable. He had spent so much of the last few months looking over his shoulder and worrying about being caught that it was hard to allow himself to relax. Being attacked on the street near Roger's house was just the newest item on a long list of reasons why he felt that this was a bad idea.

Roger assured him that they were both safe, however, and so he slowly allowed himself to think about something other than being grabbed from behind and dragged to a dark, unmarked car somewhere around the corner. The sun was bright and clear, there were few clouds in the sky, and the people who passed by all seemed oblivious to the fact that they were even there.

After an initial hour that seemed to crawl by, time began to move faster. Before Sam knew it, lunch had arrived and there had been no sign of anything suspicious at all. He tried to stay alert and at least slightly worried, but it had become harder to focus on the possible danger. Instead, Sam began to entertain himself.

As each person walked by, he found himself wondering who they were and what they were thinking about. At first, it was a casual case of people watching, but it soon took on supernatural qualities. Sam threw his mind out into the square like a net, and as people came close, he felt for the vibrations of their passing in his mind. For a while, he felt nothing, but eventually he began to hear sounds somewhere deep in his own mind.

Some people's minds were blank as they passed by. Sam noticed that most of those pedestrians were also wearing headphones, and made the assumption that the human mind stopped working so hard when it was being fed a steady stream of auditory input. Others, though, were the human equivalent of a passing car with loud music leaking out its open windows. Thoughts seemed to spill from these people, and Sam found it nearly overwhelming to keep up with.

...pay that bill today, or else I'm going to be in serious...

...wonderful last night! I hope he calls me again soon, because I...

...jerk needs to watch where he's walking. Nearly knocked my coffee out of my fucking hand, the...

...creep keeps staring at me. I knew I shouldn't have worn this skirt...

Sam snapped out of the fog for a moment and glanced around. Roger was still seated across from him and reading the book he had brought along. He held a pencil in his hand, and would stop occasionally to make a note in the margin. Other than those small interruptions, his friend was completely distracted by the book.

Suddenly the square seemed full of mental noise, and Sam was finding it hard to keep up. It felt claustrophobic to a degree. The sounds around him would close in as each pedestrian approached before fading again as they moved away in the opposite direction. Ebbs and flows, much like the rhythm of the ocean, but on a level that no one else in the square could comprehend.

It was both overwhelming and empowering all at the same time. He felt in complete control of his abilities, and yet as helpless as a piece of driftwood on top of a large swell. It became easy to listen and wander, letting his mental ear turn this way and that, but found it most rewarding when he managed to focus it, pointing it at one person for as long as possible.

Sam did not know how long he allowed his mind to do this, shifting back and forth between listening to the crowd and singling out one specific sound, but the sun began to move across the sky and past the lip of the buildings to their west. Shadows stretched across the square, cutting dark slashes across the bright green. Time moved, but Sam did not notice it.

He had just finished listening in on the thoughts of a busy middle-aged man as he hurried by on his way to meet a younger woman for a secret afternoon liaison—a meeting that the man was utterly convinced his wife was suspicious of—when something in the noise of the crowd around him caught his attention.

He did not know where the thoughts originated from, but they stood out from the typical pedestrian noise of the day like a hippie at a cocktail party. The voice was harsh and jarring and much less normal than those around it. It was the content though, what that mind was actually thinking, that drove a chill down his spine and pulled him from his psychic fog.

There he is, it seemed to hiss. *The freak is a sitting duck. Time to move.*

Sam snapped his eyes open and took a sharp breath. Roger looked up from his book and studied his face.

"Something the matter, Sam?"

"They're here," he replied. "I can hear them."

"Hear them?" Roger asked, and then he understood. "Ah, I see. Alright, this is what we hoped for. Ready?"

Sam was shaking. His stomach felt knotted and tight, and he couldn't scan the crowd fast enough. Each face began to look threatening, each figure seeming to be moving in his direction. It was a cacophony of suspicion and fear and anxiety, and he needed it all to stop.

That's when the two men appeared at their table, seeming to materialize from thin air.

"Good afternoon, Mr. Hawthorne," one of the men said in a flat, emotionless tone.

Their sudden appearance seemed to startle Roger as well, causing him to jerk back from the table, knocking his coffee sideways. The beverage, cold from siting for over an hour, toppled to the pavement where it landed with a wet pop.

"W-who are you?" Roger asked the pair of strangers.

"You know very well who we are, Mr. Sandbrook," the taller of the two men replied. He wore a dark overcoat and had pulled his hat low over his face, casting shadows across his features. "We're here to take Mr. Hawthorne into custody.

Sam instantly recognized the second man who stood back a step as the one who had attacked him just three night prior. He was clad in the same style of dark coat that hung to his calves, but he had opted for dark glasses rather than a hat. His bald head was pale and smooth in the afternoon light.

"I told your partner last week that I wasn't interested," Sam spat. "He clearly doesn't know how to listen."

The taller of the two men leaned down toward the table. When he spoke, his voice was barely more than a whisper, but that did not rob it of any intended severity.

"If you think for one moment that this crowd and setting will prevent us from upholding our mission, you are sorely mistaken, Mr. Hawthorne. We are here to remove you from this place, and if you choose to resist, things will escalate quickly."

"Nothing would make me happier," added Sam's former assailant. "So please, tempt me."

"Now, see here," Roger protested, trying to rise from his seat.

The man in the hat reached down and pressed on Roger's shoulder, pushing him easily back into the seat. Roger landed hard on the chair and gave up the struggle instantly. Sam noticed for the first time that both strangers were wearing shoulder holsters, the outer edge of the leather straps showing just beyond their open coats.

"Leave him alone," Sam demanded. "You're out of your mind, harassing us like this in public."

"You would be surprised at the level of violence the everyday pedestrian is capable of ignoring," the man in the hat replied. "Even still, the organization that we represent would have no problem avoiding any and all consequences. We have deep roots, and enjoy quite a bit of freedom from the law of the land."

"No one is exempt from the law," Roger replied. "You'll answer for this. For the death of Henry Olmsted, too."

"The old man was simply a message," the bald man replied. "His life was nearly over. We simply ended it early as a warning to Mr. Hawthorne. You can run, but you cannot hide."

He cast a glance at Roger and noticed the fear in his friend's eyes. In a moment of desperation, Sam reached out with his mind and tried to listen for Roger's thoughts. For a heartbeat he was afraid there would be nothing, and then he heard the clear message his friend was sending him.

Go with them, Sam, his friend was telling him. *Trust me, please. Go with them.*

Sam remembered the phone call that Roger had seemed so quick to dismiss, and wondered again whether he had somehow trusted the wrong man. Here was the person who had taught him everything he needed to know about the Purga Immundus—the man who had made it clear that this group was violent and destructive—and he was actually telling Sam to leave with them.

"Mr. Hawthorne," the bald one reiterated, reaching into his coat for the handgun that was strapped to his side. "Your time is up."

Roger's eyes locked on Sam's, and the man nodded.

Go, Sam. Go with him.

"Fine." Sam said it aloud to the strangers, but his eyes never left Rogers. "If you say so."

He stood, and immediately both men flanked him and hooked their arms in his. Before he could think of what to do, they had begun to lead him away from the cafe and back toward the street they had come from.

Sam glanced back over his shoulder. Roger was frozen in his seat, watching the two strangers lead him away. There was nothing in his expression that hinted at a plan of any kind, and that emptiness left Sam feeling hopeless.

They had nearly reached the sidewalk, covering the small area of grass and trees in quick, steady strides. No one seemed to have noticed them, and Sam wondered how it could possibly end. His friend had handed him over to the enemy, and now there was no way out.

Just a pace or two from the pavement, Sam pushed off both men. He did not know if it would help him at all, but as he did so, he pushed out at them both with his mind, envisioning them being thrown to the ground with a great force. As he felt their hands slip free from his arms, he bolted for the sidewalk and then turned right to round the corner of the building that abutted the square.

"Get him!" cried one of the men from behind him.

Sam did not dare to turn around to see how close they were, but he knew he needed to run. He rounded the corner as fast as his feet would let him, and was about to bolt down the sidewalk when two men in dark suits stepped out of the doorway of the first shop.

"Get down," one of them said to Sam as he approached.

Failure washed over him. He had tried to escape, but instead had run directly into the arms of the enemy. He had no idea there had been more waiting for him. How could he? It had been easy to assume the two strangers were alone, that there was no one else around to help them. Yet here he was, trapped between the proverbial rock and a hard place.

"Sam, get down!" the man said again. This time Sam looked at him, finding his eyes and studying the man's face. That was when relief washed over him.

"Agent Cabot!" he said with relief. "What are you—"

The FBI agent brought his weapon up quickly, cutting Sam off and sending him into a skid on the pavement near their feet. He turned around to glance back at the men who had been chasing him and saw them stop short just as they rounded the corner. Each man was armed, but Sam could tell that they were agitated and disheveled. Apparently his push had done more than knock their hands off his.

"Drop your weapons," Cabot commanded, never taking his own gun off the pair of men.

The attackers glanced at each other briefly before dashing back around the corner and into the square. Cabot and the other agent bolted past Sam and disappeared around the bend. Sam, curiosity getting the better of him, scrambled to his feet and followed after them. When he turned the corner, though, he stopped.

Two new agents had approached the attackers from the rear, and they were pinned between Cabot and the rest of the team. Sam arrived just in time to see both men drop their handguns and kneel on the ground with their hands behind their heads.

"You got them!" he exclaimed as he approached.

"You've done nothing," spat the man in the hat. "We are many. We wait and we watch. We *will* purge the unclean, Mr. Hawthorne. You can count on that."

Roger had quickly joined them, running over to stand between Sam and Agent Cabot.

"Are you alright, Sam?" he asked.

"Yeah," Sam replied. "I thought you were selling me out for a moment there."

"Never," Roger replied. "But for this to work, I needed you to go with them, and I wasn't entirely sure you would actually do it if I told you ahead of time."

"That was well done, Roger," Cabot said, turning to join them. "The audio came through perfectly. That confession will hold up nicely in court.

Sam glanced at Roger. "Audio?"

Roger lifted the left side of his sport coat to reveal the black shape of a listening device, complete with thin black wires snaking around toward his lapel.

"Why capture them in public if we can't come up with anything to hold them on?" he said, smiling at Sam. "Now we have them on tape admitting to Henry's murder, as well as making threats against your life."

Cabot nodded. "These two aren't going to walk the streets for a very long time. Thanks to both of you, I think we have a case. Well done, Sam." He motioned to the two men as they were led away in handcuffs to where a dark government sedan was waiting for them.

Sam smiled. "That's fantastic news," he said. "It'll be nice knowing I'm a bit safer tonight."

"I'm not sure I'd go that far," Cabot replied. "We caught two. There are at least a dozen of them that we know of. If anything, you very well could be in more danger now than you were this morning."

"Is it possible for us to join you for the interrogation?" Roger asked Cabot. "It could be very enlightening, and I wonder if Sam might be able to glean information that would be unavailable to us otherwise."

Sam glanced at his friend. "You want me to read their minds?"

"If you can, yes," Roger replied. "What do you think, Lewis?"

"Consider it done," the agent replied. "Get downtown as fast as you can, and I'll get you both set up in an observation room adjacent to the suspects. I just don't want them to know you're there. Too risky otherwise."

Roger nodded. "We'll follow along shortly."

Cabot shook their hands and then headed toward the others at the car. Sam watched him leave with a sense of dread.

"So, I'm in more danger now than I was this morning, and we're going to go back into the bowels of the FBI building?"

"Not the most enjoyable prospect, is it?" Roger said with a wry grin. "But at least this time you won't be the one sitting across the table from Agent Sharp, right?"

Sam sighed. "It's the little things, I guess."

CHAPTER EIGHTEEN

THE PRISONER IN THE sunglasses sat beneath the bright light of the fluorescent fixtures which hummed monotonously. Sam recognized the style of table and chairs, and noted with relief that the rings mounted in each had been put to use. The man sat still with his hands on the table, but the shimmer of silver chains that draped down and out of sight made it clear that he was not where he wanted to be.

Sam and Roger were seated in a dark room on tall stools a few feet from a large smokey window. The other side of the glass, as seen from the vantage point of the suspect, was not mirrored as television shows might suggest, but simply black. Sam assumed that the prisoner was fully aware he was being watched, but Sam hoped the man did not suspect it was he who watched him.

The door to the interrogation room opened, and Agent Lewis Cabot stepped in, accompanied by Agent Clifton. The suspect turned slowly toward the newcomers, but did not show further signs of interest. In fact, he seemed perfectly at peace.

"I'm Agent Cabot," they heard Lewis declare to the man across at the table. Sam noticed that a small speaker had been mounted above the window, and most of the sound came through it, rather than the window itself. "This is Agent Clifton. We have some questions for you."

The man in the sunglasses seemed to stare back at Cabot, but he didn't respond. Both agents took seats on the side nearest the window, and Clifton set a notepad and pen on the table. They seemed to be waiting patiently for the man to answer.

Sam reached out with his mind and tried to locate the thoughts of the suspect. For a moment he struggled to find his bearings, but then noticed sounds that resembled voices. Pushing farther into the room, he brushed against the familiar sounds of Agent Clifton's thoughts.

…going to put up a fight, I think. I wonder what Cabot has planned. This guy is going to be tough to crack…

Sam moved forward, stretching out and feeling for new thoughts, new minds to peek inside. A moment later he found something, but it felt different from anything he had felt before. He opened his eyes and looked into the room. He had expected to find some clue that might explain what he was experiencing, but there was nothing visible to account for it.

"Everything alright?" Roger asked.

Sam frowned. He motioned toward the window. "I was able to connect with Agent Clifton, but the suspect doesn't seem to be there at all. It's like a dead zone."

"A dead zone?" Roger repeated. "You mean, like when you lose signal from something like a radio or wireless phone?"

Sam nodded. "Yeah, something like that. He's still there, clearly, but when I reach out with my mind, I only find a patch of darkness and silence. It's weird. I can't explain it. I know he's sitting there, but all I can sense is his presence, nothing more."

Roger looked back through the glass at the prisoner and wrinkled his brow. "I wonder…" he began, but let his voice trail off. After a moment, he stood and approached the door to their room and knocked once on the metal frame.

An unnamed agent on the other side opened the door and leaned in. Sam could hear Roger murmuring to the man, who nodded in reply, before he came back over and took his seat again.

"What was that about?" Sam asked his friend.

"I have a theory that I've never been able to prove," Roger replied. "There's a tradition that dates back over five hundred years involving charms that ward off witches. The early charms were small glass bottles filled with an odd concoction of liquids and objects. They were meant to block the witch's power."

Movement caught Sam's eyes, and he turned back to the window. Agent Cabot had walked over to the door and was whispering with the man Roger had spoken with before. After a moment, he returned to the table.

Roger continued. "Glass bottles are easy to find and destroy, so charms evolved over time. Two materials are prominent in the legends as effective against witchcraft: iron and rowan. Rowan is a species of tree found throughout Asia and Europe, as well as here in the States. In our region, it's known as the American mountain-ash. It was a simple thing to take a rowan branch and affix it above a gate or a door to ward off a witch."

"Did it work?" Sam asked.

"Not sure," Roger replied. "But it was used for centuries and never discounted as a myth or ineffective gimmick. I have a feeling there's some truth to the notion. So I've asked Cabot to help us find out."

Roger nodded at the window, and Sam turned back toward it. Cabot and Clifton had stepped around to the back side of the table, and they had their hands extended toward the prisoner. There was a long, intense pause, but finally the man removed his sunglasses and handed them to the agents.

Cabot passed the item to the man at the door, who quickly disappeared from view. The suspect did not seem angry about the change, but Sam was almost certain he could see fear in the man's eyes where there had once been calm and peace.

A moment later, the door to their own room opened again, and the unnamed agent handed two items to Roger before leaving again. The glasses were there, but so was the hat Sam remembered the other suspect wearing at the cafe earlier in the day. Roger handed the sunglasses to Sam while he began to examine the inside of the black formal hat.

"It's a nice homburg," Roger declared. "Good quality, no dents, very clean. I wouldn't mind having one like it for my own collection." He grinned at Sam, but then stopped as he ran a finger along the inside of the crown near the sweatband.

"What is it?" Sam asked.

"I feel a thick band beneath the material," Roger replied. "It doesn't feel like it belongs there. Do you have a knife?"

Sam tugged a small pocket knife out of his jeans and handed it to Roger. The older man used the tip of the blade to cut a few of the stitches and then handed it back. Taking the fabric between his fingertips, Roger pulled and the material pealed back.

Beneath it, sandwiched between the outer material and the original sweatband, was a wooden hoop. It was flat and sanded smooth, but it was clearly an addition. Roger gave Sam a knowing glance.

"I'd stake my reputation on guessing that this is rowan. Did you find anything?"

Sam had not even begun to look, but when he opened the glasses up, he immediately found his answer. From the front, the sunglasses appeared to be plain black plastic. From the inside, however, Sam discovered that the entire length of the temples, as well as behind the bridge and top bar, had been lined with a thin inlay of wood.

"Are you kidding me?" Sam wondered aloud. "Who would go to so much trouble to line their glasses with wood?"

"Men who believe witchcraft is real, and want to keep their thoughts protected," Roger replied, nodding toward the window.

Agent Cabot had settled back into his seat and was asking more questions. Sam decided to listen for a bit before probing toward them himself.

"Why were you downtown today?" Cabot asked them. "Can you explain why you were attempting to kidnap someone in broad daylight?"

No response. The suspect didn't even looked at him. He simply continued to stare straight ahead toward the darkened glass of the window.

"Don't want to talk?" Clifton asked. "That's alright, we're happy to sit here until you do. Nothing better than seeing those tax dollars hard at work, you know?"

The bald man twitched his eyes toward Clifton for a moment before retuning them to the window. He seemed to seethe with anger now. Sam could see one of the veins in the side of his head rising to the surface.

"Go ahead," Roger whispered. "Give it another try." He motioned toward the suspects with the hat before tossing it onto the table behind them.

Sam set the sunglasses beside it and returned his gaze to the suspect. He was the one who assaulted Sam in public three nights before. The streets had been dark and empty, but Sam still recognized him, although he had been wearing a hat that night.

Perhaps they've suspected for a long time now that I might be capable of more than precognition, Sam thought. *It's as if they knew me better than I knew myself. Time to turn the tables.*

Sam closed his eyes and reached out again. He quickly found the familiar mind of Agent Clifton and moved past him toward the bald man. The presence was still there, just as before, but now there was shape and texture and sound where before it had only been an impression. It was if the light had been turned back on. Someone was home.

Sam pushed deeper, probing at the surface of the man's mind. He heard sounds—angry voices, shouting, loud music, and screams—unlike anything he had heard from other people over the last couple of days. It nearly broke his concentration, but he pushed back against it, all the time wondering what it was.

No one's mind has been this noisy, he thought as he probed deeper, feeling for an opening. *It's almost like the guy is creating his own mental shield. Throwing up distraction and noise, or at least accenting and enhancing the noise that's already there.*

He squeezed harder, squinting his eyes and pushing out with his mind, and felt his thoughts slip through the noise and into chaos. The voices were all coming from the bald man, but so were the screams. He could see images now, but it was like trying to watch a baseball game seated while everyone else in the vicinity stood and jumped around. It was complete and total confusion.

"He's trying to keep me out," Sam whispered to Roger. "Building a wall of resistance. I can listen, so he's giving me everything in the world to hear. I don't know what to do."

Roger reached out and put a hand on Sam's shoulder. "If it's a wall, there's an end to it. Push through the noise. Don't worry about interpreting the noise, just concern yourself with seeing what's behind it. That's what he's trying to hide. That's what we need you to get a look at."

Sam nodded and dove back in. Pressure was building on the sides of his head, the seeds of the pain that would follow shortly. Ignoring it, he pressed his mind against the cacophony of shouts and voices and then pushed deeper. He ignored everything, even when some of the words sounded understandable, and tried to find the end of it where the noise stopped.

Finally, after what felt like an eternity of probing, he felt the wall of sound slip past him and fade into the background. He could see again, and what few sounds still remained were softer and more normal. Sam did not know how long it would take the bald man to realize he had been compromised, but he had to assume the worst, and so he took in the images and sounds quickly.

Most of it was unintelligible, verging on the sort of thing one would experience in a fever dream, but Sam studied it all and committed it to memory. Repetitive sounds, images that seemed prominent, even faces; Sam soaked it all in as if he were recording it all in his notebook.

And then he was out.

It was as if a hand had reached out and pushed him firmly backwards, through the chaos of the noise and visual distraction, until he was fully expelled from the man's mind. Sam was certain that he could claw his way back inside, but the bald man was obviously trained to repel this kind of attack and he would soon find himself pushed out again.

Sam didn't make a second attempt, though. He was fairly certain that there was nothing more to learn. He had gleaned all he could, and what he had discovered left him feeling disturbed.

"We need to talk," Sam said aloud. Roger turned toward him. "Call your group together. We need to meet tonight. If we don't, I think it will be too late."

Sam sat on one of the low, firm sofas in the sitting room, waiting for the others to arrive. Roger paced in front of the wide, unlit fireplace, his hands behind his back, deep in thought. In the other room, Sam heard the clock chime as it ticked over to 8:00 PM and checked his watch to confirm it.

"I still don't understand why this meeting has to happen tonight," Roger said, stopping at the center of the mantle. "What did you see?"

"I think the Purga Immundus is planning an offensive. Some kind of attack. I saw hints of it in that man's head. I couldn't figure out the exact details, but I know it's going to happen soon. We need talk, as a group, about how we might be able to handle that."

Just then, a knock echoed through the hall. Roger turned and glanced at the door, and then gave Sam a worried expression.

Sam shook his head. "It's just Lewis," he said with a smile.

"I have a feeling I'm going to regret teaching you how to do that," Roger replied with an expression of mock sternness.

Roger headed to the door and let Lewis in, and the three men chatted briefly about the afternoon's excitement before another knock announced the arrival of two more. Robert Atmore entered the room wearing another very expensive suit, followed by a woman of roughly the same age, but a much more casual appearance.

"Helen Jacobson," she said, introducing herself to Sam.

"Good to meet you," Sam replied.

"Helen is our resident medical doctor," Roger added. "She specializes in genetics."

"Genetics is a hobby," she said with a friendly grin. "By day, I'm an Assistant Professor of Medicine at Harvard Medical School. It pays the bills."

Helen wore dark blue jeans and a pale green sweater over a white shirt. Her hair hung straight to just above her shoulders, and she had a playful sparkle in her eyes. Sam liked her immediately.

Roger motioned to the door to his study. "Shall we?"

The five of them settled into seats near the fireplace, and Lewis helped Roger build a fire to add some warmth to the room. Robert managed to locate a stash of bourbon and began handing out glasses to everyone except Lewis, who politely declined. Once they were ready, they all took their seats.

"How were your guests doing before you left, Lewis?" Robert asked.

"Quiet," Lewis replied. "They've refused to say a word the entire time they've been in custody. It doesn't matter, though, since we have one of them on tape confessing to the murder. Still, it would have been nice to get something else out of them that would be admissible in court, you know?"

Robert nodded. "Their silence isn't going to be very helpful to them when their case goes to trial, don't forget. The judge is not going to look favorably on a silent defendant. They're digging their own grave by doing this."

"Still," Roger added, "we did manage to sit through part of your attempt at an interrogation, and Sam here had some success."

"Success?" Helen asked.

"Sam's discovered his latent telepathic abilities," Robert said with a grin. "We always wondered when it would happen. Thank goodness you started testing him before this happened, Roger."

Roger turned to Sam and raised an eyebrow. "Enlighten us, Mr. Hawthorne," he said. "Tell us what you learned."

He looked around the room and studied the faces of the others. Roger trusted them, and that was good enough for Sam, but it still felt odd describing something as unbelievable as telepathy to a group of people he had only just met. He took a deep breath and then began.

"These men are highly trained," he told the others. "I expected them to be good at tracking people, and possibly even skilled killers, sure. But what I didn't expect was to learn that they have also been trained to protect themselves against witches."

"It makes sense," Helen interrupted. "I mean, they do *track* them, after all. And from what we know, they've been doing it for a very long time. Lifetimes. Their accumulated knowledge of witchcraft far outstrips our own."

"These men were each wearing something on their heads," Roger added. "Unassuming things. One wore a hat and the other a pair of sunglasses. But we discovered that these objects were lined with rowan. It was acting like a shield around their minds, keeping Sam from looking inside."

"It really worked?" Robert asked. "We've only ever speculated about it. I've felt confident the legends were true, but you've actually seen it work in practice?"

Sam nodded. "Before asking Agent Cabot—sorry, Lewis—to remove these objects from their heads, I couldn't read anything. I could tell they were in the room, but barely. They were a warm spot in the air, nothing more."

"But after?" Robert asked.

"After they took their shields off, everything changed," Sam answered. "Though, they still put up a fight. The one I tried to read managed to throw up a huge amount of noise and distraction. I have to wonder if most people, the ones who aren't aware of this sort of thing at all, would even be able to do that. It's like these men were trained in making it hard for witches to read them."

"What did you learn?" Lewis asked, getting to the point. "They clearly weren't telling *me* anything, so I hope you managed to get something out of them."

"I did, but it wasn't completely intelligible. My hope is that you guys perhaps will recognize some of the details and help me put the puzzle together. For instance, one of the prominent visuals in the bald man's mind was a wooded area. Narrow trees, very tall, and possibly some large rocks."

"Oh, that's easy," Helen said. "That's clearly an image of *the entire state of Massachusetts*." She offered a grin to highlight her sarcasm.

Sam sighed. "I know it's not a lot to go on, but it's what I saw. I also heard a name a few times. Thomas, I think."

"Thomas?" Robert asked. "That's all?"

"I feel like I heard more subconsciously. Part of me wants to say Thomas Mather, but that could just be me putting odd memories together."

"Wait," Roger said, holding up a hand. "There *was* a Thomas Mather. Your father, Matthew, was our resident Mather historian. Just about everything we know about that family was sourced by your father, although all of that was lost in the fire along with him. Still, we had numerous conversations about the things he discovered."

"I remember this," Helen added. "Matthew said that the last descendant of Cotton Mather was a man named Thomas. But I want to say he told us this Thomas Mather was dead."

Robert nodded. "Yes, died nearly forty years before Matthew learned about him. Died young, if I remember correctly. An accident in college back in the mid-Fifties, I think."

"I like to think there was a group like us back then," Lewis said. "Some group of men and women who banded together to try and stop the Immundus by killing their leader. Of course, it's all fantasy. We have no idea whether this Thomas Mather was even the leader of his fraternity, let alone a two-hundred year old secret organization."

"Sure makes you wonder, though," Helen agreed.

"The only other thing I feel confident about after digging into the man's head is that their group is planning a large offensive. It's going to happen soon, and it involves the culmination of years of planning."

"That's not too specific, though, Sam," Lewis said. "No other details to help us narrow it down and maybe search for them?"

Sam shook his head. "No. I can tell you confidently that they are based in Salem, and that their numbers are far greater than the dozen or so you guys have guessed at. They're powerful, hidden, and they have something planned that will not be good for people like me."

Everyone was quiet for a moment, and then Roger spoke up.

"Lewis, I think we should step up our search of the city tomorrow. There's no way your office could devote some resources to that, given the suspects you now have in custody?"

"It will be a tough sell to my supervisor," Lewis replied. "With these guys keeping their mouths shut, there's not a lot to go on. I'll go back over the audio tonight and see if there's a clue that might justify a team of agents. No promises, though."

"I'll call in a few favors tomorrow, as well," Robert added. "I've been playing with a theory that involves property taxes in town. I'm wondering if there's a chance of a paper trail there."

"That name still bothers me, though," Helen said. "Why would Sam hear the name of a dead Mather descendant?"

"Dammit, I wish Matthew were still here," Roger said. The moment the words left his mouth, he realized the effect they might have had on Sam, and turned to him apologetically. "Sorry, Sam. I hope that didn't offend you."

"No," Sam replied with a sigh, "I wish he was here too."

CHAPTER NINETEEN

ROGER CLOSED THE DOOR for the final time that night, and Sam watched through the sitting room window as Helen climbed into Robert's car. The evening of discussion had been a frustrating one, as well as emotionally draining, and Sam was more than ready for bed.

He had hoped for a more solid plan. They had made some progress earlier that day, of course, with the capture of two operatives from the group that wanted to kill him. Surely they had enough information to go on in order to take the fight to the enemy's door. If the meeting tonight had shown him anything, however, it was that this matter was more nuanced and delicate than he had ever imagined.

They did not know where the Purga Immundus were located. Outside of a general assumption that they were Salem-based, no other signs existed to point Roger and his friends toward them. The group had something terrible planned, but he lacked so many details about what that might be that Sam was left with an impotent frustration that boiled just beneath the surface.

At least Roger's friends were united in their goal, and Sam found some comfort in that. It was clear that the Immundus needed to be exposed and handed over to the authorities. Lewis was confident that, if brought to the light of justice, each and every member of that organization, however ancient and secret it might be, would see swift and severe punishment.

That made thinking about the situation that much more frustrating, though. Without a location, they could not be found and caught. Without being caught, the group was free to continue with plans that Sam felt would have tragic consequences. Plans that were still unknown.

Sam sighed and turned away from the window. Perhaps they just needed more time. Maybe there was one powerful discovery just waiting around the corner for them to stumble upon. Time would tell, hopefully.

The consensus was clear from their conversation, though, that Sam's father would have brought something to the table that was sorely lacking. Aside from his historical perspective and knowledge of key players from the last three centuries of this drama, Matthew Hawthorne had been the researcher for the group, a mantle that Roger was forced to pick up after his death. Whatever Sam's father had discovered, though, had been lost in the fire, along with Matthew himself.

And my mother and brother, Sam thought bitterly.

"I'm going to spend some time in the study," Roger said, interrupting Sam's brooding. "Are you headed up now?"

Sam nodded. "Yeah, I think I've done enough for one day."

"Sounds good," Roger said. "I'll lock up and take care of the kitchen. You should get some rest."

Sam stood, and then an idea occurred to him.

"I was wondering," he began. "What sort of information did my father have that was so important? It seems like so much of what you guys know is written down and easy to reference. What could he have possibly have known that was too sensitive to record?"

Roger paused in the hallway. "Well, the short answer is that we don't know. Your father was the smartest of us all. I mean that, too. Robert, Helen, and Lewis are all bright people, brilliant in their respective fields, but none of us could hold a candle to your father. His insight and discoveries made our research possible. Without him, we were just a handful of people interested in local history."

"I didn't realize that," Sam replied. "I guess he was just always my dad, you know?"

Roger smiled. "Sam, please remember that for as much passion and time as your father poured into this project, he cared infinitely more about you and your brother. He told me once that he did all of it for you. He never explained what that meant, but he said he was building a legacy for you. One of peace and safety."

"That would have been nice," Sam replied with a sigh. "It sounds like he wouldn't be too happy to know his son has been hunted for years, and is currently at risk of being caught."

"It would piss him off, for sure," Roger said with a grin. "But you're safe, and that's all that matters. We don't have your father or his research, but I'm so very glad that we still have you. His passion and vision lives on as long as you do."

"Well," Sam replied, "let's hope we can find a way out of this. The tables need to turn. I'm tired of being the one who's hunted. I'd love a chance to take this fight to their door."

"One day at a time, Sam," Roger replied. "We'll get there, though. I can feel it. We're closer now to the end than we've ever been."

Sam turned to walk up the stairs, but Roger stopped him one last time.

"Hey, this is going to sound like a random question, but your father never had an office outside of your house, did he?"

Sam shook his head. "No, he worked out of that room on the first floor," he said. "It was always a mess. I can't imagine it would have been that messy if he'd had another place to put things.

"Darn," Roger replied. "Maybe a safety deposit box, or some kind of storage locker?"

"I don't know. That doesn't sound like my dad's style. Everything always had to be within reach, easily accessible, you know? I think he felt that as long as he could see something and reach out to it, it was safe." Sam paused, and then added, "Why do you ask?"

Roger shrugged. "Oh, your father asked me to look after something before he died. It's an old key. I guess I've always held on to the hope that it opened the door on some forgotten storage room where a treasure trove of documents and notes awaited us."

Sam smiled. "It's a great dream, but I have a feeling that we lost it all when we lost him."

"And what a loss," Roger added. "I miss that man. He was a good friend."

Sam nodded but found that he couldn't find the words to reply. Instead he smiled, fighting back the warmth behind his eyes, and then began to climb the stairs.

"See you in the morning," he said.

"You bet," Roger replied. "Sleep well, Sam."

Upstairs, Sam slowly made his way to his room. It was not late by the standards of most people, but it felt like midnight. He was drained, physically and emotionally. As was typical, a more eventful day meant much more to consider and process.

He could not help but wonder how long his safety here would remain intact. The Purga Immundus had grown bold since his arrival in New England, and that worried him. Something had changed, and it was more than just his proximity to the historic area. It was as if his exile from Hollesley had been something they disliked, and that he had been driven back home for some unknown reason.

Sam knew that he presented a threat to them, though. He had experienced new things over the past few days. He had learned to accept his abilities and explore their limits. He had tested the comfort that Roger seemed to show with such unusual, supernatural abilities. He had even used those powers to help further their cause, and all of this had made him even more dangerous than before.

Yet, he thought. *I'm just learning, and I'd have to imagine they aren't worried about me* now, *but me* later.

He was too tired to think about it. He walked over to the dresser at one side of his room and reached into the ruffled bag he had placed on top. He pulled out a pair of flannel pants and a t-shirt and tossed them onto the bed, and then proceeded to change out of the clothes he had worn all day. It felt good to get more comfortable.

He folded his jeans and shirt and pushed them into the bag. He was not sure just when he would feel safe enough to unpack and use the dresser as it was intended, but for now it felt better to just stay light and flexible. He had grown so used to running that it almost seemed unnatural to consider settling down at this stage.

His hand brushed against something firm and solid at the bottom of the bag, and he reached deeper to retrieve it. He knew what it was, but seeing it again—touching it with his hands, feeling the weight of it—reminded him of its significance.

Roger's key, he realized as he pulled the box out of the duffle bag. *What are the chances that it unlocks this old thing?*

For the last twenty years, this small wooden box had always been with him. Safe, treasured, and unopened. When he had first taken possession of it, that day long ago in the front yard of his family home, he had felt numb to it. It was simply the thing his father had given him before he died. That had made it difficult to look at for a very long time.

He purposely kept it out of sight for about a year after leaving Hollesley for the Midwest. It was not until he had settled into his new life away from his past and the loss that hovered over it like a dark cloud that he gave it a second thought.

He wondered what could possibly be inside it. What had his father believed was so important that he had struggled to rescue it from the fire, even at the cost of his own life? Sam was nearly paralyzed by the significance that the wooden box represented, too frozen to even consider unlocking it.

As time had gone by, he had thought less about opening it at all and more about simply keeping it safe. He had always made sure it was ready to travel with him at a moment's notice, and that it stayed out of sight. He always knew where it was.

He was clueless to its contents, but he guarded it with his life nonetheless. Now, in light of all the things he had learned since returning home and reconnecting with Roger, he had begun to wonder if the box held more than just memories from his past.

What if it held answers? What if a solution to his troubles, and those of others like him, were hidden inside the locked container?

Roger having a key—one he received from Sam's father, no less—seemed to suggest that perhaps it *did* play some crucial role. What that was, though, remained a mystery. And would continue to do so until Sam found the strength to tell his friend about the box. Did he even know of its existence? Would he recognize it? Would he find hope in Sam's story of how he came to own it?

Sam set the box on the dresser and stepped back. It felt impulsive, but he knew that he needed to show it to Roger, and he committed to doing that first thing in the morning. He would bring it up at breakfast and then they would try to solve the mystery, beginning with the key.

His stomach felt light and full of fluttering things at the thought of finally opening the box. For a moment he considered picking it up and walking down the hall to his friend's room to get it over with now, but that would not be wise. They were both tired from the long day, and a fresh outlook would help them both approach it with proper reverence and insight.

Sam turned to walk to the bed, but decided he still wanted the box to remain hidden until then. He picked it back up, pushed it to the bottom of the bag it had come from, and then zipped it shut. He was tired, but he did not want that to lead to carelessness.

The bed was a soft, welcome experience, and as he pulled the coverers up to his collarbone, he sighed and felt the stress of the day melt from his body. The sheets were cool enough to make him shiver, and he tugged them up higher to fight off the chill.

Tomorrow had the potential to hold answers. Tonight, though, was all about rest. Sam reached over to the bedside lamp and twisted the nob. With a faint *CLICK*, the room was dark and he was falling fast and hard into well-earned sleep.

Sam was back in the woods. The grass beneath his body felt damp and smelled of fresh clippings and rotting bark. Trees, narrow and tall, stood like sentinels around him, black lines against a deep gray backdrop. Everything he could see seemed bathed in shadow. Everything, that is, except the fire.

A tall bonfire raged just a few yards from where he lay, casting orange and red light on the large gray stones that were scattered around him. It seemed to be positioned lower than his head, but even still the flames reached high into the night sky. As they flickered and waved in the darkness, Sam's eyes were led up by their orange and yellow fingers. Waiting above them and the dark silhouette of trees was a vast array of bright stars on a field of deep blues and purples.

With a sudden realization, Sam recognized the clearing. The trees, the stones, the feeling of enclosure and confinement all reminded him of the images that he'd seen inside the mind of the bald attacker.

Sam felt painful pressure around his wrists and ankles, and struggled to look at them. Try as he might, however, his body refused to obey his mind, and he remained horizontal on the damp ground. His hearing seemed muffled, but somewhere in the distance he could hear the faint sounds of traffic mixed with the low murmuring of a dozen voices. Some were closer than others, but whatever they were saying was lost on him.

The darkness seemed to shift and ripple at the edges of the firelight, and Sam watched as a small crowd appeared from the shadows on the right side of the bonfire. A handful of figures were slowly inching their way through the dark. They struggled against something, like men at a game of tug-o-war, but Sam could not see what it was.

The voices faded and silence washed over the clearing, and he returned his gaze to the fire. A lone figure stood beside it, black against the bright light of the flames. The person wore a hood over their head, and a long cloak concealed any recognizable feature.

This figure seemed to be awaiting the approach of the others, but their movement was slowed as they fought against something. A moment later it occurred to Sam what they were doing: the shapes were dragging something toward the fire. It was large and long and it writhed on the ground as they pulled and tugged and leaned forward to bring it closer.

A voice cried out. Sam could not understand what it said, if in fact they were words at all. To him it sounded more like a guttural cry of panic and fear. He could not be sure, but he guessed that the cry came from the shape behind the struggling figures. Someone, or some*thing*, was being dragged against their will toward the bonfire.

Sam struggled against his bindings and attempted to roll up onto his knees, but someone kicked out at him from behind, knocking him back to the ground. Anger flowed through his body like a powerful undercurrent and he struggled to inch closer to the fire. Again, the unseen foot struck him, connecting with his side and sending an eruption of pain and pinpoints of light into his field of vision.

He stopped moving when the small group of figures did the same. They had reached the fire, and the flames had painted their dark cloaks with bright orange light, but the deep shadows still made it hard for Sam to see faces. He tried to roll forward, but he was trapped, pinned to the ground and forced to watch the scene unfold from a distance.

The figures turned and descended upon the writhing figure on the ground behind them. Sam expected them to lift the man up, but instead they bent and found the end of a long pole. As they lifted one end of the wooden post from the ground, the struggling man rose with it. Sam could not see them, but he knew there were ropes binding the man to the post.

Then, with slow deliberation, the figures guided the post toward the fire. Two of them lifted the lower end of the long wooden pole and moved it into the smoldering coals at the base of the bonfire. With a heave, they tossed their end of the post into the flames, kicking up a cloud of embers and sparks that rose into the darkness like fireflies.

Panic rose in Sam's chest. He did not know who the men had tied to the post, but something inside of him cried out against their actions. He opened his mouth to scream, but something prevented sound from escaping. No one turned toward him or even acknowledged his presence. They simply moved ahead with their plans.

With the foot of the post planted in the heart of the bonfire, all of the figures gathered at the other end and began to lift and push. The screaming man, still tied to the post against his will, kicked and struggled with impotent rage as he was brought closer to the fire. The higher the top of the post rose, the fewer feet remained between him and the blistering flames.

Sam struggled to his knees before falling forward. He landed on his chest and began to worm his way toward the light of the fire. He did not know how he planned to help the man, but every fiber of his being cried out for the figures to stop. He needed them to put the man down, whoever he was, and pull him back from the flames, but there was nothing he could do to stop them.

And then the pole shifted, rotating as the men struggled to stand it upright without stepping into the flames themselves. As the post spun on its foot, the orange light of the fire spilled across the man's face, and for the first time since waking up on the wet, filthy ground of the clearing, Sam could see who it was.

Roger.

His old friend, and the man responsible for helping him come to terms with his gifts and challenges, hung from his place on the post. His feet were already smoking as the flames licked at the leather, and there were blackened edges on the cuffs of his pants. He only had moments before the rest of his body would be in the flames.

Sam screamed and Roger looked up. He expected his friend to cry out for help, to yell to Sam from the fire, but the older man instead turned to the lone figure just out of reach and began to shout. Roger kept nodding toward Sam as his screamed, but Sam could not tell what his friend was saying.

The figure, who had waited beside the fire as the others dragged Roger closer and closer, finally approached the flames. The hood fell back to reveal the pale face of a man crowned with a head of white hair. A hand rose from the dark folds of his cloak, and Sam could see firelight glint off a polished edge.

The man had a knife.

Sam struggled again but hopelessness quickly washed over him. There was no chance he would break free. No chance he could reach Roger in time. As the flames began to singe more and more of his friend's clothing, the strange old man stepped closer, bringing the knife up high.

With one swift motion, the man brought his blade down toward Roger's body. Sam screamed again, but as he did the darkness swallowed him. In an instant, everything was gone; every sound and scent and splash of brilliant orange, so powerful and real one moment, simply vanished as if they had never existed in the first place.

CHAPTER TWENTY

SAM SAT UP, AND as he opened his eyes, the darkness faded away. He was relieved to find that he was still in his bed, the white sheets tangled around his legs and early morning light pouring in through the windows. Whatever he had experienced, whether a vision or a nightmare, was gone now. All that was left to do was to act upon it.

He pulled at the sheets to free his legs and swung them over the side of the bed. The floor was cold. Sam reached for his watch on the nightstand and checked the time as he fastened it around his wrist.

Quarter to eight, he thought. *I might just beat Roger to the kitchen today.*

That was a good thing, considering how much he wanted to discuss with him. The conversation about the key returned to his mind as he gathered his things for the shower. He was bracing himself for disappointment, but hope always had a way of creeping in.

I might find out today. Two decades of wondering what's in that box could end today.

Sam could tell from the moment he stepped into the bathroom that he was the first to use it for the morning, which seemed odd. Roger was always out of bed early. The man had an annoying knack for getting an hour or more of work in before breakfast. The previous night had certainly been a late ending to an exhausting day, though, so perhaps Roger had decided to sleep later than usual.

After his shower, Sam headed downstairs and made his way down the hall toward the kitchen. It was colder downstairs than it had been in his bedroom, and he made a mental note to grab a sweatshirt after breakfast. The light that filtered in through the windows had the weak tone of an overcast sky. Sam wondered if it might rain before long.

He found the kitchen as it had been left the night before. Glasses sat beside the sink with traces of bourbon still at the bottom of some. The plates from the dinner he and Roger had eaten before the meeting were still in the sink, and their silverware lay in a pile beside them. There was, however, no sign at all that Roger had made coffee or breakfast for himself.

Sam filled the carafe with water from the tap and pulled a package of ground coffee out of the freezer. After setting up the machine to brew a full pot, he decided to check the library for his friend. Roger was allowed to sleep in whenever he wanted, but something was not sitting right with Sam and he felt compelled to check.

The hallway outside the kitchen was still cold, and as he stepped into the sitting room he discovered why. One of the long, sheer curtains that covered the windows was billowing into the room. How the window had come to be left open, and for how long, was a mystery that Sam immediately wanted to solve, but in the meantime he wanted it closed.

He stepped around the armchair and bent to reach for the open window's bottom edge, but drew back in shock. The window was closed and locked, but the glass had been smashed inward. He looked down at the floor between the sill and the end table and saw the sparkle of hundreds of tiny glass fragments.

Shit, this isn't good.

"Roger?" he called out with mounting panic in his voice while turning toward the study door. Sam did not approach it right away, but he could tell from where he stood by the window that the door to the other room was slightly ajar. He called out louder this time, "Roger, are you in there?"

The was still no answer, and the silence filled Sam with dread. He stepped away from the window and jumped when a piece of glass cracked beneath one of his shoes. A gust of wind rushed in through the shattered window, sending a chill down his back.

It was beginning to make sense to Sam now, and his mind was racing toward a horrible and frightening conclusion. Roger had told him he was staying up late to work in the study. Something had clearly happened before his friend had made it upstairs.

What confused him, however, was the absence of any sign of struggle in the sitting room. Everything that had happened, from the moment the window was broken until now, had taken place elsewhere. If he was a gambling man, Sam would bet all his money on the study as the scene of the crime.

It occurred to Sam that if someone was still in the room, they would have heard him shouting for Roger already. He had effectively announced his presence to anyone waiting for him. The question now was whether or not there really was someone still in the study.

He moved across the room with a slow silence, keeping his eyes on the small gap between the door and the frame. When he was close enough, he reached toward the knob, fingers flexed to grab it, but stopped before doing so. Another idea occurred to him.

Rather than touch the door, he pushed with his mind. He had levitated a spoon just days before, and assumed the principles were the same. Moving the object in his mind would be mirrored in the physical world.

Sam skipped closing his eyes this time, and instead focused intently on a small part of the door and pushed out at it. For a moment he wondered if it would work, and then suddenly the hinges creaked as the door slowly swung inward. As it did, he braced himself for an attack, for something or someone to crash through the doorway and strike out at him.

Nothing happened, though.

Sam counted silently to ten and then stepped through the open door. Inside, his suspicions were immediately confirmed. Whatever had happened last night, it had happened in this room. Furniture had been overturned near the table and papers were strewn everywhere. He saw no sign of anyone still being in the room, however.

That included Roger.

Sam stepped deeper into the room. He skirted the overturned sofa and approached the large work table. Roger's papers had been pushed off the surface, as if a struggle had taken place right in this very spot. He checked for blood, but after a brief search he decided there was none to be found.

I guess that's a good sign, he thought. *If he's uninjured, he's probably safe. For the time being, that is.*

He could not help but wonder what Roger had been doing before the break-in. Who had attacked him, though, was clear enough. The only people who would have had a need to remove Roger from the picture was the very group that Sam was trying to avoid: the Purga Immundus.

Sam picked up one of the stools and stood it back up. Taking a seat, he paused to think everything through, to process what had happened and what it meant. The biggest questions he had involved the purpose of this attack, and how it served the greater purpose of the people pursuing him.

It was clear from the events of the past few days that the Immundus wanted to take Sam into custody. They had been close for years, biding their time until the best opportunity came about. When Sam moved back to the area, effectively returning from exile, he unknowingly moved right into their seat of power.

It was not as if he had planned to do so, he had simply been unaware. He wanted nothing more than to avoid the people who had harassed and stalked him for years. It was deflating to realize he had fled to the one place where they were most deadly: Salem. There was no other location where this group was more protected.

Sam rested his elbows on the table and planted his face in his hands. Roger had been protecting him. He had been teaching him, and together they had been forming a plan that would remove Sam from danger. Roger, his oldest friend and most powerful ally, had been the proverbial basket that Sam was stacking each and every egg into.

Now he was gone.

Not just gone; Roger had been kidnapped, and though Sam had yet to find confirmation of what he suspected, there could be no other explanation other than the Purga Immundus.

Sam opened his eyes and scanned the table. He hoped that figuring out what Roger had been working on might offer a clue that could could keep him safe and hint at his friend's whereabouts. But it was one massive jumble of paperwork, hand-written notes, and scans of historical documents. It blurred together into a field of white.

Everything, except for one item in the center of the table, looked the same. When Sam's eyes landed on it, he practically leapt from his seat on the stool. He snatched up the paper and turned it until he was sure of what he found. That's when his stomach knotted up with fear.

GRAVITER SUSPECT. UNDE OMNIA AD ITER NOCTE.

He didn't know what it said, but he read the Latin over and over until it was committed to memory. Then, reaching into the front pocket of his pants, he pulled out a business card. Robert's business card was still there.

With the Latin note and the card both in hand, he went to find a phone.

⸺⸺ ⧢ ⸺⸺

Lewis and Robert both arrived at almost the same moment, just before noon. Sam opened the door and immediately walked them over to the window in the siting room.

"Shit," Lewis said, bending down to examine the shattered glass on the wood floor. "It didn't even occur to me that Roger would need protection."

"You're kidding," replied Robert. "He's got a man living with him who is the prime target of a secret organization, and you never thought to post an agent or two outside? Good God, Lewis, you even had just cause!"

Lewis shook his head. "I know," he said. "I'm just as pissed at myself as you are, believe me. It's obvious in retrospect. Dammit!"

"What do we do?" Sam asked, attempting to bring some focus to their conversation.

"Show me the study," Robert replied.

Sam led the men into Roger's study, and both men began to examine the scene.

"He put up a hell of a fight," Lewis said, uprighting the sofa. "Have you found any blood or signs of a weapon?"

Sam shook his head. "Nothing," he said. "Except the note I found."

"You mentioned that on the phone," Robert said. "What's the significance? You sounded as if a note was almost predictable."

"It's how they harassed me over the years," Sam replied. "A few small notes left inside the apartments I lived in. Subtle ways of communicating how unsafe I really was, that they wouldn't be stopped by locked doors and privacy. The last two notes, though, were written on my walls. In blood."

"Blood?" Lewis repeated. "Damn, why didn't you tell us this earlier?"

"I told Roger," Sam replied. "I figured that was enough. Maybe he forgot to pass it along. Maybe he felt it wasn't as important as the messages themselves."

"What were they?" Robert asked.

"I was being accused by them according to some level of suspicion found in the *Malleus Malificarum*. The first bloody message declared me to be under 'light suspicion', and the second one bumped me up to 'strong suspicion'. Which is why the note they left is so frightening."

Sam picked the paper up from the table and handed it to Robert. Lewis stepped closer and read over his friend's shoulder.

"Did you translate this yet?" he asked.

Sam nodded. "While I waited for you guys to get here. Roughly translated, it says, 'grave suspicion, travel tonight to the place where it all began'. Any idea what that could mean?"

"Where *what* all began?" Lewis asked.

"That's a good question," Sam replied. "One that I'm sure Roger would have had an easy time answering, too."

Robert nodded. "Looks like we're going to have to figure that out without him, though." He motioned toward the workspace. "Clear some room and get some blank paper for me. Let's start listing off any and all possibilities that make sense."

"Possibilities for what?" Sam asked.

"Where they have Roger," Robert replied. "They've taken him, and left a message for you to travel to his location. A location they've left in code, unfortunately. We need to find 'the place where it all started', and quickly."

"You guys are going to help me, right?" Sam felt like he had been set adrift in a vast ocean with no hope of survival. "I can't do this on my own."

Robert smiled, and the sight of it gave Sam hope. "Of course we will," the man said. "We'll figure out where you need to be, and then I think Lewis can accompany you. He's a trained law enforcement official, after all."

"You both realize that I can't call the branch for backup, right?" Lewis was pacing beside the table. "There's little I can do other than come along for the ride. If I called this in, it would open the whole thing up to the other agents in my office. And I know Sharp would simply *love* to crack this thing wide."

"Sharp is a prick," Sam added. "No offense meant, but that guy couldn't have been more aggressive and mean-spirited during my time with him."

Lewis grinned. "Yeah, he and Clifton have that Good Cop, Bad Cop routine down pretty well. It helps that Clifton is actually a really great guy, and Sharp is an asshole through and through."

"Where did everything begin?" Robert asked, looking down at the blank piece of paper on the table. "What in the world does 'everything' encompass, though? Are they talking about the genetic origins of people like Sam's family, or are they referring to something more specific, like the birth of Mather's little hit squad?"

Sam and Lewis were silent, each man processing the questions and running through the possible answers. It was Sam who spoke up first.

"It would have to be local," he said. "If they really expect us to come to this location, and if they really did take

Roger there, then it's near by. Whatever began, it had to have begun here."

"Well then, the answer is pretty easy," Lewis added. "The 1692 trials here in Salem pretty much kicked everything off that we're dealing with today."

"Right," Sam replied. "So where did that begin? I mean, we're in Salem, aren't we?"

Robert shook his head. "I thought you majored in American history in college, Sam?"

"I did," Sam replied. "That was twenty years ago, and I never finished the degree. You see, my family died, and I went on a walkabout through the cornfields of the Midwest."

"Don't be a smart-ass, Sam," Robert replied. "I know what you've been through. I'm not playing a game here. Neither are they. We need to figure out the right answer, and soon. They want us there by tonight."

Lewis began pacing again, and Sam leaned on the table beside Robert, staring at the empty page with him, willing an answer to appear. He ran through all of the details he could remember about the Salem witch trials, but that list was very short. Robert was right, it was too short for a lover of history who was born in the area. He had never felt more ignorant.

"They would be places that are still accessible after three centuries," Lewis said. "What about the Rebecca

Nurse homestead in Danvers? It's still there. Hell, the cemetery out back is still accessible too. Maybe there?"

Robert nodded and wrote the name of the location on the page. "What else?"

"Gallows Hill," Sam suggested. "It's a park now, right? I suppose they could be expecting us to meet there. It's big and much more private after sunset."

"I'm not sure about that one," Robert said, writing it down anyway. "One could say that Gallows Hill is where it all *ended*, not began. Still, worth listing. Next?"

"The Witch House," Lewis said.

"The Corwin place?" Robert asked. "I never thought of that." He scribbled the name on the list.

"I thought it was just a museum in an old house," Sam said. "Is it connected?"

"Indirectly," Robert replied. "Jonathan Corwin was one of the nine ruling Magistrates that presided over the trials. One of the other nine, by the way, was John Hathorne, who you are a direct descendant of, Sam. Corwin was from Salem, and his home is now known as the Witch House."

Lewis stopped pacing and returned to the table. "So, we've got the Nurse homestead, Gallows Hill, and the Corwin house. Which one is it?"

All three men stared at the page, reading the locations over and over. It was finally Robert who broke the silence.

"I vote for the Corwin house," he said, leaning back from the table. "It's of the period, and the man who lived there was part of the trials. It's locked up at night, and run by a non-profit. I'd be willing to bet that the Immundus are somehow connected to it."

Lewis slapped the table and stepped back. "That settles it, then," he said firmly. "Let's get ready for tonight. Do you agree, Sam?"

Sam, though, was lost in thought. Something about the list, and their decision, did not sit right with him. There was something older, something deeper in the past that seemed to be scratching at the back of his mind. He struggled to find the name, but in his mind he could see it.

It was surrounded by trees.

A shiver ran down his spine as his dream from the previous night rushed back. As it did, everything lined up. He knew what they must do.

"Parris," he said.

Lewis and Robert exchanged confused glances.

"Sam, nothing about the Salem trials has any connection to Paris, France," Robert said. "Wrong continent, wrong culture."

"No, not Paris, P-A-R-R-I-S," he spelled out. "Reverend Samuel Parris, the Puritan minister here in Salem during the trials. His daughter Betty was one of the two girls who started it all, remember?"

Robert's eyes grew wide. "Good God, you're right," he muttered. "Parris and her cousin Abigail. They had been spending time with the Parris slave woman, Tituba. Some people think she was teaching the girls magic."

Sam nodded. "Exactly," he replied. "In the Parris home, which isn't even in Salem. It's in Danvers."

Lewis nodded enthusiastically. "That's right! Danvers was Salem Village back then, and most of the accused came from that area. Danvers hasn't taken the same approach to those events, though. They've distanced themselves about as vigorously as Salem has embraced it. That means most of the key places from the 1692 trials are hard to find these days. The Parris home is still there?"

Sam shook his head. "Nope, but the foundation is. It's in a clearing in the woods behind a residential street. A clearing that matches the images I pulled from one of the suspects during his questioning. And it also matches the clearing I've been seeing in my dreams."

"Dreams?" Robert asked. "Dreams of the premonition kind?"

"I hope not," Sam replied with the image of Roger being carried to the bonfire still fresh in his mind. "I can tell you more about them later, but for now I think it's safe to say that we're supposed to meet them there tonight."

"It's settled, then," Robert pronounced. "Lewis, what can you do to prepare Sam for this meeting?"

Lewis smiled. "Oh, I have some ideas."

CHAPTER TWENTY-ONE

THE SIGN WAS BARELY visible beneath a shroud of leaves and deep shadows. It stood beside a low stone wall that ran perpendicular to the street before disappearing between a large white house and a small, worn-out garage. An unkept path followed the wall into the shadows, and a wooden fence lined the opposite side of the path.

Sam stopped and looked at Lewis. The older man wore a worried expression on his face, and Sam could empathize. They had no idea what awaited them at the end of the path, but considering the harassment and attacks that he had endured so far, it was likely to be an unpleasant experience.

Still, they needed to find a way to free Roger. If his dream was a glimpse of the future, it told a story that he did not care to live through. The Purga Immundus planned to kill Roger while he watched, and Sam was not ready to let the last remaining friend from his childhood die. If the future could be changed, he was ready to do whatever it took to save his friend.

"Ready?" Lewis asked. Sam could not see the man's handgun in the dark, but he heard the FBI agent pull back the slide to chamber his first round.

Sam nodded, afraid to speak aloud in the dark, and then stepped onto the path. At some point in the distant past, someone had edged the pathway with large, flat stones. They were irregular and inconsistent, but every footstep resulted in a sound that was too loud for Sam's comfort. After a moment of experimenting, he finally moved to the inside of the path and walked on the grass that grew there.

A few paces in, the trail passed between two trees, and the sky immediately vanished, taking the dim starlight with it. Sam could hear Lewis beside him, the low and steady rhythm of his breathing matching the soft plodding of his feet. Ahead, only darkness and shadow awaited them.

After walking a dozen yards down the path and into the trees, Sam heard a sound to his left. He turned to look into the shadows of the wooded area beside the path, but as he did, two men dressed in dark clothing and black cloaks stepped over the fence and leveled their handguns at him.

"If you have a weapon, drop it," came a cold, harsh voice from the shadows ahead. "Your friend as well."

The two strangers stepped closer, and Sam saw a faint reflection of light glint off one of their guns. Lewis, behind him and to the right, tossed his own weapon on the ground, where it clattered against one of the paving stones.

"You're making a horrible mistake," he told the strangers.

"Are we?" one of them asked. "I think you underestimate our power. There is very little we cannot get away with."

"Tell that to your friends sitting in a cell in Boston right now," Lewis spat.

"Ah, yes," the other man replied. "Those men knew the cost of their involvement. They willingly chose their mission, and are fully prepared to endure the consequences. But they will never talk. You may count on that."

The other stranger approached and picked up Lewis's gun, and then patted both men down to check for other weapons. Sam nearly recoiled with indignant anger from the man's touch, but managed to remain still. When they were done, the man pressed his handgun against Sam's low back, and guided him forward into the shadows.

"Where are you taking us?" Sam pleaded.

"Be silent, witch," his captor hissed. "Keep walking forward until you see the light."

"I'm with you, Sam," he heard Lewis say from somewhere behind him. "Take care of Roger!"

Sam set his eyes ahead. Everything was darkness and shadow, the black vertical lines of the tree trunks cutting through the deep gray of night. But as they stepped farther down the wide path, he began to see what his captor had told him about.

A small lantern seemed to float among the shadows that filled the clearing at the end of the path. To his left he could make out the faint outline of the edges of the stone foundation, all that remained of the old parsonage from centuries ago. It was surrounded by a low fence, and the silhouette of a sign stood before it, black against the deep shadows.

The light of the lantern illuminated the bare hand of a figure who stood alone in the clearing. The pale glow of the flame behind the glass revealed the shape of a man wearing a dark cloak or robe. He was broad-shouldered, and light flickered off the cut of his jaw, which was set with a grim firmness.

"Mr. Hawthorne," came a voice, but not from the figure. Sam looked farther into the clearing to see another dark shape moving through the shadows toward him. The light of the lantern crept up the newcomer's features as he approached. "Welcome to our little gathering. We've been waiting for you for a very, very long time."

"Let Roger go," Sam demanded. "He's done nothing wrong. He's innocent."

"Your friend, Mr. Hawthorne, is guilty of aiding a witch," the man replied. He stepped to within a pace of

Sam. "We do not think he is as innocent as you would have us believe."

"He's guilty of nothing," came the sound of Lewis's voice from behind him. "You're nothing more than a thug, a self-righteous prick who kills what he doesn't understand. And you're most certainly not going to get away with this."

The older man smiled with an expression that reminded Sam of an amused child. Without a word, the man nodded once in the direction of Lewis, and Sam turned just in time to see one of the cloaked men swing his fist quickly toward the back of Lewis's head. As if the power had been cut inside a house, the FBI agent instantly crumpled to the ground.

"Who are you?" Sam asked, turning back to the old man while struggling against the one who held him. "Why are you doing this?"

The man smiled and pulled back the hood of his cloak. His skin was pale and weathered, and his white hair was held back with a thin, simple band of dark wood. The man's clean-shaven face twisted into a grin, revealing teeth too perfect to be real. Instantly, Sam recognized him as the old man from his dream.

He's the one with the knife! Sam thought.

"Mr. Hawthorne," the man replied. "Sam—can I call you Sam?—do you still not understand what it is that we want? It is very clear, and from what your friend has told us, you are fully aware of all the pieces. Have you truly not yet put them all together to see the full picture?

"Our goal is very simple. Humble, I should say. We believe that people of your kind are a curse upon this world. You always have been. Throughout history, those like you have caused trouble across the globe, instilling fear in the hearts of everyone around them. Some have worshipped your kind, committing blasphemy and idolatry. The Church understood for centuries that people like you were unclean —impure, adulterated, and twisted imitations of God's creation—and they deserved to die."

"You're insane," Sam growled. "I didn't ask for this. I didn't sign a contract with some dark power. I was just born this way."

"I understand that," the old man replied. "My family has understood that for centuries. Ever since this group was founded. We have always understood your flaw—your *sin*— to be unintentional. But that does not preclude it from being dealt with. As I said, it is a humble calling, but one that I and my followers are prepared to follow through with."

"Who are you? What family?" Sam's body shivered with fear.

"I am Thomas Atherton," the old man replied. "Thomas Atherton *Mather*. Direct descendant of the Reverend Cotton Mather, a man who once stood on this very plot of land and discussed similar matters with Reverend Parris. A man who knew that people like you needed to be stopped, lest the Devil's foothold in this world grow too powerful."

"You?" Sam said. "But you died sixty years ago. An accident in college, they said."

Mather grinned, and Sam could see delight dance in the old mans eyes. "Oh, I died in my own way. Our organization was under intense scrutiny in the 1950s. We had been very careful for nearly three centuries, but the advent of McCarthyism created a harsh environment for secret organizations. People were overly suspicious of everyone, neighbor or relative, and it quickly became too risky for a man of my lineage and social standing to have clandestine activities.

"So I died," he continued. "I put my old life to death and slipped into obscurity. The Mather family fortune was donated to a non-profit shell organization that was run by the remaining members of my compatriots, and I went into hiding. I have successfully directed the activities of this noble organization for sixty years. Believe me, there was much work to do.

"My forefather began a mission at the turn of the Eighteenth century that has been carried on by every generation since. The slow, systematic eradication of each and every witch from this world. They knew, of course.

They knew and they ran. Hid among the rest of the world like dogs hiding from punishment. Some were found and dealt with, while others managed to survive, passing their curse down through the generations of their own families.

"Families like yours, Sam. Yours is an ancient lineage, you see. One that we have pursued long and hard, across many centuries. But your parents made a fatal mistake when they aligned themselves with your friend's little club. It exposed them, and we took advantage of that."

Sam staggered. Confusion and dread welled up inside him, and he took a deep breath, struggling to maintain control. "What do you mean, you 'took advantage of that'?" he managed to ask through gritted teeth.

"Come now, Sam," the old man said patronizingly. "You truly do not understand what I mean? Your friend Roger knows. I'm surprised he has not told you already. We have watched his small group of sympathizers for nearly three decades. They have been a wealth of information, unwittingly exposing others like you through the course of their research, and deepening our understanding of how and why those of your kind exist.

"When your parents decided to work with them, they stepped into the spotlight. I personally led the team that burned your home to the ground. That is, after we killed your family. A pity you couldn't have been there with them that night."

Sam lunged forward, but the man behind him held him back, twisting one of his arms farther upward. The pain brought Sam to his knees, but the rage inside of him did not subside. He pushed his mind out toward the old man, but it crashed against nothingness.

Mather tipped his head down toward Sam and tapped the wood ring around his brow. "The old legends conceal many truths," he said cheerfully. "Some, such as the truth about you and your kind, have provided us with a mission. Others have aided our efforts. Rowan is one of those wonderful tools."

"Bastard!" Sam shouted, struggling against the man behind him. "My family was harmless. They didn't need to die."

"Oh, but that is where you and I disagree, Mr. Hawthorne," Mather replied. "Your family was more dangerous than any other witch of their generation. They might not have known it themselves, but I was very much aware of it. I did what was necessary, and it was most rewarding."

"You're a psycho, you know that?" Sam cried out. "There's nothing wrong with people like me. I didn't ask to be born this way, dammit. You have no right. I didn't even understand who or what I was until your people pushed me to desperation. I could have remained blissfully unaware if not for you. What do you want from me?"

"We want you to burn," Mather replied with cold confidence. "Did you think you were coming here to rescue your friend? Your friend is already as good as dead, Sam. His sentence has been cast, and soon he will enter the flames. After his corpse is nothing more than charred bone and blacked earth, we will repeat the process with you. Tonight, you will pay for your crimes."

Mather smiled again, and Sam struggled to regain his feet. The man who held his arm, however, twisted it more firmly and forced him to the ground. The soil was damp from the rain earlier in the day, and the scent of it was fresh and thick in his nose. He remembered it from the dream, and as those two worlds overlapped and combined, he redoubled his efforts against his captor. At least there was no bonfire here.

"Oh, no," the man warned him. "You aren't going anywhere."

The man pressed a knee hard against Sam's back, and he felt rough cord being wrapped around his wrists. When the rope had been knotted, the man repeated the process around Sam's ankles, despite his kicking and thrashing. Then, when he had been thoroughly bound, he was hoisted up to stand on his feet to watch as a small group of new figures began to approach. They were clustered around another dark form, but this one seemed to walk with less freedom, less energy.

Sam knew exactly who it was they had brought with them, and he cried out. "Roger!"

"You shouldn't have come after me," Roger's voice cut through the darkness. It was soft and tired. "You can't save me, Sam."

As the group of men led Roger into the dim circle of light cast by the lantern, Mather stepped toward Sam's friend and raised a long knife to the older man's neck.

"Stop!" Sam shouted again. "Let him go! I'll do anything, just leave him alone."

Mather stopped. He turned away from Roger and set his gaze back on Sam, the corners of his mouth creeping slowly upward as a smile threatened to appear.

"You will do anything?" the old man asked. His voice was filled with curiosity. "Tell me, Sam. What reason could I possibly have for letting your friend go?"

Sam paused to collect his thoughts. He had little to bargain with, and he was in a very disadvantageous position. He needed something that Mather would desire more than the death of one man. Something he did not know existed. Something that he might fear. Something to provide enough leverage to free his friend and end this.

When the answer finally came to him, he clenched his jaw. It was simple, but would be costly. Still, Roger's life was more important.

"My father," Sam replied. "You thought you killed him, along with the rest of my family."

"Thought?" Mather echoed. "I *know*, Sam. I pressed the knife into his flesh myself. I watched as his eyes darkened and flickered out. I left him dead on the floor of his study just before setting flame to your home. I *know* your father is dead because I killed him."

Sam shook his head. "You're wrong," he said. "I arrived at the house before the fire department did. A vision —my first, if you care to know—told me to go home as quickly as possible. Maybe I barely missed you and your thugs. I don't know, and I don't care. But what I do know is that when I got there, my dying father crawled out of the house."

"Impossible," Mather spat.

"I'm telling the truth," Sam said. "Yes, he did die, but not in the house. He died right in front of me, there on the lawn outside my home. But not before he gave me something."

"He what?" Mather's face twisted with confusion. "What could your father have possibly thought was that important?"

"I wondered that myself for a very long time," Sam replied. "But after talking with Roger and the others, I'm now convinced I know the answer. You see, everyone in my father's group has a role. His, along with being the resident witch, was to watch *you*. I think that my family has done that for generations, you see. And that they kept meticulous notes."

Mather took a step back. Fear had washed over his features, and his eyes were now open as wide as they could. "I don't believe it," he whispered.

"Is that a risk you're willing to take, Thomas?" Sam asked. "Because my father felt that whatever was inside the box he handed me was worth more than anything else. He could have tried to save my mother, or my brother. He could have followed after you. He could have tried to save the house. But instead, he crawled outside, bloody and dying, to make sure a simple wooden box didn't burn in the flames."

"And you are offering me this box?" Mather asked.

Sam nodded. "It hasn't been opened yet. My father did not give me a key along with it, but I learned just yesterday that the key has been in Roger's possession for decades. Release him, and I will give you both; the box and the key to unlock it will be yours to do with as you please."

"Where are they?" the old man asked, stepping closer to Sam. "Tell me now, or there is no deal."

"Oh, no," Sam replied. "I'm not stupid. Their location is my last bit of leverage I have in this conversation. No, you're going to have to keep Roger alive for that."

Mather turned toward his audience at the edges of the light. "And what say you, Mr. Sandbrook? Your friend here has offered his own life in exchange for yours. He tells me that in addition, you will lead us to a box in his possession, as well as the key that opens it. All this in exchange for your freedom."

"Don't do it, Sam," Roger moaned in reply. "Please don't do it, not after everything we've accomplished."

Mather turned back to Sam. "Actually, I believe I have a slight amendment I would like to make to your offer," he said with a grin. "I think it would be more advantageous to simply kill both of you this evening, and then go search your friend's house ourselves—before we set fire to it, of course. I would like to destroy any evidence that might come back to haunt me."

"No!" Sam tried to lunge forward again, but the bindings at his feet prevented it. "You bastard!"

Mather's smile widened. "I do thank you, Mr. Hawthorne. That was a helpful bit of information to receive, and at the eleventh hour, no less. Marcus?"

The old man nodded and then walked away from the lantern, back into the dark clearing. For a moment, Sam did not know what to expect, but as he turned to look for his captor, he saw movement out of the corner of his eye.

As the man's fist collided with his temple, Sam felt intense pain. Then, blackness filled his vision. The ground disappeared from beneath his feet, and a moment later he was unconscious.

CHAPTER TWENTY-TWO

WHEN SAM AWOKE, THE world was sideways. Slowly and carefully, he lifted his head to look around. Pain throbbed in his temple from the punch that had knocked him unconscious, but he strained against it to focus.

A few yards in front of him, an enormous bonfire had been constructed, and it roared and flickered in the night air. He had been dropped into wet grass and he could smell the soil beneath it. For a moment, he was convinced it was the dream again, yet another dip into the pool that he had already been in before, but there were too many sensations for this to be mere fantasy.

He rolled onto his back, expecting to find the face of the man who had bound him staring back at him, but he was alone. The man—had Mather called him Marcus?—had disappeared, leaving Sam bound and unconscious where he lay.

It took a moment for Sam's eyes to settle on the tree line, the deep blue and black sky filled with pinpricks of starlight overhead. Something about it did not sit quite right with him, but it took a few seconds before he realized why: they weren't in the same place as before.

He and Lewis had arrived at the historical site of the parsonage earlier, but the clearing where the foundations had been dug out and fenced off was much smaller, and with many more branches covering them overhead. This clearing was at least twice the size, with an unobstructed view of the night sky. But where this new location was, Sam had yet to discover.

At the center of the clearing, gathered around the raging bonfire that seemed to lick at the stars with deep hunger, were each of Mather's cloaked followers. Many seemed to be waiting, but a few were off to the right, trying hard to move something toward the fire. Sam stared at it, his mind translating what his eyes were seeing, before gasping. Roger, it appeared, had been tied to a long pole, and a dozen or so men were struggling to maneuver him into the fire.

"Sam!"

Someone called out to him with a harsh whisper. He rolled until his back was to the fire and looked into the darkness near the edge of the clearing. After having stared into the brilliant orange of the fire, it took his eyes a moment to adjust. As they did, a dark shape came into focus and suddenly Sam realized that it was Lewis.

Lewis dropped to his knees and began to work at the ropes that bound Sam's hands.

"God, I thought you were dead," he said.

"I thought the same about you," Sam replied. "I figured we were both trapped and scheduled to die tonight."

Lewis grinned while he tugged at Sam's bindings. "Not a chance," he said. "I might be old, but I'm not *that* old."

"Where are we?" Sam asked, glancing over his shoulder back toward the fire. "They've moved us."

Lewis grunted as he worked one of the knots loose. "No clue," he replied. "But I planned ahead. Small GPS tracker in my pocket. I've activated it and help should be on its way within the next thirty minutes or so."

"How did they not find that and take it from you?" Sam wondered aloud.

"It's thinner than a credit card and half the size," Lewis replied with a wink. "You think the federal government only spends the big bucks on fighter jets and expensive toilet seats?"

The FBI agent gave up trying to tug the rope free and reached into his sock where he had hid a small blade. Sam raised an eyebrow and Lewis grinned.

"Always come prepared," he said as he cut through the thick cords.

As soon as the last of the ropes fell away, Sam sat up and rubbed at his wrists. They were chafed and raw from the friction caused by his struggles. His ankles felt just as bad.

"What's the plan now?" he asked. "They still have Roger, and I doubt we'll stand a chance if they spot us and head our way."

Lewis nodded toward the line of shrubs and trees and the edge of the clearing. "I'm thinking we can hide in there," he whispered. "It should provide enough cover to hold our ground."

Sam didn't need to be convinced. Both men bent and slipped through the bushes before kneeling behind a small cluster of maple saplings. Once hidden, they both turned and studied the scene around the bonfire.

Mather had begun his approach, and light reflected off of the knife that had appeared in his hand. Sam remembered this moment from his dream. He remembered where that knife would be in a matter of minutes. But he also knew that he had not slipped his bindings in his dream. The future wasn't set in stone, and Sam was highly motivated to change it.

"I've seen this," Sam told Lewis, who's head tipped sideways in confusion. "In a dream. Their leader is going to cut Roger with that knife."

Lewis peered back through the low branches and leaves. "I don't know what I can do," he said, shaking his head. "I don't have a weapon anymore, other than this knife, and I doubt it's going to do us much good against that crowd. I think we need to be more creative than that, though."

At first, Sam didn't understand, but the meaning quickly became clear. Lewis was suggesting Sam do something with his abilities. But Lewis didn't know about the headbands.

"Their leader is a Mather," he said, letting the significance of that sink in. "When he spoke with me earlier, he was wearing a wooden headband."

"Rowan," Lewis said with a grimace. "Dammit. So we have no options at all."

"Not quite," Sam replied. "I might not be able to read their minds, but I can still hurt them." He dug at the leaves around the roots of the trees and searched until his hand struck something solid. When he pulled his hand out, his fingers were wrapped around a stone the size of a softball.

"Let's see if I can send them a gift," he said with a grin.

Lewis furrowed his brow. "Sam, Roger told me that you could barely move a spoon. Do you honestly think you're going to be able to push a rock through the air? They've got to be ten yards away."

"If I can't, Roger dies," he replied. "I have to try."

"Fine," Lewis replied. "But we need an alternative in case that doesn't work." He paused and glanced through the leaves again, scanning the trees across the clearing. "There," he said sharply, pointing at a darker patch in along the wall of deep green shrubs. "That's most likely the path they used to get in here. If I think things might go south on us, I'll try and lead them out of here so you can help Roger."

Sam nodded and then tossed the stone through the bushes. It landed silently in the grass at the edge of the clearing before rolling to a stop about ten feet from where both men crouched in the shadows. Then Sam closed his eyes.

He imagined it flying through the air and connecting with Mather. He willed it. He pushed so hard with his mind that his head immediately began to ache and throb. Then, with everything he had, he forced it all to happen.

Lewis raised his head to watch the stone levitate off the ground where it hovered for a moment, rotating slowly as if dangling from some invisible cable. He was more than impressed, and was about to tell Sam that it was working when the stone rocketed away in the direction of the bonfire.

Sam's eyes slammed open and he looked for the rock. He found it just a few feet from Mather, and pushed one last time with every fiber of his being. As if shot from a cannon, the rock connected with Mather's hand, knocking the knife free and sending it into the fire.

"Ah!" the old man cried out, clutching at his injured hand as if it had been smashed with a hammer. He turned his twisted face toward where Sam had been just minutes before, and then began to scan the rest of the clearing.

"They're gone!," he shouted. "Find them! Don't let Hawthorne get away!"

Everything erupted into chaos. The men who were hoisting Roger toward the fire dropped the pole and spread out, the vast majority of them heading toward Lewis and Sam's direction. There were more shouts from near Mather, and three of the larger figures converged on his location, surrounding him.

Sam reached out with his mind to knock the closest man backwards, but it felt like pushing through smoke.

Those damned headbands, he cursed silently. *How the hell am I supposed to stop them if they're all shielded?*

Before he could act, Lewis jumped out of the bushes, raising his knife into the air.

"Hey!" he shouted at them. "I'm over here!"

Lewis bolted for the path across the clearing from where Sam was still hiding and, just as he predicted, the majority of the cloaked figures followed after him. As they disappeared into the darkness, Sam heard gun shots, and he couldn't help but worry for the man's safety.

He glanced back toward the bonfire and located Mather and his small cadre of bodyguards. Four others milled about edges of the clearing, systematically moving in Sam's direction as they inspected the shadows and foliage. The closest had already come within five yards of his hiding place.

I can't control them, he thought. *But I can certainly control objects near them.*

Sam reached out with his mind and found something that he could use and a plan took shape in his mind. He concentrated, and within seconds, one of the ropes that had bound his hands flew out of the darkness and wrapped itself around the man's neck. With a final surge of will, Sam yanked at the rope, pulling the man into the bushes with him.

Sam swung out and struck him on the head with a small rock. Every muscle in the man's body relaxed and he collapsed like a puppet without strings. Then, Sam carefully removed the rope and climbed out of the undergrowth and into the clearing.

He stayed low to the ground and as far behind the sparse foliage as he could, but he knew that he would eventually need to step closer to the fire, and doing so would expose him. It did not matter, though; he needed to save Roger, and from what he could see it was clear that

Mather's men were helping him finish what the others had started.

Sam continued along the edge of the shrubs and shadows, and when he had come within a few yards of the next figure, he tossed the rope and guided it to the man's neck. It struck him around the throat and mouth, and when Sam pulled with his mind, the man nearly rocketed to the ground in front of him. Another quick blow with the rock he gripped in his hand and the man stopped moving.

The other two members of Mather's cult were on the far side of the clearing, and Sam closed his eyes and reached out to find something near them that could be used as a weapon. A fallen limb rose from the shrubs near one of the men, who turned to see it floating in the air beside him. He opened his mouth to scream, but before a sound could exit his mouth, the branch rotated with ferocious velocity and crashed against his forehead.

Three down, one more to go.

He flung the branch toward the last man at the edge of the clearing and heard a wet crunch before seeing the man's silhouette crumple to the ground, melting into the shadows. After a quick glance around, Sam realized that the only people left were the three who were assisting Mather.

A sound interrupted his thoughts, and Sam turned toward the deeper shadows that marked the entrance to the path. He caught a brief flash of light, first red and then blue, punctuated by the chirp of a siren. Whether Lewis had called for backup, or a resident of one of the nearby homes phoned the police about a disturbance in the woods, Sam knew that help was on its way.

Turning back to the bonfire, Sam saw Mather waving his arm at one of the men beside him before pointing a finger toward the path. Immediately they dropped Roger's post and one of the figures walked toward the fire. Sam watched in horror as the man pulled a large burning branch from the base of the bonfire and began to poke at the flames.

He's looking for the knife!

Sam bolted out of the cover provided by the shadows and low branches. He held the rock in one hand and the rope in the other, and as he crossed the gap between himself and the fire, he tossed the rope at the man near the fire.

For a moment, Sam expected it to connect just as it had done before, but one of the other bodyguards saw what was about to happen and threw himself between Sam and his target. The rope collided with the newcomer, and as it did Sam pushed at each end of the rope, wrapping it securely around his body.

The impact of the blow knocked the man backwards. He was a tall man with broad shoulders, but the speed of the rope must have created more force than Sam expected, and the momentum carried him toward the fire. Even though it meant losing the rope as a weapon, Sam pushed again, and the man stumbled into the blazing fire.

As the man toppled into the fire, the other managed to catch sight of the knife. Completely unaware of Sam's presence, he stooped and batted at the base of the flames, knocking the blade free from where it had come to rest beneath one of the logs. The hot knife gave off a wisp of smoke when it landed on the grass, and the man hurried to kick dirt over it to cool it down.

Still in possession of the element of surprise, Sam dashed toward the man and pulled his arm backward, the rock gripped tightly in his hand. The large man glanced up and tried to dodge the blow, but Sam swung with the precision of a man who had used a hammer daily for twenty years. It connected with the larger man's head with a thud, and blood immediately poured from the wound.

"Freak!" the man cried out, staggering from the blow. "You will be the next to burn!"

The last remaining member of Mather's bodyguard broke off from Roger's position and turned to help his partner.

The injured man—Sam now recognized him as Marcus, the one who had tied him up earlier—lunged at him. Sam backpedaled to get away, but stumbled and fell to the ground. Just as Marcus was about to stomp down on his chest with an oversized boot, Sam spotted something on the ground near the knife.

His headband! he realized. Immediately, he knew what to do.

Sam lashed out with the raw power of his will, forcing Marcus to back away. The larger man staggered toward the fire before righting himself and shaking his injured head. It reminded Sam of a boxer who had been driven to the ropes by a haymaker, but was intent on staying in the fight.

The second man was running toward them, but before Sam could act, the man dove at the spot on the ground where the knife had been dropped. He grasped at the wooden handle, all black and cracked now from the fire, and then scrambled to his feet.

"Hurry, you fool!" Mather shouted at him from the other side of the fire.

The man, now carrying the implement of Roger's execution, bolted past him. Sam tried to reach for the man's legs to trip him, but Marcus, now in full possession of his wits again, lashed out with a kick that sent a wave of pain up Sam's arm.

Get up! he urged himself. *You can't win a fight laying on the ground, you idiot!*

He rolled away from Marcus as the man attempted to stomp on his arm, as he did, he passed over the rowan headband that had fallen off the man's head. Sam snatched it from the grass and tossed it into the fire, and then spun around to prepare for the fight.

Marcus was faster, though, and Sam turned his head just in time to see the man crashing into him. Sam flew backward again, but as he landed he tried to roll with the momentum and get as far from his attacker as he could.

Marcus hit the ground just as hard, but his larger size prevented him recovering as quickly. The man's eyes seemed to glaze over, and he shook his head as if a daze had washed over him. When he finally did return to the fight, Sam found it easy to elude the man.

Sam glanced over his shoulder toward the fire, checking to see if Mather was still there. The old man was standing over Roger with the long curved knife clutched in his hand. The flickering light of the fire had thrown sharp shadows across his face, and he looked practically demonic. He was clearly enjoying himself, his thin lips pulled back in a wide grin.

The last remaining member of Mather's cult was kneeling beside him, turning the post enough to expose Roger's chest and face. Sam glanced over at Marcus and decided he needed to act. He had lost the stone he used as a weapon earlier, but Marcus had also lost his headband. Hopefully, that was enough to give him the upper hand.

He jumped to his feet and kicked out at the large man. Despite being addled and more than a little confused,

Marcus managed to grab at Sam's foot, something he had not expected. The man twisted at his leg, and Sam toppled over, landing closer to the fire.

Sam could still see the figures standing over his friend, and froze with panic as he watched Mather raise the knife high in the air. His dream rushed back again, and the hope he had clung to—the hope that had whispered seductively to him of free will and his power to change what he saw— slipped from his grasp.

He was climbing to his feet as the knife was brought down. He did not remember screaming, but as the sound of bitter anguish and pain rang out through the clearing he realized that it was his own mouth that had been uttering the cry.

"No!" he shouted, turning to run toward Mather. The old man turned toward him, and when Sam saw the grin on the man's face, his fear boiled over into rage. "You bastard!" he shouted.

"We purge the unclean, Mr. Hawthorne," Mather intoned. "Only the innocent shall stand when this is over."

An immense weight struck Sam from behind, and he was thrown to the ground just two yards from Roger and the others. He rolled as quickly as he could, bringing his arms up to protect his face, and saw Marcus standing over him.

The man's eyes seemed wrong somehow, as if he had lost his mind. Rage was painted across his face and he held a burning branch high above his head. Something inside of Marcus' brain had snapped, and Sam's life was now firmly under the man's control.

When the branch began its vicious arc toward him, Sam curled up reflexively, throwing his arms over his head. Just when he expected the burning limb to strike, a shot rang out through the clearing. Sam opening his eyes to see a circle of dark red blood blossoming in the center of the man's chest.

Marcus dropped the fiery branch and collapsed to his knees. He remained there for a moment longer, his eyes and mouth wide with shock, before toppling sideways. Sam turned to see who had fired the shot, only to discover Lewis running toward the bonfire.

Sam gathered his legs beneath himself and stood. Marcus had hit him hard on the previous attack, and he was struggling to find his balance. With Lewis in the clearing, he felt safe letting his guard down, but he didn't stop.

Roger needed help. Sam glanced toward where his friend had been left tied to the post, and was surprised to see that he was alone.

Mather and his lackey had vanished into the night.

CHAPTER TWENTY-THREE

SAM DROPPED TO HIS knees beside Roger and immediately began to grope for the bindings that fastened him to the post. The knife had left a ragged opening in his chest, and blood soaked the front of his shirt. By the soft light of the bonfire it looked almost black.

"Sam," Roger coughed at him. "Stop. It's too late."

"No," Sam replied, moving his hands frantically up and down the wooden post to find the knot. "Dammit, where's that knife!" He scanned the ground but there was no sign of the blade that Mather had used to stab his friend. Panic was welling up inside him.

"Sam," Roger said more weakly this time. "I don't have long. You have to listen...before I can't talk anymore."

Sam froze. His mind flashed back to the front lawn of his childhood home twenty years prior, to the image of his father crawling across the grass toward his feet. That wet, choking sound of lungs filling with blood. The tight voice speaking painful words. It was as if his family were dying all over again.

"Roger, we've got an ambulance on the way," Lewis said, squatting down beside them. "Hold on another five minutes, old friend."

Roger's eyes closed and he shook his head. "Not quick enough," he coughed. "Sam, you did well. I'm proud of you. Know that. Remember that."

Sam's eyes felt as if they were on fire. Tears began to fill the edges of his vision, and he reached out to find his friend's hand. "I didn't plan for this," he said through a throat tight with emotion. "You weren't supposed to die."

"Listen," Roger said. "The key is on the mantle in my study. It's..."

A fit of coughing interrupted his words. Sam leaned closer. "Where?"

"The clock," he managed to say. Blood was beginning to dribble from his mouth and down the side of his face. "On the mantle. There's a key in the winding hole. That's the key your father gave me."

Lewis had stepped over the post and pulled the knife from his sock. With a quick motion he sliced through the bindings and Roger spilled off the pole and onto the ground.

"Sorry about that," Lewis said quietly.

Roger grimaced from pain and squeezed his eyes shut again. Sam put his hand on the man's chest and closed his own eyes. He had been able to heal a little girl once. Perhaps he could do the same for his friend. He concentrated and pushed with every bit of strength he had left, but no matter how hard he tried, he could not feel Roger's pain.

"Don't," Roger struggled to say. "There's no way to heal this. Sam, you must listen. I have more to tell you."

Sam pulled his hand away reluctantly and then placed it on Roger's arm. "I'm listening."

Roger coughed again, blood pulsing out of his mouth with each expulsion of air. "Mather has a plan to end it all. He wants to kill every last person like you, Sam. You need to do everything you can to stop him. All of you do."

"How?" Sam asked. Roger's skin was so pale now, his breathing growing more shallow with each breath. "Is he hunting them?"

Roger shook his head and then coughed again. "No... the genetics...oh God, this hurts."

Sam cast a panicked glance at Lewis. "Do something!"

"Sam, there's nothing we *can* do," Lewis replied. "I think it's a miracle that he's lasted this long."

With a sudden surge of movement, Roger reached out and grabbed Sam by the front of his shirt. The dying man pulled him close, reaching up to guide Sam's head to his own. Sam could feel his friend's breath on his ear, and the scent of blood was heavy in the air.

"Don't trust...anyone...they've gotten...to us..." but Roger's words cut off.

The man's hands slipped off of Sam's head and fell to the ground. Sam leaned back to look at his friend. He held on to a dim hope that Roger had just gotten too tired, but his eyes were open and glassy now. He touched his friend's wrist, but there was no pulse to be found. The rise and fall of his chest had stopped, and with it, his last message.

Sam sat himself back on the grass and looked at Lewis in disbelief.

"He can't be," he said. "He's all I had left." Sam's head fell to his chest as the emotional tsunami began to roll over him.

"I know, Sam," Lewis said, putting a comforting hand on Sam's shoulder. "I know."

———

Lewis guided Sam across the clearing toward a rough path. Sam's body ached, but it was nothing compared to the blinding throb behind his eyes. He had needed the agent's arm to support him as he rose from the ground beside Roger's body, but halfway across the clearing his head cleared enough to focus.

As they walked down the path into the darkness, flashes of blue and red lights flickered through the leaves and small branches with a hypnotic rhythm. Each time the lights pulsed, they were stronger, growing as they moved closer to what Sam hoped would be the exit. Lewis steered him around the body of one unlucky man who had been shot through the neck.

"Careful," he told Sam. "I'm anxious to get ID's on all of these guys, and I don't want to disturb the evidence any more than we have to."

Sam nodded and carefully walked around the body, skirting the edge of the path. The night had grown cooler now that they had moved away from the bonfire, and a shiver ran down his back. He could not help but wonder if his loss of hope had anything to do with it, though.

At the end of the trail, they stepped into a small parking lot. The source of the flashing light was a single police cruiser that had been parked a couple of yards from the entrance to the path, but there were at least four other unmarked sedans beside and behind it. On the opposite side of the parking lot from the trees stood a tall building. Sam wasn't positive, but he was fairly certain it was a Walgreens.

A handful of men in dark cloaks stood along side the trees, each one paired up with at least two law enforcement officials. Sam noticed that all of them had their hands behind their backs, presumably having been restrained. He wondered if they would be as silent during their interrogations as their compatriots had been the day before.

A pair of men dressed in suits broke off from the confusion and approached them. Sam immediately recognized them as they approached.

"Agents," Lewis said with a nod.

"Lewis, glad to see you're alright," Agent Clifton said with an expression of genuine relief. "I'm very glad you talked me into sending you with that tracking card. We lost you in Danvers shortly after you arrived there."

"Get him?" Sharp practically barked at them. "Their leader? Did you catch him?"

Lewis shook his head. "By the time I made it to Sam's side, they were gone. Can you get a car out into the neighborhoods around this area and search for any signs of their whereabouts?"

"You bet," Sharp replied before heading in the direction of a small cluster of uniformed police officers.

"Agent Clifton, I'm going to get Sam home. He's had a rough night."

"Get a statement, that's all I ask," Clifton replied. "By the book, Lewis."

"I wouldn't have it any other way," he replied. "But tonight, he just needs to get home and get some rest. And listen, the body by the fire is someone I knew personally. Can you be sure the medical team treats him well, and get me a copy of his autopsy report when you're able?"

"A friend?" Clifton asked. "Is there a deeper story that I should know about?"

Lewis shook his head. "No," he replied thoughtfully. "No, I think we've already covered everything pertinent to the investigation. Thanks for asking, though."

"I need a car," Lewis said. "Any chance I can borrow one of yours?"

"Take mine," Agent Clifton replied with a grin. "I won't enjoy the drive back to Boston with him, but hey, no partner is perfect, right? Keys are in the car."

Lewis smiled and nodded before the other agent slipped back toward the crowd of captives. Sam followed his friend to one of the cars and climbed into the front seat. As he did, his body seemed to let go of every ounce of stress it had managed to accumulate. Within seconds, he was weeping.

Lewis climbed in and started the car, but did not interrupt Sam. He tapped a button on the car's dash and a GPS program came to life. One tap on the compass icon delivered a surprising result, and he read it out loud to Sam.

"We're in Salem," he said with wonder. "They brought us all the way back to were we started this evening. We're literally half a mile from home."

Sam didn't respond, though. He simply stared out the window at nothing in particular, the dark line of trees and bushes blurring together into a green haze.

Lewis pulled the car out of the parking lot and began the short drive back to Chestnut Street. The presence of another adult in the car would have normally made Sam self-conscious about his tears, but Lewis knew Roger. Probably better than he himself did, when he really thought about it.

No, the emotions were a healthy expression of his loss. Still, releasing it all did not seem to be as cathartic as he had hoped. There was more to focus on than his grief and hopelessness. More important matters than simply venting his emotions.

Roger's killer, the man who had murdered Sam's entire family, as well as orchestrated the harassment and threats that he himself had experienced for years, had slipped away. He was gone, and if there was one truth he believed tonight, it was that Mather would not be caught.

Not by the FBI or the police, and not tonight. Their net was being cast too late. Someone like Mather, the mastermind behind this century's incarnation of an organization older than the United States itself, would not allow himself to be caught. His entire life had been an exercise in evasion and secrecy.

"What now?" he said, breaking the silence. "Roger is gone and Mather got away. I can't imagine he's planning on letting me live in peace. Or anyone else like me, for that matter."

"No," Lewis replied, shaking his head. "But don't forget, a good number of Mather's people are now in FBI custody. Whatever his plans are, they're going to be severely hampered by tonight's events."

"We don't even know how many people he has working for him," Sam said. "Tonight could have been catastrophic for him, yes, but it also could have been incidental. What if there's another three dozen fanatics waiting for him back at his lair? I could be dead tomorrow, Lewis."

The FBI agent forced a friendly smile. "Not tonight, Sam. You'll have a half-dozen of Salem's finest watching your house the rest of the night. And I'll be staying over as well. I'm not about to take any chances. Still, my intuition tells me that he's through for a while. His people are going to need to regroup and reassess everything after their loss tonight."

Sam looked out the window at the buildings as they passed through town. "Both sides lost tonight," he said softly to himself. "There are no winners."

⟨⟨⟨∞⟩⟩⟩

Rain arrived with the morning, matching the mood in Roger's study. All of the members of the group had shown up to discuss what had happened the previous night, as well as what it all meant for the future. The conversation was difficult, in the face of the loss they had all suffered, but no one was more silent than Sam.

His sleep had been fitful, with dreams of long, sharp knives and cloaked figures dancing around a raging fire. He awoke frequently throughout the night, and when he did he was left with an overwhelming feeling of dread and hopelessness.

Helen had arrived first, bringing a half-dozen cups from a local cafe. One of the cups held milk, another had packets of sugar, and the rest were filled with piping hot coffee. Sam sipped his quietly at the large work table while Helen paced and explored the room, neither one willing to break the silence first.

Lewis, who had slept in one of the guest rooms upstairs, was the last to arrive, having been beaten by Robert by about ten minutes. Once they were all assembled, they took care of polite condolences and pleasantries while Sam brooded at the table, facing away from the fireplace, his hands resting on the smooth, worn surface of a small wooden box.

Lewis filled everyone in on the exact details of what had transpired in the clearing, and fielded a few questions. When they were done, everyone turned to look toward Sam.

"There are matters which must be discussed," Robert said, interrupting Sam's thoughts. "I know you aren't interested in talking, but it can't be helped."

Sam turned from the table and looked at the others. "I know," he sighed. "It's just so weird to be in here without him, to be gathered as a whole when there's such a large part missing."

"Believe me when I say," Helen said from her seat in an antique chair beside the fireplace, "that we are all feeling the exact same emptiness, Sam. I won't pretend to know exactly what you are going through, but I have a feeling all of us can make fairly accurate guesses."

"We don't need to talk about anything painful," Lewis added. "But there are some small details that we need to discuss."

Sam ignored Lewis and stood up, facing the cold fireplace. He stepped around the sofa and slowly approached the wide, thick mantle.

"Sam?" Helen said.

Sam put his hands on the clock that sat in the center of the collection of items Roger had gathered there, and turned it around so that he could see the back. There, protruding from an opening like a knife from a corpse, was a key. Sam pulled it out and returned to the table.

"What are you doing, Sam?" asked Robert.

"I've had this box in my possession since the night my family died," Sam replied, holding up the box for all to see. "It's locked, and I've never had the courage, or the reason, to try and open it. I didn't know if there even *was* a key until two nights ago, when Roger mentioned that my father had given him one."

Helen's eyes opened wide. Robert stepped closer to the table.

"What do you think is inside?" Lewis asked him.

"Proof," Sam replied. "Proof that Mather didn't die sixty years ago. Proof that his group has been around for centuries. Proof, I think, that his group has been stalking and hunting my family for generations."

"That would be a monumental piece of evidence," Robert said. "I didn't know such a thing existed."

"Neither did I," Lewis added. "But then again, that was your father's realm. But I'm not sure we knew he was building a case to prove it all. How did you even come by this box?"

Sam closed his eyes. Reliving the fire and smoke of his ruined home wasn't something he enjoyed doing under the most normal of circumstances. But doing so just hours after losing Roger—a man who had been the last remaining piece of Sam's past—felt like torture.

"I made it to the house just as the fire was beginning to rage," he told them. "It was a vision that led me home. When I got there, I found my father crawling out of the fire. He was carrying this box."

Helen brought a hand to her mouth. "Oh my God, Sam," she said with a wet glimmer in her eye. "I had no idea. I'm so sorry."

Sam did not respond. Instead, he turned back to the box and looked at the key. It was simple and unremarkable, but for two small characters engraved in the flat bronze end.

MH, he thought. *My father's initials.*

He pushed the end of the key into the opening on the box and turned it. There was a soft CLICK from inside, and the front opened slightly. As he placed his hands on either side of the lid, the others walked toward the table and craned their necks to watch. Then, after taking a deep breath and closing his eyes for a second, he lifted it open.

Empty.

The box had nothing inside. Nothing at all to greet him after two decades of wondering. The inside of the lid, as well as the bottom of the box, were both lined with old scraps of wallpaper, but other than those small bits of color, there was nothing waiting for them to see.

"There's nothing in it?" Lewis asked incredulously. "How can that be?"

Sam shook his head. "I have no idea," he replied. His hands were trembling as he set the box back on the table. Suddenly, an overwhelming wave of rage swelled up within him. He wanted to throw the box against a wall, or smash it on the floor and grind the pieces with his feet. But he just pushed it away slowly, as if it were an empty plate after a big meal.

"So that's that," he declared. "After all this *shit*—every last bit of harassment and pain and loss—the last bit of hope that we had is nothing more than a lie. It's empty, and now I have nothing left. Nothing." He lowered his head and closed his eyes as numbness creeped through his body.

Robert stepped closer and placed a hand on Sam's shoulder. "I'm sorry, Sam," he said in a fatherly tone. "Honestly, we all are. This has been difficult for each of us in our own ways, but you have suffered considerably more, and for that I am truly sorry. I hope that I can offer you one final bit of news, however. One that should be easier to handle than all the rest of this mess."

Sam looked up from the table and turned to Robert. "What do you mean?" he asked.

Robert glanced at the others before answering. Sam saw Lewis nod once toward the attorney, and then Helen did the same.

"Roger had a will," he said. Sweeping his hand to include the others, "All of us do, actually. One of the benefits of having a lawyer in the bunch, I suppose. We never expected to need it so soon, but Roger had left plans for how his estate would be dispersed should anything ever happen to him."

"I knew it," Sam sighed. "I'm going to have to leave the house, too. Is that it? He's left the house to some organization and I need to get out by tomorrow?"

"Not at all," Robert replied. "In fact, you can stay as long as you'd like. The house is yours, now."

"It's what?" Sam did not seem to understand, a result of having to deal with much more than any normal person should over the past few days.

"The house is yours, Sam," Robert repeated. "Roger left it to you. It's yours, free and clear, as well as a sizable inheritance."

"Why would he do that?" Sam asked, but the question was aimed more at himself than the others. "I abandoned him twenty years ago. Why would he do something like that for me?"

"Because he truly cared for you, Sam," Lewis replied. "He had no children of his own, and even when we weren't sure where you were, he spoke of you often, and fondly. Yes, you are the last of the Hawthornes, and that holds a lot of significance to our research. But more importantly, Roger felt you were family."

Robert placed his hand back on Sam's shoulder before extending a white envelope to him. "It's all in here," he said. "Read it when you're ready. There's no rush. We'll be checking in on you every day for a long while. When you've read through the documents and are ready to accept Roger's gift, just let me know. I'll draft up the paperwork and make it official.

"In the mean time, get comfortable, rest up, and know that you are safe here. The others and I have hopes that you will consider joining our cause at some point in the near future, but that's up to you. Your father was incredibly gifted and immensely helpful, and I think I speak for all of us, including Roger, when I say that you would fill his shoes nicely."

Sam opened his mouth but nothing came out. Robert gave his shoulder a squeeze and smiled warmly at him before walking away. Helen leaned over and gave him a kiss on the cheek, although Sam saw sadness in her eyes. After Lewis patted him on the back and flashed a quick, painful smile, all three of them walked quietly to the door and exited the study, leaving Sam to process everything without interruption.

He turned back to the table and picked up the old wooden box. He had placed so much hope in it over the years. He had guarded it, escorted it from state to state, and treasured it as the last thing his father had ever given him. Yet here it was, empty and useless, and he could not help but feel the same about himself.

For the first time in hours, though, Sam felt something else. It was a nagging feeling that he finally had real work to do. A feeling that the group's invitation to work along side them, to further their cause and carry on Roger's work, could provide him with meaning beyond the confines of a small wooden box.

It was purpose that he felt. Intention. There were new goals to aim for, and he was finally in a position to work toward them. It was what Roger would have wanted him to do. His father, too. That was all Sam needed, in the end. A calling.

For the first time in a long while, Sam smiled. Maybe things *would* get better. He could move forward and go on because he had a role to play now. Perhaps that was the true gift his father had given him, and it was Roger's gift as well.

Sam would mourn, of course. He knew that was the first hill on the horizon that he must climb. After that, though, the future felt more hopeful.

It was time to get to work.

EPILOGUE

SAM COULD SEE SNOW falling outside through one of the windows that faced Chestnut Street. There was something magical about the way it covered the cobblestone sidewalks and tops of the black shutters of the other houses. If Salem had been built for a season, most would say it was autumn. Sam, though, would strongly disagree.

He set down his worn copy of *The House of Seven Gables* and reached for his coffee cup. It had finally cooled down to a temperature that his tongue agreed with, and he took a long drink. Setting the cup back down on the small white saucer, he was about to reach for the book again when a knock at the door broke the silence.

Sam glanced at his watch. He was expecting Lewis for lunch, but it was barely half-past nine. He leaned to peer out the window toward the driveway. A small green sedan was parked behind his truck. It was far from new, and nothing like the kind of vehicles the FBI, with their deep pockets and penchant for sophistication, tended to provide to Lewis.

He stood and walked to the door, and although an unscheduled visitor had the potential to represent trouble, he had a feeling that this was nothing to be concerned about. Whether that was a result of some subconscious telepathic sweep of the house or just wishful thinking remained to be seen.

Sam opened the door to find a tall, slender woman standing on the porch. She wore a dark wool skirt, leather boots, and a green top, but her posture told him that she was not wearing enough for a day as cold as this.

"Hi," he said. "What can I do for you?"

The woman wrapped her arms around herself and glanced back toward the street.

She's not looking at her car, he though, following her gaze. *She thinks she's being followed.*

"Are you Roger Sandbrook?" she asked, turning back to lock eyes with him.

A pang of sadness rippled through Sam's chest, but he tried his best to smile. "No," he replied. "Mr. Sandbrook passed away six months ago. He was a dear friend of mine, though. I'm Sam." He extended a hand in greeting.

"Rebecca," she said. "Rebecca Howe."

The woman, perhaps only a few years younger than Sam, reached out and politely gripped his hand. Her fingers were cold, and Sam immediately felt concern for her.

"Please," he said, stepping back from the door. "Come in and get warm. I may not be Roger, but I would like to see if I can help you."

Rebecca studied him for a moment. Her eyes seemed to scan his face, but Sam felt as if she were processing a vast array of information, taking in every detail and examining it all. There was a brief moment, no more than a second or two, where he would have sworn he heard a soft voice, but then she smiled weakly and nodded.

"Thank you," she said, entering the house timidly.

Sam closed the door. "It's much warmer in here. The snow is beautiful, but it has a way of chilling me to the bone."

Rebecca nodded in agreement, but her eyes were taking in the wonderful features of the house. "What a beautiful home," she said. "You live here?"

"Indeed," he replied. "Please, why don't we take a seat in there." Sam gestured toward the elegant sitting room.

Light filled the small space, streaming in through the two windows that looked out on the front lawn. Sam returned to the chair where he had been reading moments before—the chair beside the brand new window that had been installed after Roger's abduction—and offered the nearest armchair to Rebecca.

She took a seat and looked out the window. Sam noticed that it was an intense glance rather than a casual one. She was afraid and suspicious of everything. Sam thought he understood why.

"So, Mrs. Howe—" he began, but she interrupted him.

"Ms.," she said.

"Ms. Howe," Sam corrected himself with a polite smile. "What can I do for you?"

Rebecca quickly looked back out the window, and this time Sam cast a brief glance himself. There was nothing out of the ordinary to be seen. It took her a moment to gather her thoughts, but eventually, she replied.

"Mr. Sandbrook had offered me protection," she said before pausing. The silence was pregnant with meaning. "I'm not sure you would believe me if I told you why. It's difficult to understand. I'm not even sure I fully understand it, myself."

Sam glanced down at his coffee cup. Almost on impulse, he pointed to it, watching her eyes as he did. When she was watching it, Sam did something that he knew would either help break the ice or frighten her out the door.

"I think I understand better than most," he said, levitating the cup about about six inches above the table.

Rebecca's eyes opened wide, but it was not fear or disbelief that Sam saw in them. It was a look of recognition.

"You," she stammered. "You're like me."

"Am I?" Sam replied.

For a moment, he was not sure if she would answer. Her icy blue eyes drifted away from his own and scanned the room. She finally settled on the mantle of the cold fireplace across the room.

Like the one on the opposite side of the wall in the study, this mantle was covered in an odd collection of objects, including two silver candlesticks. Rebecca pointed toward them, and almost immediately one of the wicks ignited into a bright orange flame.

"I am," she said with a playful smile.

52968196R00197

Made in the USA
Middletown, DE
23 November 2017